SHADOW'S MYSTERY

SHADOW ISLAND SERIES: BOOK NINE

MARY STONE
LORI RHODES

MARY
STONE
PUBLISHING

This book is dedicated to our teachers, those tasked with illuminating young minds. Please know that your lessons echo far beyond the walls of the classroom, igniting dreams and molding futures. Even a little girl with dyslexia who thought she could never be a writer. Thank you.

DESCRIPTION

No good deed goes unpunished.

Reeling from guilt and haunted by the recent loss of one of her deputies, Sheriff Rebecca West doesn't have time to recover before Shadow Island delivers yet another blow. The island's most beloved teacher has mysteriously disappeared on the night of her retirement party, her wallet, keys, and cell phone still in her unlocked car. If Rebecca doesn't want the missing woman to join the island's growing list of corpses, she's got to focus on the present.

Even as the past tries to rip her apart.

When the woman's body is found with a cryptic, blood-spattered note—penned in her own handwriting—stuffed in her blouse pocket, one thing is clear. Not everyone loved the veteran schoolteacher. But who would hate her enough to slit her throat?

With suspects that span the length and breadth of the island, from a potentially violent husband grappling with early-onset dementia to almost every islander the victim once taught, Rebecca finds herself immersed in a web of deceit and vendetta. The more witnesses Rebecca interviews, the more rumors and conflicting stories arise—and the bigger the pool of suspects grows.

But when another, even bloodier murder occurs on school grounds, Rebecca must work faster. A killer with a grudge against people who worked at the school is lurking...and he's escalating.

From its confounding beginning to the heart-stopping conclusion, Shadow's Mystery—the ninth book in the Shadow Island Series by Mary Stone and Lori Rhodes—uncovers how a love turned obsession can cast the darkest shadow of all.

1

It was only a few days until school started again, and for the first time in three decades, Amy Washington wouldn't be there to greet the year's new batch of students. It was both sad and exciting as she looked around the school's gymnasium where her former colleagues had gathered to say farewell.

Her party had been pushed to late summer since many of her fellow teachers had scheduled professional development classes and seminars to keep their licensing current. She understood that all too well. That was definitely one aspect of the position she wouldn't miss.

As she peered around the room with its balloons and crepe paper bunting, her gaze landed on her dear husband of twenty-five years. Richard—or Buzz as he'd been dubbed by his parents as a child—seemed desperate to escape a conversation with the very talkative Pamela Radcliffe.

Buzz scanned the room, searching for a way out.

Amy's heart clenched as she realized she needed to intercept their interaction before it was too late. Almost a year ago, Buzz was diagnosed with early-onset Alzheimer's disease. It was the reason she was retiring, and it was a secret she held close.

Of course, her coworkers were under the impression Amy and Buzz were about to embark on a grand adventure, crossing off all the items on their shared bucket list. Lying to her friends had been difficult, but protecting Buzz's pride was Amy's priority.

After all, it *was* going to be an adventure. Just not the one she'd described. There would be no Fijian bungalow rental, no trip to explore their English roots in the UK, no Alaskan cruise. At best, she hoped for long walks with Buzz and spending time with their sons while he still knew who they were.

With her years of service to the school, Amy had been able to retire with her full pension at only fifty-two years of age. Many of her colleagues chose to retire as soon as they were eligible. They often cited unruly students, impossible helicopter parents, or onerous, short-sighted state mandates as the main reasons for running for the door. But that hadn't been Amy's experience.

She loved teaching and adored her students almost as much as she did her two adult sons. Although the students could create problems, they were all good at their core.

Amy knew many kids had struggles that were bigger than school and their latest assignments. Some of them were dealing with dysfunctional families, cyberbullying, sexual identity issues, and intrusive peer pressure. The issues facing kids today were more complex than many of her colleagues seemed to understand.

Which was what made walking away so difficult. Her kids needed her understanding ear and open-door policy. They needed an adult who tried to offer perspective and wisdom instead of judgment and generalizations about how lazy their generation was. Sometimes, they just needed a hug and a shoulder to cry on.

But as much as those kids needed someone like Amy on their side, Buzz needed her more. At just fifty-five, Buzz's early-onset diagnosis was grim, and his symptoms had become increasingly concerning. Just last night, he'd grown agitated when he couldn't find either of their boys in their room.

He'd searched the house, frantically calling their names. It had taken Amy more than an hour to convince him that the boys didn't live there anymore and were actually adults. The pictures she'd shown him of their oldest son's wedding had been knocked out of her hand in anger.

Finally, well after midnight, he'd fallen asleep. These challenging nights were becoming increasingly normal.

Yes, Buzz needed her more than the students, and she was going to be there for him. She'd already made arrangements with a very nice care center on the mainland. The house on Shadow Island would soon be listed for sale, and Amy would move into an apartment near the facility so she could be close to her husband.

So, yes…a new adventure. Just not one she ever expected.

After opening her gift basket filled with thoughtful presents for her "Bucket List Adventure," as they'd called it—gifts she didn't have the heart to tell them she and Buzz would probably never use—the partygoers began excusing themselves.

Principal Hill had steadfastly refused to allow any alcohol at the celebration, so many of the teachers, despite it being after nine, were headed to Pamela's home to continue the party without the wet blanket administrator dampening their fun.

With Buzz safely at her side, Amy lingered behind the last of her colleagues streaming out the double doors of the gym.

"They're going to miss you here. You're one of a kind, you know?" Buzz slipped an arm around her waist.

Amy leaned against his shoulder, taking in one final glance around the empty bleachers. "Spending every moment with you is the best retirement gift I could get." She lifted the oversize gift basket off the table, but Buzz took the heavy package from her.

He kissed her forehead before taking a step toward the exit doors. "Why don't you turn off the lights, and I'll put this out in the car? I'll give you a moment to tell this old building goodbye."

Buzz always understood her. They'd been high school sweethearts and married only a few years after she'd begun teaching in this very school.

Heaving a big sigh, Amy spun in a small circle. She could almost swear she smelled the faint aroma of burnt popcorn sold by the pep club. Her years here had included chaperoning dances in this gym, watching countless students compete in various sports, and participating in thirty graduation ceremonies. She could almost hear the girls' heels as they clomped across the varnished hardwood of the gymnasium floor and onto the stage to snag their diplomas—their whole lives laid out before them.

She shook her head as she made her way to the metallic box that served as the light switch for the whole gym. When she inserted her key and flipped the switch down, the room fell into an eerie darkness. She pocketed the key and rushed toward the illuminated exit sign to join Buzz outside.

The night was dark and quiet with only the stars watching her. Even the moon was hiding, the barest sliver faint in the sky.

Crossing into the employee parking lot for the last time, Amy spied her faded green Civic. Since she'd come with Buzz, she hadn't parked near a light. Of course, after decades of experience, she knew every bump and dip of asphalt as she passed the vehicles of her friends and coworkers to reach hers. They'd all walked to the after-party at Pamela's home just down the street, so the lot was still rather full.

Amy's hand lifted to her neck and lightly tapped the delightful locket she'd received, dangling from a rope chain. On one side was her first yearbook photo. On the other was the one taken this past year, her last one. Her entire career was encompassed in those two pictures.

She'd stared at the first picture, almost unable to recognize herself. Her smile was still white and beaming. But seeing the two faces side by side was a stark reminder of how much had changed. Buzz had always reassured her that her wrinkles were evidence of a life well lived, and he loved every single one of them.

The locket had been hers for only a few hours, but she already knew she'd cherish this gift from her colleagues for the rest of her years. It signified the chapter of her life as a devoted teacher. And now, Amy could turn the page and devote herself to being a wife to her beloved husband. With his failing memory fueling her guilt, she regretted not being there for him more throughout their marriage.

Tomorrow was the last weekday of the summer before classes began on Monday. It was an optional workday for her former colleagues, but not for her. That idea put a skip in her step, and she giggled a little. Her laughter fell silent as she reached her car and realized Buzz wasn't there.

Amy scanned the parking lot, searching for her husband. "Buzz, honey, where are you? I'm here now. Place is all locked up."

Her voice drifted out over the isolated expanse with no reply.

Sweat began to bead on her forehead despite the slight coolness of the evening air. Glancing inside her car, she noticed her lovely gift basket resting on the passenger seat. On the floor was the spare set of keys Buzz had used to open the door.

"Okay, think. He obviously made it to the car and put the basket inside. That shows cognition. Where would he have gone after that?"

Panic rose in her chest, and she tried desperately to squelch it.

"It's fine. His episodes don't last long. If I just keep calling his name, he'll return once he comes to his senses."

But what if he doesn't?

Maybe the excitement of the party had been too much for him. Amy probably shouldn't have dragged him along. Now he could be wandering the streets, getting injured or lost.

Dammit, Richard!

"Richard Buzz Washington, you answer me right now!" Her voice cracked as she shouted her command, silencing the crickets.

Think, dammit, think. Where would he go?

And then it hit her. As classmates at this very school, Buzz and Amy had often cut through the dune grasses at the end of the parking lot to gaze out at the ocean together. Sometimes, they'd sit on the shore and study the distant mainland, discussing their dreams for the future. If Buzz was anywhere, it was on that shore.

Worried about sand or water ruining her cell phone, she dropped the device on top of the basket, knowing she could still get to it if she needed.

Please don't need it.

Grasping onto that sliver of hope, she headed toward the tiny path that led into the grassy dunes that rose up behind the school grounds.

This was the same path she'd led her students down innumerable times, inspired by her trips down it with Buzz. She might even have been the reason that trampled trail existed among the thick, wild grasses and rushes that grew tall enough to brush her shoulders.

The beautiful weather that came with spring was normally hard on her students. She'd learned early in her career that taking them outside to enjoy the sunny days was a better way to get them to focus than forcing them to stay inside while they all stared out the window.

And every time, even as she trudged outside with a stack of blankets, she swore that going out was only for her students, allowing them a chance to relax and refocus in the much-needed sunshine after the rainy, dreary days of winter. Taking them to the beach would've been frowned upon, but there were plenty of sandy hills covered in tall grasses where they could sit as she taught the day's lessons. So long as they didn't "get caught" by the administration, no one minded. It was the worst-kept secret of the school, but harmless.

There was no warm sunshine this evening, though. No students to teach, no Buzz by her side as she stepped onto the sandy trail.

The tiniest rustle of dried grass in the faint breeze was the only sound aside from her calling out to her husband. As the sand ate up her fervent pleas, she worried that Buzz couldn't hear her even if he was in his right mind.

Amy searched the familiar path for his footprints or anything to indicate he'd come this way. For a moment, she debated going back for her phone. The flashlight would've been a useful tool. But a silvery crescent moon was reflecting off the waves, making the world brighter than it should've been after nine at night. Her eyes adjusted easily to the shadows.

Her inspection was cut short when she hung a right on the trail and met a pair of shoes facing her on the path.

"Buzz...oh!" She jolted to a halt, her hand still stroking

her locket. The man, a shadow standing near a thick bundle of rush, didn't move or speak, causing shivers to run down her spine. "I'm sorry. I was looking for my husband. Did you happen to see anyone else pass this way?"

Amy waited, but the man didn't reply. Worried about how much time had passed since she'd last seen Buzz, she tried to step around the stranger, but he moved in front of her again.

She tittered nervously as her heart beat loudly in her ears. "Sorry about that. Just trying to get around and continue my search." She stepped the other way, and he, yet again, moved with her. "I'm…" Peering closer at his face in the dim light, she recognized the man before her, though his name wasn't as quick to follow.

He was glaring at her, though, which was odd.

"What are…how have…" Amy's mind raced as she tried to remember his name. It was no use. Every one of her thoughts was devoted toward finding her husband. "I'm sorry. I'm trying to get out of your way. Just let me get around you, and I'll be on my way."

She stepped left.

The man's hand shot out for her throat before she could utter another word. She was so startled she jerked back. Her brand-new necklace snapped.

"What are…?" The words lodged in her throat as her silver chain swung from his fingers, the same hand wielding a long metal blade.

He lifted the charm to his face, and the knife glinted in the moonlight. She froze.

"Scream, and I'll make this so much worse for you." He pried open the locket, sneering at the pictures inside.

The familiar voice from Amy's past was one etched into her memory like her first day of teaching. She strove to keep her voice calm. "What do you—"

"Don't talk to me."

Like lightning, he threw the locket over her head. It glinted in the starlight and was gone. He grabbed her upper arm. His grip was like a vice.

Before she could even try to twist away, a terrible burning sensation seared across her neck. Her knees weakened as warmth trickled down her chest. She tried to raise her hand, to touch her throat, but her arms hung uselessly at her sides. What little air she had in her lungs seemed desperate to leave her, and when she tried to call to Buzz, she couldn't form the words. The ground rushed up to catch her as she fell, collapsing into the tall, dry grass.

Why was this happening?

Even as life drained from her body, her biggest concern wasn't for herself.

Oh, Buzz. Where did you go? Who will look after you? I'm so sorry, honey. I promised I'd take care of you, and now I'm leaving you alone.

She looked down at the blood saturating her blouse.

As life slipped from her grasp, Amy Washington remembered the young man's name.

And she also remembered why he wanted her dead.

2

Out of the frying pan and into the fire.

The old adage played on repeat through Sheriff Rebecca West's mind as she stared at the phone in her hand. She'd only just returned home after visiting Arlington Cemetery, where Deputy Darian Hudson had been laid to rest. She hadn't even managed to reach the front door of her rental and unlock it before receiving a call from the office.

Instead of going inside and collapsing on her bed like she desperately wanted to, she cleared her throat to steady her voice and answered. "Hello?"

"Sheriff West..." It was Melody from dispatch, her voice soft and hesitant.

"Yes, what can I do for you?"

"I'm calling your cell instead of radioing out because I wasn't sure if...well, if you were working today. And I knew you'd want to hear about this either way."

That doesn't sound good.

"What's going on?"

"We have a report of a possible missing person at the Shadow Island School."

Rebecca pressed her fingers to one temple. *Please don't be a child.*

"What are the details?"

"Amy Washington, fifty-two-year-old retired teacher. Last seen at the school last evening for a retirement party."

And just like that, instead of having time to decompress after the long and emotional drive, she had to investigate a possible missing person at the local K-12 school.

"I'm on my way." Rebecca hung up, giving a small thanks that this time it wasn't a missing child.

Maybe it was because she was emotional, maybe it was because she was still racked with guilt and grief, but she couldn't stop second-guessing her decision to stay on Shadow Island.

Is Darian dead because of me?

Since she'd woken in the hospital two weeks ago, she'd been questioning all her decisions. The long, quiet days of her recovery had given her plenty of time to think and rethink every decision that had led to where she was today.

Going against the FBI to find her parents' killers. Leaving DC to come to the island for vacation. Agreeing to help the local sheriff search for a missing teenager, then staying after he'd been killed in the line of duty. Taking on a high-powered organized crime group called the Yacht Club. Going up against a couple of local politicians time and again in the search for justice while digging up old cases and solving new ones.

And letting a good man get killed.

Bracing herself, she stepped off her porch and climbed into her SUV. It was white and tan with *Sheriff* emblazoned across the side of it in big, shiny letters. An honor, to be sure, except when it felt like a cage. Or like today, when it was more like the sword of Damocles.

It was because of Rebecca that she and her small band of

deputies had been on that island, trying to take down a drug ring. In the end, they'd won the battle. The war, though?

We lost that...and so much more.

She had an assortment of injuries she was still recovering from, but she didn't care about herself. Images of Ryker, a civilian caught in the cross fire, floated through her mind. Deputy Trent Locke had been shot in the thigh. And Darian...

Tears burned her eyes for the thousandth time that day as images of the young deputy flashed through her mind.

Darian had been hit in the lung, a freak shot that went in through the armpit hole of his bulletproof vest. Rebecca learned about his death when she'd gain consciousness in the hospital, and the pain of his loss hurt more than any of her physical wounds ever could.

Lilian Hudson was a widow now, and three-month-old Mallory would have to grow up without ever getting to know her amazing father.

It isn't fair.

At first, it looked like everyone might be safe when Ryker Sawyer brought his small boat out to retrieve them. Ryker, the man she'd confessed to loving mere hours before the shoot-out, ended up getting shot as well, leaving him in a coma for days. So many people were hurt that night.

Because of me.

And it was all because Rebecca had been hell-bent on getting justice for a small-time drug mule who'd nearly been killed by a cartel for trying to get an "in" around the island.

Rebecca glanced down at her right arm as she turned off her street and merged with the crush of late-summer afternoon traffic. Her newest scars were visible below the short sleeve of her newly acquired uniform. Ryker and the deputies weren't the only ones shot.

During the standoff, a bullet went straight through her

bicep, leaving her nearly helpless against a man determined to give her a painful death. He was the leader of the group that'd laid in ambush, waiting for her. And she'd led her men —her friends—right into that trap.

His plan, and that of whoever had paid him, hadn't succeeded. Instead, she'd managed to get all her men off the island while she stayed behind to hold off the shooters, ensuring the others could reach safety and medical care.

It had been a close call. So close, in fact, that when she'd passed out trying to bandage her wounds, she was certain she would die. She remembered it so clearly...

The night faded away as her body grew cold and heavy, her heart slowing as the blood drained from her body. Surrounded by dead enemies, alone and covered in blood, she succumbed to darkness with no strength left to fight back.

As her body twitched and cramped in pain, her only source of comfort was knowing she'd told Ryker how she felt. And it hadn't been a heat-of-the-battle declaration. They'd both been safe and clearheaded. Even better, he loved her too. That memory was the only warmth she could cling to as her limbs went numb from blood loss.

Except she hadn't died. Instead, she'd been saved, only to wake up to an even more painful reality.

One where she had to live every day knowing Darian's death and the injuries to those she'd grown close to were all on her. She'd put her people between two warring groups— the Yacht Club and the Amado Cartel. While the cartel had effectively been neutralized, she figured the Yacht Club still had a grip on local drug running and human trafficking. One threat had been taken out, but the other remained a thorn in her aching side.

She pulled into the parking lot of the school, grinding her back teeth together as turning the wheel put additional strain on her healing ribs.

The shooting pain in her rib cage and the pounding in her fractured cheek and eye socket were a welcome distraction compared to the emotional pain. Two and a half weeks of healing wasn't enough to allow the bones to fully knit back into place, though.

Hell, a solid blow to her chest might still be able to kill her if it landed right. Because of the locations of the breaks, she couldn't even rely on casts or braces. A competent tape job of the area seemed mostly like placebo-effect bandaging at best.

The stitches from the knife wound in her side had come out two days ago. Now she only had the wound glue holding the inner part of it closed. One more reason for her to move slowly and carefully, so the pain wouldn't send her to her knees and the cut wouldn't tear back open.

She'd been cleared to go back to work only because she'd lied to her doctor about her pain levels. Sitting at home with nothing to do but think about everything had been a new kind of hell. The first few days, she'd relied on pain pills to get her through. They'd knocked her out both physically and mentally.

But they were a grim reminder of how easy it could be to fall into the trap of addiction with the garbage she was going through. Dependency on a narcotic wasn't something she wanted to manage on top of everything else. After that realization, she tossed the pills and relied on over-the-counter painkillers.

Rebecca checked her face in the rearview mirror. The skin around her eyes was still slightly puffy and discolored from the beating she'd taken. 'Most every resident of this small town knew exactly what had happened to her. If, by some miracle, they didn't, the fading bruises on her face and stiff movements would clue them in pretty quickly.

In the back parking lot, Hoyt and Viviane watched her as

they waited beside an old faded-green Honda Civic. On the sidewalk that wrapped around the building, a woman dressed in leggings and a tank top paced while talking on her phone.

Rebecca pulled in a few spaces away from her deputies and opened the door. Taking a deep breath and holding it, she spun on her butt in her seat—keeping her back straight—and slid out of the Explorer. The air in her lungs was supposed to cushion any jolts to her body, but a twang of pain thrummed up and down her torso as her feet hit the ground. Thankfully, the broken bone in her foot was minor and barely caused her any pain.

There had to be a less agonizing way to get out of her cruiser, but she hadn't found it yet. Stretching one leg down at a time pulled even more viciously at the new scar across her side. Releasing her breath slowly, she shifted her feet to turn and face her two deputies, careful to control her breathing with the exercises her doctor had recommended to help her heal.

"Hey, Boss." Viviane smiled, fresh-faced and entirely too chipper. "We're looking pretty snazzy in our new uniforms, aren't we?" She eyed Rebecca up and down while twisting back and forth to show off their nearly matching, starched-stiff garb and gear. Rebecca even had the hat, but rarely wore it since it wasn't required, per the dress code.

Despair filled Rebecca instead of the joy she usually experienced seeing her friend.

Fresh meat for the grinder. But Rebecca knew nothing that'd happened would be enough to make Vi reconsider taking on the deputy sheriff role.

Not even all my new bruises and scars could talk her out of this. How can I protect her when she's out here with us?

Darian's face as he crumpled after being shot flashed

through Rebecca's mind, blinding her to the two living people standing in front of her.

Come on. Get your shit together.

She took a deep, fast breath and winced as the pain of her expanding ribs drove away the last of the flashback. Her recovery time was over, no matter what decision she made in the future. She was on the job now and had to act like it.

"What do we have, Frost?" She ensured her blond hair was secured in her low ponytail.

Hoyt shook his head and nodded toward Viviane, arms crossed. He possessed the demeanor of a drill sergeant or a school principal, waiting for the student to mess up. As far as hazing went, it was minor. Still, Viviane gulped as her two superior officers waited for her to give the report.

"Miss Washington, age fifty-two, had her retirement party last night." Viviane pointed at the car they were standing beside. "This is her Honda Civic, and she hasn't been seen since last night. The woman who reported it, Marjorie Lamb over there, has already called everyone who was here last night to ask if anyone has seen Miss Washington since or knows where she might've gone. So far, nothing. We've checked the whole building. It's clear."

"Has anyone checked her house yet?" Rebecca peered into the car through the closed window. She noted that Viviane had addressed the woman as most people did with their teachers. Regardless of their age or marital status, students and parents tended to refer to them as *miss* or *mister*.

"Marjorie did before she called us. She spoke with the husband, and he thought she must've gotten up early to run errands before coming here for a meeting." Viviane checked her notes. "Marjorie wasn't sure why he'd say that, though, because Miss Washington's not working at the school anymore. He told her the kinds of places she frequents, so we called around, but Miss Washington isn't there either. We even patrolled the streets near here, asking if anyone had seen her. It was a no-go. That's about where we're at now. And you can see why we didn't bother calling her cell phone."

A basket filled with tissue paper and small gifts sat in the passenger seat with a set of keys on the floorboard and a cell phone on top of the basket. On the cell phone case was a sticker that read, *Making a Difference, One Student at a Time.*

Rebecca glanced around, surprised the car was still there. It was a car thief's wet dream. Keys, phone, and even a present, all sitting there for the taking.

"The car isn't locked, correct?" She reached for her gloves even as she asked.

"It's unlocked. I checked. We've only been out here a bit longer than you." Viviane moved her hand close to the glass but stopped before touching it so as not to taint any potential evidence. She might be new to the position of deputy, but she'd worked with the police and been around them since she was a girl. Hopefully, that meant she wouldn't make a lot of the rookie mistakes so many first-years did.

Rebecca pulled on her gloves and opened the car door to check inside, noting that Viviane copied her action and donned her own gloves as well.

Exhaustion etched into Hoyt's face like a second set of fine wrinkles. "We called her house phone. No answer. Washington didn't answer that call either. Marjorie Lamb, our witness, confirms that's Amy's cell phone sitting on the basket there. She recognized it by the sticker."

As the only one on the force who wasn't wounded in the island ambush, the poor man had been forced to cover all the shifts for the first few days, with only Rhonda Lettinger and her force from the state police in Norfolk helping out as they could. Locke had come back after the first week, the gunshot wound in his leg—life-threatening at the time—having healed quickly enough once the wound was stitched closed.

Viviane had gotten her promotion and was sworn in last week. Rebecca had managed to drag herself in for that, since all she had to do was stand there and look pretty in her brand-new dress uniform, which had come in at the same time as Viviane's. As the sheriff, she was there only as part of the backdrop, not wanting to mess up the pictures with her extra-colorful face.

She'd only succeeded in being presentable thanks to Meg Darby, Viviane's mother. The older woman had been her ride and showed up two hours early to help her get ready with a color palette specifically designed to hide bruises. The ones on her face had faded to that horrid yellow-purple combination by then and were ultimately impossible to conceal.

Wesley Garrett, the man who'd been paid to kill her, had focused on her head and face during their fight. And he'd been an expert at inflicting suffering. His hands had been as hard as rocks, slamming into her cheeks and eyes. The crack of her orbital bone still echoed in her mind.

Dammit, woman! Get your head in the game. Garrett is dead. Darian is dead. Ryker is healing. You're healing. Stop focusing on the past and focus on making sure Amy Washington doesn't join the growing list of corpses.

Rebecca jerked her focus back to the job at hand. Viviane was going to be out on her own all too soon. And Rebecca would make damn sure she had everything she needed to stay alive and as safe as possible.

She attempted to take a breath without drawing attention to the wince on her face. "There are no obvious signs of a struggle. But she could've been forced to leave her things behind. Or left them of her own volition. We need to keep both possibilities in mind as we move forward. Did you already take pictures?"

Viviane nodded vigorously. Behind her, Hoyt gave a single nod. Rebecca started to lean into the car but stopped as the strain hit her healing bones, forcing out a wheezing groan.

"Let me get that for you, Boss." Viviane darted forward, and Rebecca gladly stepped out of the way.

"Still hurting?" Hoyt eyed her up and down, a knowing and suspicious gleam in his eye. "Did your doctor really sign off on you coming back to work?"

"Yes, to both." Rebecca didn't look at him as he sighed gustily.

"You lied to him, didn't you?" His tone was dour but had a tiny hint of amusement too.

Knowing she wasn't going to get away with another lie while he was studying her face, she ignored the question completely. It didn't matter if she'd lied to get released. She was on the job now. "Viviane, what did you find?"

"Cell phone's dead. The keys fit the ignition, so they're for this car. The gift basket has a bunch of gift cards, a bottle of wine, a coffee mug, an apple, some art supplies, and an empty jewelry box." Viviane lifted everything from the vehicle and showed them, stacking the items in the basket that she held up.

"We gave her the gift basket last night." An unfamiliar voice reached Rebecca from the other side of the car. "The art supplies were because she planned on taking up painting for her retirement."

Rebecca peered over the roof at Marjorie Lamb as she joined them. "Did you find anyone who saw Amy after the party?"

"No." The woman shook her head while scowling at the phone in her hand. "I tried calling her house again too. This time, her husband didn't answer."

Hoyt nodded. "Same when I called him a few minutes ago. But we have the contact information for Amy and Buzz, so we can try the house again later."

Rebecca took a slow turn around the car, looking for signs of forced entry. "Can you please walk me through what happened last night that led to your discovery of her car today?"

"Amy retired at the end of the last school year, and we had a pretty big to-do for her last night." Marjorie tossed her phone back and forth between her hands. "She'd been a teacher here for thirty years. All of us showed up. The teachers and admin, at least. It was the usual, watching a slideshow, sharing stories...we gave her that basket, she gave a speech. But we called it just after dark. We spend enough unpaid hours in this place. I can get the list of everyone who came, if you want."

"That would be useful. Thank you. What time did the party end?"

"Around nine. Then most of us went over to Pamela Radcliffe's house for a few drinks afterward. We're not allowed to drink on campus, no matter the time of year. Some of the staff still party when they have an excuse."

"Was Amy's car still here when you left?" Rebecca poked through the items in the basket. It would've been more useful if the phone was still charged, but they could plug it in back at the station if they needed to. Maybe an elderly school-teacher wouldn't have bothered with little things like pass-codes or facial identity.

Yeah, right.

Marjorie frowned and glanced around. "Yes, I'm pretty sure it was. I remember seeing Buzz walk past Pam's house and thought maybe Amy and Buzz had changed their minds about joining us. But Amy wasn't with him, so I guessed she wanted to hang out at the school a bit longer."

"He was walking alone?" Rebecca confirmed. "Not in a vehicle?"

The teacher nodded to no one in particular. "Yeah, he was

walking alone. And I'm sure the car must have been here when we left. Pam lives down the street, so I walked over. So did most of the others. I had my husband pick me up, since I'd had a few drinks."

That put another wrinkle in things. *Why didn't Amy and Buzz drive home together?*

There was no telling yet if Amy had left the school last night after Buzz had decided to walk home and then simply come back earlier today. She could have left the gift in the car for any number of reasons. None of the contents seemed to be perishable. Other than that, there was nothing out of the ordinary in the car.

"Is there a chance she came back for some reason? Perhaps to go to her old classroom? Maybe she was missing the school more than she thought and decided to visit while everyone set up their rooms?"

"Not too many people would've been working early today after the party. It's an optional extra workday if we're behind in setting up, so I doubt she'd come by for that. I don't even know why I got out of bed to get here today." Marjorie gave a rueful smile. "Besides, a few of the other teachers walked back here after Pam's party and mentioned they'd seen Amy's car in the lot."

"Do you have any pictures from last night of Amy? Preferably where we can see what she was wearing?"

"Of course. I can text you one." Marjorie lifted her phone and typed in the number Rebecca gave her, then turned her screen around to show them the picture. "She's even wearing the necklace we got her. It was in the basket, but she put it on right away. We all chipped in for it." She zoomed in on the picture of the woman beaming with pride next to her husband, showing off the jewelry she'd mentioned. A silver oval hanging from a matching rope chain necklace.

The phone in Rebecca's pocket buzzed, indicating she'd

received the picture. "I can see the security camera for the parking lot. Can you tell us who could get us access to that footage?"

"It only covers the entrance, so I'm not sure it'll help. But I can ask the principal for it."

Rebecca nodded. "Please do." She watched as Marjorie headed for the building.

Viviane shifted uneasily. "Are we waiting for something?"

"Yup." Hoyt nodded, then moved to the back of Amy's car, pulling on his own set of gloves. "We're waiting for her to get out of earshot."

"Why?" Viviane dropped her voice to barely above a whisper and sidled closer to Hoyt.

Rebecca knelt and popped the trunk release. "So she won't have to see what might be hidden in the back."

The trunk swung open. Hoyt caught it partway and carefully raised it. "It's clear. She's not in here. Nothing is. Not even a jack."

"You were worried someone had stuffed Miss Washington in there?" Viviane swallowed hard.

"Or she fell in there. Both were possible. Especially when the keys are sitting in the car like these were. In cases of falling, the sudden weight drop can cause the trunks on older cars to drop and close, trapping people inside. Always check the trunks."

"She used to take us on excursions into the field during the spring." Viviane blushed. "Miss Washington was one of my favorite teachers when I was in school."

Considering Viviane's age and how long Amy Washington had worked at the school, that made sense.

"She was a great teacher. All the kids loved her." At Rebecca's frown, Hoyt explained. "Miss Washington taught my boys. They liked her too."

"Since you two are familiar with her habits and this location, go check if she went for a walk. I'll swing by her residence and see if she's there."

Hopefully, this would turn out to be a silly misunderstanding. Rebecca could go for a nice simple case to ease her back into the job. And it would be good for Viviane's first time too.

But something nagged at her, a whisper in her mind that refused to be silenced. The haunting doubt lingered, casting a shadow over what should be a straightforward investigation.

Something felt terribly wrong.

3

Before Rebecca left, Hoyt had filled her in on Richard "Buzz" Washington, Amy's husband. At fifty-five, he was a few years older than his wife and already retired. By all accounts, he was a nice gentleman who kept to himself, taking the occasional trip to the docks to fish and sporadically attending the local Baptist church with Amy.

It took him awhile to answer the door, and Rebecca was starting to worry before it swung open, revealing a man with receding brown hair, a slight hunch to his shoulders, and a ready smile. His pale-blue button-down shirt was wrinkled and partially untucked from his black trousers.

"Hello, my dear. Can I help you?"

"Are you Richard Washington, Amy Washington's husband?"

He nodded. "Yes…why?"

"I'm Sheriff West. We found your wife's car parked at the school, but we can't seem to locate her. Do you know where she could be?"

His smile widened, showing off perfect teeth. "Well, she does work at the school. It only makes sense her car is there.

She probably had to go in for a meeting or something. And, please, call me Buzz."

For a moment, Rebecca was puzzled. "Sir, she's retired, and school isn't in session yet."

His smile dropped slightly, then he laughed, patting a palm on his forehead. "Oh, that's right. It's a new reality for us so it can be hard to keep it all straight."

While his confusion made some sense, that didn't fully address her comments, and her eyebrow crept up. "Mr. Washington, when was the last time you saw your wife?"

"Well, not since I woke up. I was napping in my chair."

Rebecca shifted her weight, looking around him to try and see inside the house. "When was—"

"Would you like to come in? If you'd like to see Amy, I'm sure she'll be home soon. I know she's retired now, but you can never tell with those school board people. They always come up with some emergency at the last minute. I'm sure you know all about that, what with being a sheriff and all."

In a show of absolute innocence, Buzz stepped back and motioned for Rebecca to come inside. She took him up on his offer.

It was a neat, if spartan, home. Two recliners sat side by side across from the television, one with a lap blanket tossed haphazardly over an armrest. A love seat was nestled under the window at the side.

Mr. Washington strode over to the closest recliner, leaving Rebecca to close the door and follow him.

"You just saw her when you woke up? When did you wake up, Mr. Washington?"

"Oh…" he eyed the clock on the wall, "about an hour ago, I think. I fell asleep in my chair watching a show."

An hour ago. He hadn't seen his wife in an hour? That didn't make any sense. They'd been at her car for longer than that. But why would he lie about something so easily disproven? His confusion didn't add up. "Did you see your wife this morning?"

"I'm sure I did." He frowned and chewed on his lip.

She could see his mind working. The question was, was it because he was trying to remember or because he was thinking of the best story to tell her?

He picked up the television guide and set it back down without opening it. "No. This morning, I didn't see her. I remember waking up and being surprised she wasn't there. The bed was made, and her car was gone. I figured she'd woken early to run errands."

Or it could've been because she'd never slept in it the night before. Maybe he'd been sleeping so heavily, he simply didn't notice she hadn't returned the previous evening. None of this was making sense. "Did your wife come home last night?"

"I'm sure she did. After I got home, I fell asleep in front of the TV, watching my shows. She usually wakes me up to join her in bed, but sometimes she can't." He chuckled and patted the arm of the chair. "This recliner is so comfortable. You understand."

She did understand. Recently, she'd been sleeping on her couch because it was easier to get up and down from, and she'd been surprised by how comfortable it was. Of course, she'd made a virtual nest of pillows to sleep on, so she wasn't lying flat. Maybe she should try a recliner instead. "Where were you last night?"

"I told you. I was sleeping in my chair."

"Yes, but you said you fell asleep in the chair after you got home. Where were you before you came home?"

"Oh! That." He scratched his temple. "Um, let's see. What day is it?"

"It's Friday, sir. August twenty-first."

He frowned and glanced around the room. "I was..." A

look of confusion knitted his eyebrows. "Are you sure it's Friday?"

"Yes, sir."

"Okay, let me think." He sat on the edge of the recliner.

Not knowing the day of the week was a bad sign. "Sir, have you had anything to eat today?"

"Huh? Oh, no. I'm waiting for Amy to get home. We always eat together."

There was something so certain in his voice, but Rebecca wasn't convinced he knew the time of day or what meal he was waiting for. "I'm going to get you a glass of water."

She excused herself to the kitchen, noticing that Buzz Washington didn't seem to even be aware of her actions. First responders were trained to check refrigerators for vital medical information. Sure enough, a small piece of paper labeled *In Case of Emergency* was stuck to the stainless steel appliance with a World's Best Teacher apple magnet.

Removing the paper, Rebecca skimmed the limited information. Amy apparently suffered from high blood pressure that she was taking medication for. If she was out there alive and unable to get her meds, Rebecca now had a new concern to deal with.

Below, in the perfect handwriting of a schoolteacher, was an ominous statement of fact. *Richard Washington receives an infusion therapy of aducanumab to remove amyloid beta every four weeks at Coastal Ridge Hospital and also takes donepezil to help with memory and judgment issues.* The note went on to list his doctors and their contact information, along with the phone numbers for their two sons, Austin and Brandon.

Observing the man's behavior and cognitive issues combined with the medical notes brought clarity to the situation. Buzz was battling dementia. But he was awfully young to have cognitive issues. Early-onset, however, would explain Amy's retirement. She'd needed to take care of her spouse.

Rebecca snapped a photo of the emergency information with her phone before returning the note to the refrigerator. Grabbing a clean glass from the cupboard, she filled it with water and took it to Buzz, who was staring absently out the front window from his recliner.

"Mr. Washington, here's some water."

He stared at the glass for what seemed like an eternity before accepting it and setting it down without taking a drink.

"Sir?" Rebecca waited until he was looking at her. "Are you aware that you have been diagnosed with early-onset Alzheimer's disease?"

Buzz waved his hand in the air as if batting at a pesky fly. "You'll have to ask Amy about that. She takes care of all our affairs."

Rebecca didn't need to remain here and ask him a list of questions to confirm what she'd already learned. The priority here was to get someone to the house to keep an eye on him. She moved to the far side of the room and quietly cued the mic on her radio.

In a near whisper, she asked Meg Darby to contact social services to have someone come out to stay with Buzz. Meg was filling in until their new dispatcher could begin. Rebecca then relayed the contact information for his two sons and asked Meg to reach out to them as well.

Rebecca couldn't leave the man in his home alone. Her training had taught her that people with dementia could sometimes have episodes of wandering, hysteria, and even violence, especially against those closest to them. They could then carry on with no recollection of their actions.

Though she needed to get back to the scene and figure out what happened to Amy Washington, for now, she would stay to watch over the missing woman's husband.

4

The sun was still fairly high in the sky as her deputies roamed the school grounds. Rebecca knew the approximate time for how long someone could survive outside in the heat with no food or water. What she didn't know was how that translated to Amy Washington with her high blood pressure and fitness level.

It'd already been fifteen and a half hours since she'd last been seen.

Rebecca wished they had the resources for a search and rescue dog. If they didn't find anything in the next half hour, she vowed to call Rhonda Lettinger and get some canine backup.

There was a well-worn path leading to the shore as well as several less distinct offshoots. The deputies had cleared twenty yards on either side of the main path by the time Rebecca returned. Almost immediately, they found the locket from Amy's coworkers.

Marjorie, who was still on scene, had identified it—though it'd been clear from the pictures the locket belonged to the woman. There was no sign of its chain, so they were hopeful it was merely a faulty clasp that dropped the locket.

When she learned of the discovery, Rebecca'd gone ahead and called in Deputy Trent Locke and Greg Abner, a sheriff's department retiree who still consulted. Greg was currently playing home base and relay in the parking lot. She'd also reached out to the state police to set up an Adult Rescue alert. The alert, along with the recent picture of Amy, had been sent to every cell phone in the area.

As Rebecca crept through the tall switchgrass, rushes, and spindly trees, casting left and right for clues, she ignored the claustrophobic similarities to what grew on Little Quell Island. Experience had taught her she needed to push through this anxiety and get to the other side.

Right now, someone needed rescue. She couldn't deal with yet another PTSD trigger, especially one she would encounter so often on this island.

Like how the sand had triggered Darian.

Dammit.

A large part of what was making this easier was Viviane walking beside her. Not close enough to crowd Rebecca as they shuffled through the drooping tendrils of rough grass stalks, but a calming presence letting her know she wasn't alone.

Which was the exact opposite of Rebecca's earlier concerns about Viviane being in the field. Further proving how out of whack her emotions were right now.

Maybe I should've taken more time off.

The yellow glow of the midafternoon sun got brighter, and Rebecca lifted her gaze. It wasn't the angle of the sun that made the difference. Ahead, the grass wasn't quite as tall as what she was walking through. After a few more steps, Rebecca saw why. There was a small trail ahead.

"Reb…I mean, Boss. I found something."

Rebecca moved over to where Viviane was squatting.

"This is the chain from the picture. Isn't it?" Viviane pointed to something in the sandy soil.

Sure enough, there was a silver rope chain, broken at the clasp. Although Rebecca was keeping an open mind about how the chain could've become separated from the locket, one theory was that it had been ripped loose and thrown.

"That's the one. Take some pictures and call it in." Out of reflex, Rebecca spoke softer, and her hand drifted to her holster. The broken necklace was only a tiny sign of violence but enough to set her nerves afire.

Viviane's gaze followed the movement. "Better safe than sorry?"

Rebecca nodded, her eyes inspecting every swaying blade, reed, and seed head. "This is a perfect place to stage an ambush. Don't get caught unaware."

"Frost, Locke, we've got the chain." Viviane mimicked Rebecca, keeping her voice low as she spoke into her mic. The woman who'd worked dispatch for so long knew how dangerous loud communication over their radios could be.

As Rebecca peered at the scene around her, Viviane freed her own weapon but didn't draw it.

"There." Rebecca pointed to a spatter of blood. Dried, it was a dusky brown and blended with the variegation of the plants. But she knew blood when she saw it. Now that she'd seen one spatter, her eyes jumped to another, and the next.

These weren't drips. They were castoffs, flung here from somewhere nearby. The trail pattern of the blood droplets directed her to their point of origin.

Stepping sideways, she twisted her head until the separate splatters made a solid arcing line. Combining the trajectory with the patterns of the drops themselves, she carefully moved to their point of origin, following the trail like a rainbow leading her to the pot of gold at the end.

A flash of white caught her eye.

Moving forward, one steady step at a time, she minimized the sound her feet made on the dry grass until she was just a foot from the patch of white.

Spreading the tall grass apart with her free hand, Rebecca found Amy Washington.

Her white blouse was twisted and bunched on her chest, its collar stained with red from the long gash across her throat. She was slumped on her side, lying in a pool of dried blood. Her cloudy eyes stared sightlessly, her mouth hanging open. Insects, attracted by the smell of death, crawled over her face.

"Miss Washington!" Viviane bolted up beside Rebecca and tried to rush to her old teacher.

Rebecca stopped her short. "We can't do anything for her now. She's gone." Holding her deputy in place, she checked the ground that had been trampled, hoping no evidence had been lost in the rookie's unthinking reaction. "Watch where you're walking."

Viviane gulped, swallowing a cry, and nodded. "We need to preserve the crime scene so we can figure out what happened and who did this to her."

"That's right. Stay right there for now and start taking pictures of the scene, so we'll have everything on record before we approach. Once you're done, head back the way we came and keep taking pictures 'til you get to the parking lot."

Rebecca slipped into the role of teacher and friend. There was no reason to make Viviane stand over Amy's dead body. Especially not on her first case. Her bias was already starting to show. Rebecca couldn't risk it contaminating a crime scene.

She let go of her deputy and raised her radio to her lips.

"We found her. Abner, can you call Dr. Flynn and forensics? Frost and Locke, get the tape so we can secure the site. Over."

"Copy."

Rebecca stood for a moment, listening to the wind brush through the coastal grasses.

Only hours before, Amy Washington had been preparing to start a new chapter of her life. Rebecca tried to imagine Amy walking down to the beach last night, with stars twinkling overhead. Perhaps the teacher—after being surrounded by so many people feting her—had wanted a moment to herself to reflect.

Staring into the woman's sightless eyes, Rebecca mourned the loss of a community pillar who seemed to be loved and respected by all who knew her.

5

S tanding in the copse of trees and grasses, Rebecca surveyed the scene.

This was Viviane's first time seeing a murder victim, and it'd been someone she knew and cared about. While there'd been plenty of dry heaving, Viviane had managed not to puke on the crime scene. Rebecca wanted to keep it that way.

Let the rookie have something else to focus on other than her dead teacher while she deals with the aftereffects of her first murder scene.

It was expected for a first-timer to lose their lunch, and Viviane always hated the "icky stuff" that came with the job. She'd actually managed it surprisingly well.

Darian would've had a blast giving her a ribbing about the dry heaves. Probably would've compared her to Hoyt. Though he'd have hated this scene with all the sand and blood.

The random thought floated through Rebecca's mind as she shifted on the balls of her feet to take another picture from a different angle.

Or maybe he would've appreciated it as a way to help him get over his trigger. It could've been just the thing he needed to work past that part of his PTSD that kept him from enjoying time at the beach with his wife and child.

Not that he would ever be able to do that now.

Grief blanketed her again as she thought about Darian and the baby rattle she'd tucked against the man's headstone earlier that day.

That was this morning. Feels like a lifetime ago...

Deputy Darian Hudson would never be able to recover from his PTSD now. He'd worked hard to get past sand being a trigger so he could accommodate his wife's love of picnics at the beach.

The photo Rebecca was trying to line up went blurry as tears wet her eyes. She had to take a moment to wipe them with the back of her wrist while holding the camera.

"Pollen is starting early this year." Hoyt moved up behind her as he noisily pushed his way through the rushes. "It's probably due to the hurricane and the nightly rains we always get this time of year. In a week, this whole area will look like a fairy village with all the seeds and pollen floating in the air. Ya know, I've always wondered if the stories about fairies were actually people seeing dragonflies in the dusk. It makes sense if you think about it."

"Dragonflies?" Rebecca didn't look at her deputy and tried to focus her mind on the scene in front of her, instead of wallowing in what might have been.

"Yeah. You ever see them up close? When they're perched on the side of something, they look a little bit like a tiny person with wings. Add in some thick pollen and blurry eyes, a person could easily mistake them for a fairy."

It was a whimsical image, and Rebecca smiled. "That's a nice thought."

"Tape's all up. Bailey and forensics are on their way. You want me to finish up the pictures? I know squatting down like that has got to be playing hell on your ribs and the stitches in your side."

"Getting down here was the hard part. I may as well finish before I try to stand up again." Rebecca shifted to the side again. Her knees were splayed wide, so they didn't touch her torso at all. The pose probably looked obscene, and it was hell on her ankles, but she was doing a damn sight better than the murdered woman in front of her. "Why would someone drag someone into the brush and slit her throat?"

"No idea. My boys hated school, but they still loved Miss Washington. She was one of the favorites for everyone." Hoyt leaned forward, looming over Rebecca where she was crouched. "You done with the pictures yet? I think there's something in her pocket."

"Not quite. And I noticed that too. Those blouse pockets aren't really meant to hold anything. I don't even understand why they still put them there right on the breast. It's ridiculous."

"Most things about women's clothing are," Hoyt grumbled, and she would've laughed if she wasn't afraid of doing further damage to her cracked ribs. "Angie's always complaining about pockets and ends up buying a ton of purses because none of her pockets are usable."

"If she ever figures out the pocket thing, let me know." Rebecca shifted her weight back onto her heels and flipped through the pictures to make sure she'd gotten everything.

"She already did. I told you, she has to buy a ton of bags because of the useless pockets. The manufacturers make you buy more things to do a simple job."

That made a sadistic and capitalistic kind of sense. She appreciated her senior deputy's attempts to distract her from her grief over Darian.

Hoping to give him a silent nod of appreciation, she looked up, but he glanced away. His desire to obliquely comfort her was so fitting with his character that she couldn't help but smile at his back while he pretended to inspect the crime scene around them. He'd obviously guessed she was thinking about Darian again.

He probably was too.

"We're clear to approach the body now. Just stay out of the blood."

"Not my first crime scene, Sheriff." Hoyt grinned and shook his head while bending over the body. With a gloved hand, he carefully removed the item tucked into the breast pocket of the white blouse.

"But it *is* Darby's, so we need to get into the habit of double-checking everything and saying the basics out loud. I don't want a deputy who doesn't know how to work a crime scene properly."

They both knew she meant *another* deputy, as Locke still wasn't allowed to get too close to anything that could be evidence.

His training had been rushed, his instructors possibly paid off, so he needed to be reeducated. Despite having worked on the force for years, he was still green when it came to such things. Wallace, she'd finally figured out, had never let him handle evidence either. Now it was up to her to instill the proper techniques in him so he could be a viable part of their team.

Or fire his ass.

Which was why Locke walked through the grass with Greg Abner at his side, watching his every move. The semi-retired deputy had volunteered for the job. After it came to light that most of Locke's on-the-job issues were due to poor training, Greg had considered it his responsibility as the "old guard" to help correct the next generation of deputies. As he'd instructed Darian and Hoyt, that worked well for Rebecca.

They really couldn't afford another poorly trained officer in their ranks. Viviane was supposed to be their fourth deputy. Instead, she'd ended up replacing Darian, which left them at their original number and below the manpower they really needed.

Rebecca would have to put out a hiring notice for a new deputy.

It was like an uphill battle in the sand, fighting to gain ground only to end up slightly worse off.

Darian was supposed to be showing Viviane the ropes.

Rebecca sighed. It was useless to pretend she could think of anything else. "I wish Hudson were here."

"That's a bit morbid. We don't need another corpse at the scene, Boss."

Rebecca stared at Hoyt, horrified.

He chuckled sadly. "Darian would've thought that was funny."

She realized he was right and smiled. Darian had never fully relaxed around her, not like he did around Hoyt, but she'd overheard their back-and-forth plenty of times and knew the ex-soldier had a dark sense of humor.

"I miss him too. I tried calling him earlier when you said to call in searchers. Lilian answered, and I realized what I'd done. So did she, before I could even come up with some excuse." Hoyt chuckled again, and there was a dark tinge to it. "She told me to stop being a slacker and do the job myself. It's not the same without him."

As bad as it was for Rebecca, she knew it was worse for Hoyt. Not only had they been closer and known each other longer, Darian was the second friend Hoyt had lost this summer. The third, if she counted Rebecca Munroe, who'd been murdered by her jealous husband then dressed up like a mermaid. And they were now standing over the body of someone who'd been a teacher to both his sons.

She studied Hoyt...really looked at him for the first time that day.

His wrinkles weren't the only new thing. He'd already had a few grays showing in his dark hair when they'd met, but now there were streaks of it. Pain showed in his eyes with every calculated movement. Maybe it was the stress of working so many hours, but she thought it was more likely his heavy heart weighing him down.

In the days that'd followed her parents' murders, Rebecca had also been slow, and every movement felt like she'd been fighting her way through chilled molasses. And that'd been when she was still in her twenties. Hoyt was in his fifties. This couldn't be easy for him.

"Nothing will ever be the same again. We have to find a new way to be." Rebecca took a slow, deep breath and stood. She wobbled for a moment as her lungs struggled against the tight grip her ribs had on them.

Hoyt reached out and caught her by the upper arm, steadying her. "You sure you're ready to be out here? Working, I mean."

"It's better than sitting alone on my couch all day with nothing but my thoughts."

Hoyt grimaced and nodded. "I hate getting sidelined too. Just...don't push it too hard, okay?"

"You mean like you did after your surgery?" She smirked.

"Exactly. Learn from an old man. Don't do the stupid shit I do."

"Like pick up a piece of evidence, then stand there holding it while chatting about random things?" Rebecca pointed at the folded paper in his gloved hand.

He glanced down. "Touché. Though, maybe I was waiting on you to take pictures while I unfold it."

"Sure." Rebecca took rapid-fire pictures as he straightened out the paper, focusing on how it was splattered in blood. Her eyebrow quirked in response to the writing. "'Please meet me after school.'" She frowned. "I was just at the Washington house, and this handwriting is nearly identical to what I saw on their fridge. Here." Rebecca found the photo saved to her phone and held it up for Hoyt.

"Huh. Do we think she asked someone to meet her here? After her party?" He looked as confused as she felt.

"Who knows? Why wouldn't it say, 'after my party'? I think the more important question is if the person who received the note could've killed her." The scrap of paper had been torn off a larger piece. It was yellowed with age and Rebecca wondered if the killer had held on to it for some reason.

"No way that was in her pocket when her throat was slit. There's no blood on that pocket."

Rebecca nodded. "It looks like blood was dripped on the paper before it was planted on her. So what's the significance?"

It was late August, and school wouldn't start until Monday. Still, Rebecca guessed the teacher had asked numerous students over the years to meet her after school. But Amy had retired in May. This didn't make any sense.

"A romantic tryst? Maybe her husband?" Hoyt frowned at the words on the scrap of yellowing paper as if they'd answer him.

Buzz Washington's dementia might have induced Amy to leave him notes so he'd remember basic tasks. But the phrasing of the note didn't feel like what a woman would say to her husband, even one with memory issues.

Considering that the note appeared old, maybe there was a personal story to it that only the victim and killer knew.

6

The walls were closing in. I counted my steps as I paced the length of my bedroom. Each time I got the same number, but I could swear the room felt smaller with every circuit. It was like a tiny rabbit cage, one that hadn't been cleaned in months and only had more hay tossed down on top of the old.

Stretching and flexing my fingers, I squeezed them into tight fists again and again. Something had to give. It should've already. I'd killed the Washington hag. I should've felt better. Things should've gotten clearer, the situation easier to deal with. Instead, I felt worse.

My gaze came to rest on her smiling face. "I took from you what you took from me. We're even."

I had no regrets. That woman got what she deserved. Maybe a little less than she deserved. She'd gone quick and easy. Not slowly, as I'd fantasized.

I'd spent a long time obsessing over her. When I saw her, I simply couldn't hold back any longer. Amy Washington had trashed my future, my life. Now that she was gone, things were supposed to be better.

"When you remove the infection, the wound is supposed to start healing. So why doesn't it feel any better?" My head felt like it was going to explode from all the pressure building up in it.

I snatched up one of the bottles of beer sitting on the nightstand. I shook it, but nothing sloshed, so I launched it at Amy's picture tacked to the wall. Instead of breaking, the container merely bounced off her smiling face and fell harmlessly onto the floor.

I checked for another bottle. One of these had to have something left. My life couldn't be that sad and messed up.

"This is all your fault, ya know. Now everything's an even bigger mess. No matter how much I try to clean it up and fix things." I threw the third bottle I tested against the wall. The glass shattered and mixed with the kitty litter that'd gotten knocked from the box and was spread across the floor.

My wife stared at me with wide eyes but didn't say a word. Her guilt must've finally stilled her tongue. She never had anything good to say to me, always criticizing everything I did. Nothing was ever good enough for that bitch.

"None of this is my fault, and yet I'm the one who always has to clean up the mess. The mess you made. The mess *she* made. The mess my life became all because of bitches like you who stand in the way of what's rightfully mine!"

Finally, one of the bottles gave a reassuring slosh, and I snatched it up. There were only two swallows left, but it was enough to wet my whistle.

"You bitches don't know what you want. You tell me you want me and then you act like you don't. Well, I'm done with people jerking me around. I'm taking my life back, and no one's going to stand in my way. Especially not whores like you and Amy Washington."

I tossed the bottle onto the stack of empties. "Do you think you could at least clean up around here? You're completely useless. I swear, you're only good for one thing, and even that you're not very good at."

I smirked and slapped her thigh. It jiggled softly, enticingly, as she continued to stare at me.

Her phone rang. It was somewhere mixed in with the pile of bottles that had spilled. She never even looked at it.

Just as I thought. Women were drawn to a man who was confident and willing to do whatever it took to get what he wanted. Men knew what women wanted, but we just had to remind them that we knew best. Some of them needed more convincing.

Before I could do anything about the look she was giving me, the house phone started ringing right as her cell phone stopped.

Dammit. I knew I should've gotten rid of that damn thing.

Who even used a landline anymore? I waited it out until the machine finally picked up.

"Hey, Crystal, it's Chloe from work. You've missed your last three shifts. This isn't like you, and I'm starting to get worried. You need to call me, or I'm going to have to write you up."

"There's no rest for the wicked." I kicked the useless hag, who wouldn't even get out of bed to save her job. She jiggled again. Red-flecked foam bubbled out of her mouth and spilled over her lips. For some reason, that made me smile. Even though it was yet another mess I'd have to deal with.

I'd already dumped kitty litter over her and the floor around her to soak up the mess that'd poured out of her slit throat after our last fight. She kept staring at me, her once-brown eyes glazed gray with judgmental anger. And her boss, that nag, just kept talking with that nasally whine older women seemed to develop.

Reaching over, I picked up the receiver. "Hey, this is Crystal's husband. I can't believe she didn't call you. Her mom was in an accident Monday evening. Crystal had to get a last-minute flight out there to act as her medical proxy as next of kin."

I listened to her boss ramble on as I rolled my eyes at my wife.

"Yeah, she was in such a rush she left her cell phone here. She's up in Nova Scotia with our son and super busy making arrangements. I'll let her know she needs to call you to get FMLA set up."

Finally convinced, the woman agreed to hold off on the write-up until she heard back from my wife. After she hung up, I threw the phone across the room, making sure it wouldn't interrupt us again.

My house was finally a quiet retreat. I was loath to leave it. But there was work to be done if I was going to make my life into what it should've been. Amy Washington hadn't been the only one to screw it up, and it was time to teach the others they couldn't look down on me anymore.

7

A my Washington's temporary resting place was anything but peaceful as Rebecca and numerous technicians busied themselves with the tasks at hand.

Bailey finished tucking Amy into a body bag and motioned for her assistants to take it away. "I do love the summers, but I have to admit, I can't wait for the fall when all these bugs start to die. Working in the cold sucks, but at least I don't have to worry about them."

"Maybe it'll get cold enough that people'll stop killing each other?" Rebecca glanced up from the notes she'd been taking.

According to the body temperature Bailey obtained, Amy had been killed shortly after she'd left her retirement party. The sad irony of that had not been lost on either woman. She'd died before she could enjoy her first fall without being stuck in school all day.

"I don't think it can get that cold. At least, not 'til it reaches perfect zero and all life stops moving." Bailey twisted to stretch her back and legs. "So long as people can move, they'll find a way to kill each other or themselves. Now that I think about it, the out-of-state drivers will probably kill themselves on the ice."

"That's a reassuring thought." Rebecca reached down to help Bailey get to her feet, then winced as the movement, once again, pulled on her ribs.

"I can make it up. Don't worry. You need to be careful. Broken bones are no joke." Bailey took her time inching up and backing out from under the gnarled branches of a scrubby tree overhanging Mrs. Washington's remains.

There were lights set up all around them despite the present daylight. Additional lighting was essential as the techs worked to find and bag even the smallest bit of evidence. Rebecca stepped aside so the M.E. wasn't trying to find a path in her shadow.

"Ah, much better. Thank you. I don't want to think about how tricky it must've been for you to get low to the ground beneath that tree and examine the scene, not able to lean forward and all."

Rebecca didn't respond and instead looked down at her notes.

"West."

"Hmm?" She pretended to flip through her pages, looking for something.

"You've been avoiding leaning forward, haven't you?" Bailey moved closer. "A knitting bone can break again. That'll set you back weeks in your recovery. And with the type of rib fractures you sustained, you're running the risk of puncturing something if you screw this up."

"I'm being as careful as I can."

Bailey touched her arm. "Take a deep breath for me."

"Bailey, I'm fine. I—"

"Don't make me poke you. I will."

Rebecca pulled back slightly at the threat. She sometimes forgot that Bailey was a full-fledged doctor and not only the medical examiner. Keeping her shoulders squared, she took a slow, deep breath. "I've been doing my exercises."

Bailey nodded, her gaze jumping from Rebecca's face to her chest as it slowly expanded. "Any coughing?"

The M.E. was keeping her voice down and being as discreet as possible, which Rebecca appreciated. She'd already caught several people staring at her—the sheriff who was nearly beaten to death and lost a man on an operation gone wrong. While she hadn't heard anything yet, she knew people had to be talking.

"Not since the first week."

"That's good. If you develop a cough…" Bailey trailed off, but her pointed look said everything.

Besides being a doctor and M.E., Bailey was also a mother to five kids. She had the "mom look" down pat, and Rebecca wasn't going to push her luck. "I'll go to the ER immediately. I promise." She held up her hand in the Girl Scout sign, pinky and thumb tucked, with the middle three fingers pointing up.

"Good. I'm not sure Frost can handle you being out for another two weeks. The man's running on fumes."

Guilt filled Rebecca. It was more motivating than even the threat of getting poked in her broken bones. "I have leaned forward, but I stop as soon as I realize what I'm doing. I'm keeping my back straight and using my legs more than ever. I really don't want to set back my progress."

Bailey studied her face, clearly searching for any hint of lies or deception. "Wearing a vest will help with that, if you can handle the weight."

That sounded like a brilliant idea to Rebecca. The bullet-proof vests did force the wearer to keep their back straight and shoulders squared, or it would dig in. "I'll give that a shot. Thank you. Can we talk about our victim now?"

"Sure, but let's walk while we talk."

Rebecca turned on her heel, aware that Bailey was still

watching how she moved as they made their way through the grass toward the parking lot. "Did you find anything else useful to us?"

"Not much more than what it appeared to be at first glance. Middle-aged woman was grabbed forcefully. That's what left that pattern of bruises on her arm. Her throat was sliced, cutting deep enough to hit the larynx. Thankfully, she bled out before she could drown as the blood filled her lungs."

As they emerged from the dune grasses and neared the parking lot of the school, she motioned to her people, who were barely in view, to begin loading up Mrs. Washington.

"I can't be certain until I get her back and do a full autopsy, but the cause of death looks pretty cut-and-dried. We'll do the full workup. It looks like she's got something under her nails. And with the way her clothing is twisted, I'm going to check for sexual assault and body fluids as well. If nothing else, we might get some sweat from the unsub. If anything unusual crops up, I'll let you know."

"I'll be looking forward to your call, as always." Rebecca stepped down onto the asphalt.

They went their separate ways from there, Bailey toward her van and Rebecca to where the cruisers were parked together.

"Viviane, Hoyt, what did you find out?"

The two deputies looked over at her arrival, Viviane from the woman she was speaking with and Hoyt from the laptop in his cruiser.

"Nothing obvious on the camera." Hoyt climbed out of the cruiser as she walked up. "I can take it back to the station and get plates and run them." The wrinkles on his face were even deeper now, and his eyes had dark bags under them.

"Don't worry about that. Do you know Buzz Washington?"

"Yeah. You want me to go do the notification?"

"Yeah, if you're up for it. Did you know anything about him having Alzheimer's?"

"Mr. Washington? No. What makes you suspect that?"

"Not really a suspicion. He was exhibiting many of the signs when I was there. I also found information on the fridge for first responders. Remember that picture of Mrs. Washington's handwriting I showed you? That's what the note was about. It clearly states he's being treated for early-onset."

"Damn." Hoyt pressed the heel of his hand into his eye. "I had no idea. Hard to keep a secret like that on this island. Must've been important to them to keep that under wraps."

Rebecca nodded. "I'm not saying I suspect the man, but he was at the scene with his wife last night, so he had opportunity. The cryptic note left on her body appears to be an invitation from her to someone. And there are documented cases of people with dementia harming the people closest to them." She rubbed the back of her neck. "Go see him and tell me if you think he's capable of something like this, if he wasn't in his right mind."

"Will do." He started to climb back into the cruiser, but she stopped him.

"If he has any lucid moments, see if he can tell you what he did when he left the party. One account has him walking home alone. Her car was still in the parking lot, and given the time of death and witness statements, it's likely been here all night. Once that's done, call it a day. It's just shy of five, and you've been working since eight this morning."

"Yeah, Boss." Hoyt saluted her, pulled the door shut, and drove off, not giving her a moment to second-guess her decision.

"Sheriff." Viviane indicated the woman before her using

her note-taking pen. "This is Pamela Radcliffe. She's the one who helped organize the retirement party last night."

The woman's eyeliner was smeared, and her reddened eyes were surrounded by blotchy skin where she'd been scrubbing away tears. "I also put the gift basket together. Marjorie said that might have something to do with what happened?"

"We're not ruling anything out at this point. We do know she was wearing the necklace."

Fresh tears welled up in Pamela's brown eyes. "She...she said she loved it and was going to wear it all the time. She was going to tease any former students she ran into and show them what they'd done to her, the 'before' and 'after' photos. The gray hair and wrinkles and...Amy was quite a looker when she was younger. Still pretty now, of course." She gulped. "Or she was."

The woman dissolved into another bout of tears. There was no way she was going to be able to withstand a full interview.

"Can you look at something and tell me if it looks familiar?"

"Sure. Of course. I'll do anything I can to help."

Rebecca motioned to Viviane, who pulled the evidence box from her cruiser. There weren't many bags in it, and she quickly pulled out the one Rebecca wanted.

"Can you tell me anything about this note?"

When Viviane held up the blood-stained scrap, Pamela gasped and clapped her hand over her mouth. She didn't say anything but shook her head. Viviane dropped the bag back into the box and closed it out of sight.

"We're sorry you had to see that, Ms. Radcliffe. But since we found it on her, we had to ask."

She nodded, gulping convulsively. "I understand."

"Can you think of anyone who she might've been meeting?"

Pamela shook her head. "No. Sorry. I don't know who…" Her eyes unfocused for a moment.

"Did you think of something? A connection to Amy?"

"Well, not a tie, really. But…it is an invitation. It's just a rumor, though."

"Rumors tend to be based on a version of the truth." Rebecca nodded gently, hoping to ease the woman into speaking.

"I'm not sure this one does. There was a rumor. It keeps coming back. It's stupid, though. And I've never seen anything that supports it." She was clearly uneasy about sharing. "Amy's not the kind of woman I ever thought would be unfaithful to her husband. She loved Buzz. But people have said she had something, some kind of relationship beyond professional, with the janitor. Sebastian Drysdale." Her words came out in a rush as she shook her head in denial. "I never believed them."

Rebecca nodded but wrote it all down anyway. A romantic tryst would explain why Amy hadn't gone home with her husband and had, instead, slipped off into the nominal privacy of the field with such tall grasses.

"Was Mr. Drysdale present at Mrs. Washington's retirement party?"

"Oh, no. They were friends, but it was just for teachers and a few admin. And Buzz, of course."

"One last thing, then we'll let you go home. Do you have any pictures from the retirement party?"

"I do." Pamela started to dig her phone out of her purse, then frowned. "Can I email them to you once I get home? There's a lot of them, and data packages are so expensive on phones. Teachers don't get paid a lot, you know."

Rebecca weighed extra data charges against the unexpected death of a friend and coworker, briefly wondering about Pamela Radcliffe's priorities. Nonetheless, shock did strange things to people.

"I totally understand. And emailing them will be fine." She reached into her pocket and passed over a business card. "If you could get those to us ASAP, that would be great."

"Yeah. I can do it tonight."

"Tonight would be very helpful. And thank you for talking to us."

Pamela clutched the business card and nodded sporadically as she turned and walked away.

"That was rough." Viviane blew out her breath and leaned against her SUV, resting her head on her forearms.

"This part gets a tiny bit easier." Rebecca patted her back. "We also need to go ahead and call off the missing persons alert."

Viviane's head popped up as she gave a sassy wink. "I already did that."

"Great. That was a test. There's another part that gets easier with time. Or at least, it will when a new rookie gets hired on."

Viviane narrowed her eyes at Rebecca, who was grinning like a Cheshire cat. "What part?"

"The part where the newest rookie has to sit at the scene all night 'til the techs are done."

Viviane wilted against the side of the cruiser and sighed. But she offered a quick smile. "Maybe I can learn something from the techs while they're working."

It wasn't Viviane's nature to see the negative side of a situation.

Rebecca just hoped that becoming a law enforcement officer never changed that.

8

Hoyt raised his hand to knock on the door, but paused as a fierce yawn took over his body. Rebecca had been right. He'd been in the office at eight that morning. That was after he'd left the office at three a.m. Not that it mattered much. He'd been having a rough time sleeping anyway.

Now that Rebecca was back at work, he hoped it would get better. At the very least, the office wouldn't sound so damn empty when he walked in every morning. Maybe tonight he could get a decent amount of sleep. Or at least more than four hours of nothing but nightmares.

He knocked on the door and waited. It took a few minutes and another knock before Buzz Washington came to the door.

The man was disheveled, looking as if he'd just woken up, with his shirt twisted and wrinkled and his hair a mess and standing up in back. "Can I help you, Officer?"

Taking his hat from his head, Hoyt held it at his waist. "Mr. Washington, I'm not sure if you remember me. I'm Deputy Frost. And I have news about your wife."

"Amy? Oh, she's not in right now. Is something wrong?"

His eyes held a hint of worry in them, but a smile was trying to pull up the corners of the confused man's lips.

Hoyt frowned at the question. Even though Rebecca had briefed him on Mr. Washington's dementia, it was disheartening to witness in person. Here he was, about to notify this man that his wife had been murdered, and he wasn't sure if Buzz would comprehend the news.

What he couldn't decide was if that was a blessing or a curse. Would Lilian be better off forgetting that Darian was dead and never coming home to her and Mallory again?

Mentally shrugging off the philosophical thoughts, he focused on the task at hand. He smiled weakly in the doorway. "May I come in?"

"Oh, of course. Come in. Have a seat. Amy isn't home now but should be soon. I think she went out to get groceries." Buzz turned and made his way to a chair covered with a lap blanket. It was hard to see the rest of the room, as there were no lights on, just the TV casting a flickering glow.

With one foot in the door, Hoyt froze. "Um, sir, Amy isn't at the store."

"Oh? Is she at another PTA meeting? Don't tell me she got a ticket." Buzz sat in his recliner and pulled the blanket over his legs.

Hoyt walked into the house, closed the door behind him, and glanced around. The place was spotless, as far as he could tell in the dim light.

He hated this part of his job more than any other, and one thing he learned long ago was that it was better to rip off the bandage and get straight to the point. "Sir, I regret to inform you that we found your wife's body earlier today."

"Her...body?" Buzz went pale, and his hands started shaking where he clutched his blanket. "Amy is dead?"

"Yes, sir. I'm very sorry."

"That can't be right. She was fine when I last saw her."

"And when was that, sir?"

"Oh…I'm not sure." He scratched his temple and actually chuckled. "Do you need to talk to her? She should be home soon."

Death notifications were never easy. But talking to someone who simply couldn't grasp the reality of the news was like punching that person over and over. Except Buzz Washington wasn't even crying. His grasp of the information was so fleeting, he didn't have time to register his own grief.

Hoyt didn't understand how Amy and Buzz had kept his condition secret from everyone on the island. He was at a loss with how to proceed. His wife would've embraced the man and known all the right things to say. Angie was stronger than him in so many ways.

Before he could decide on a course of action, a car pulled up to the house.

Buzz didn't seem to notice, even though he was sitting by the window. As the woman exited her car and made her way to the door, Hoyt opened the door to greet her.

Surprised by the sudden presence of a deputy on the threshold, the woman startled. She sized up Hoyt's uniform before producing her state ID. "Is this the home of Richard Washington? I'm Lenora Hatterly from Coastal Ridge Social Services. Our office received a call from your dispatcher. May I come in?"

Hoyt stood to one side. "Mr. Washington, this is Lenora."

"I don't know anyone by that name. Do you work with Amy?"

The social worker's red hair was loosely woven into a long braid that ran down her back. Hoyt didn't want to hazard a guess at her age, but her freckled face made her look about fifteen.

Lenora turned on a table lamp, then moved to Buzz's chair and crouched beside him. "No, sir. I'm here to visit with you." She patted his arm. "We've contacted your sons. They're coming to see you. Won't that be nice? But until they get here, I'm going to stay with you."

Hoyt noted she didn't pose it as a question. The man couldn't be left alone and would be given no choice in the matter.

He moved to stand in front of Buzz's chair. When the man looked up at him, Hoyt tried again. "Sir, as I said earlier, I regret to inform you that we found your wife's body. She's dead, sir."

An array of emotions played across Buzz's face, contorting his features as he scanned the room. "Amy? She can't be dead. She was just here."

Hoyt and the social worker exchanged a knowing glance, confirming the inaccuracy of his claim.

The person seated before Hoyt looked more like an eighty-year-old man than someone only a few years older than he was. He doubted he'd get any useful information out of him.

As to Rebecca's question about aggression, he just couldn't see it. But he did have an idea about his alibi.

"Sir, I was wondering if you'd mind if I snapped a picture of you with my phone." If Buzz Washington was wearing the same clothes he'd been wearing the night of the party, then the complete lack of blood and mud anywhere would be a pretty clear indicator that he hadn't been the one to take Amy's life.

Lenora moved out of the way so she wouldn't be in any of the photos.

Technically, Hoyt didn't need the man's permission, but he felt better asking just the same. When Buzz didn't protest, he snapped several photos, some zoomed in on his pant cuffs and shirt and some of his full body. Comparing the images to photos of the couple at the party would either exonerate Buzz in his wife's death or keep him as a suspect.

As Hoyt finished up the mini-photo shoot, the social worker returned from the kitchen with a sandwich and a glass of water.

Buzz brightened at her arrival and began nibbling on the sandwich as he stared at the television.

Hoyt hadn't known Amy Washington personally, but repeatedly informing Buzz of the death was like Amy dying over and over, except only Hoyt was affected by the information. He didn't think it was possible for his heart to feel any more shattered.

If Buzz Washington didn't kill his wife, that meant the killer was on the loose. And if he'd kill someone as kind as Amy, then no one on the island was safe.

9

"Are you not hungry, dear?" Angie Frost stood in the doorway to the dining room, concern etched into her features.

Hoyt jerked his head up to stare at his wife. She'd set a plate of dinner aside to warm in the oven, and he'd been slowly picking away at it. He glanced down at the plate and noticed he hadn't managed to eat more than a few bites in the last fifteen minutes.

"I am. I'm just..." He couldn't find the words to continue as dementia's grip on Buzz Washington replayed in his mind. "I love you. You know that. Right?"

Angie frowned and sat across from him at the table. She was always willing to listen while he unburdened himself. Even when he dragged his sorry butt home in the wee hours of the morning, his wife was always waiting for him.

"I know you do. But you don't love me so much you'd pass up on my shepherd's pie without a good reason." Reaching forward, she took his hand. "What happened, dear?"

"Amy Washington was killed. It appears it happened last

night. We found her body today. I had to tell Buzz about it just a little bit ago."

Angie gasped, and her hold on his hand tightened. "Oh, that's terrible. That poor, sweet man. Weren't he and Amy going to be traveling and such now that she'd retired?"

"I'm not so sure." Hoyt scooped up a bit of food and mindlessly put it in his mouth.

"What makes you think that's not true?"

"Were you aware that Buzz Washington has dementia?" Giving up on the food, he pushed the plate away.

"Oh no." Angie sniffed and used a napkin as a tissue. "I had no idea. Though, since he retired, I haven't really seen him around the island much. I just thought he was busy living his best life in retirement."

"Both Rebecca and I visited with him today. He definitely has dementia and is even receiving treatment for it. While I was over there giving him the news of Amy's death, a social worker showed up."

"That's good news. He shouldn't be alone. Without Amy, his whole routine will be broken. She probably took care of all the little things to try to cover up…" A sob racked Angie's body.

Even Angie was taking the news hard. She was always stronger than him in these situations, not that she wasn't empathetic. But she always helped Hoyt see things clearly. Like Amy must've been doing for Buzz. And now she was gone.

He squeezed his wife's hand as she dabbed at her tears. "Are you okay?"

She cleared her throat and nodded, composing herself. "Yes. I was just overwhelmed by the tragedy of it all. Every day, I face the reality that you might not come home to me. But I've never dared to entertain a thought that you might be here…but not really *here*. I can't imagine how horrible it would be if you didn't know who I was."

"I had to tell him more than once."

"Oh, honey. That must've been awful."

Hoyt intertwined his fingers with his wife's, holding her hand tight. Turning his head, he saw the pictures of their sons. From babies to adults, Angie had displayed their lives on the walls of their home.

"We should tell the boys. She was their favorite teacher."

"Later." Angie stood and shifted around the table, pushing him back so she could sit in his lap.

Hoyt closed his eyes, wrapped his arms around her, and rested his face on her chest. Letting her hold him, absorbing her warmth, his scattered thoughts stopped swarming, and he was finally able to catch them.

"I hate this shit, Angie. I hate it."

"I know you do, love. I know." Her fingers soothed through his hair and pulled him close.

With her gestures, Hoyt knew his wife understood this was more than just about a death notification. This was about life's curveballs and the future, which was never guaranteed.

Her words, as always, reminded him of the reason he'd become a deputy. "You do the best job you can, making sure the people who do these horrific things don't get the chance to do it again."

Sighing, he finally released the tension in his shoulders he hadn't even realized he'd been holding. But just as quickly, it returned. His arms tightened around his wife's waist as she curled herself over him.

"Is this about Darian?" Her soft question so close to his ear startled him.

"It's always about Darian. And Rebecca. And Alden. I'm worried. About the ones they've left behind. How we're supposed to rebuild and move on after losing so much. About what would've happened if that had been me who'd been mortally wounded."

"Well, for starters, you wouldn't have been buried in Arlington." Angie's nails lightly scratched over his scalp as he laughed.

"I'm being serious."

Though West hadn't left them behind, when she'd pushed the boat away, they'd left *her* behind. That wasn't how it had felt at the time. It felt like she was both abandoning them and sacrificing herself for them simultaneously. He just couldn't figure out how to make that make sense.

"So am I." She pulled his head back and looked down into his eyes. She was as serious as he'd ever seen her. "You wouldn't have been buried in Arlington. You'd have been buried here. The house would be spotless, because I clean when I'm emotional. Darian and Lilian would've been here every day, just as we've done for Lilian and Mallory. And I'd have gotten rip-roaring drunk at your wake, the likes of which you will never see this side of Heaven."

She spoke so simply, so matter-of-factly, he was nearly entranced by her calm demeanor. And oddly a little hurt.

"You've thought about this."

"Every day since you first put that badge on. Every night when you don't come home. Every time the phone rings when you're not here. Every time Wallace knocked on the door and I couldn't see you."

A lump of pain and understanding filled Hoyt's throat, nearly choking him.

He shook his head, rubbing his face against her soft shirt. "I can't stop worrying. When we left Rebecca on the island that night, when she pushed us away, I was certain I'd never see her alive again. Since then, it's like I'm always out of breath. Always a step behind, a moment too slow. Because I don't know what the next moment will bring."

She kissed his cheek. "Oh, honey."

He hung his head. "When I step into the bullpen, I can feel the emptiness. I thought it would be better today, with the boss coming back. But when I saw her, all I felt was fear. There she was, up and walking, and what if she pushes us away again, puts herself in the line of fire to keep us safe again?"

"This is what all the spouses of all the heroes go through every day."

"How do you do it? I've only been dealing with it for two weeks, and I'm about to go insane."

"Easy. I'm stronger than you." She gave him an extra squeeze and laughed with him.

"God knows that's the truth." He pulled away so he could gaze into her smiling eyes.

"What about Mallory? It was hard enough for us raising our boys together. How much harder is it going to be for Lilian to raise Mallory on her own?"

"It's going to be challenging. But she has good friends, close family, and the determination she needs to keep moving forward. She'll make Darian proud. I'm sure of it."

Hoyt sighed. "I suppose I need to do the same. And stop crying about things I can't change."

Angie frowned, then glowered at him. "Strong people cry. It's part of self-care. You're never going to get through the really rough times unless you take care of yourself."

As Hoyt held his wife, the lingering doubts and fears were still there, but now they were tempered by determination and a sense of purpose. This was a new beginning, a chance to honor those who were gone and to protect those who remained.

But as he stroked Angie's soft hair, the shadow of an

unanswered question hung over him, a mystery that tugged at the edges of his mind. Something still felt unresolved, a piece of the puzzle still missing.

What was it that he was overlooking? And what might it cost them all?

10

Despite the late-evening hour and the exhausting day Rebecca had put in, she was determined to do all her physical therapy exercises. Wiping a tear from the corner of her eye, she took a shaky breath, held it, then exhaled as she counted through the last set of shoulder blade squeezes. The pain wasn't as bad as it had been, but every now and then, she'd get a sudden sharp sting, which was so miserable, her eyes watered every time.

"Tears are just pain leaving the body, so strength has a place to grow." She couldn't remember who had told her that line, but it made perfect sense in times like this.

Her exercises complete, she allowed herself to collapse gently and with great care against the stack of pillows on the couch behind her. The little nest she'd made in the living room was the only place she was truly comfortable.

If that's true, I have plenty of room for strength with all the tears I've shed recently.

It was hard to believe that just that morning she'd been in Virginia, visiting Darian's grave.

Rebecca missed Ryker and the comfort she knew he'd

offer as she grieved for her fallen deputy, but that sentiment was overshadowed by the guilt she carried over her boyfriend's current condition.

When she'd still been a patient at Coastal Ridge Hospital, she'd managed to convince the nurses to load her into a wheelchair for a quick visit down the hall to his room. He'd been in a coma then, and all she'd been able to do was hold his hand. Unfortunately, she'd been so messed up on painkillers, she'd initially failed to notice his parents were in the room, holding vigil over their son.

His parents had just sat there, silently staring at her. She guessed his mom's sandy-blond hair had been styled at a salon. She was very attractive. But Vera Sawyer's gaze could've melted an iceberg.

Quickly averting her eyes toward Ryker's dad, Jim, she'd hoped for a friendlier reception. Dads always liked her, though she wasn't sure why. But the deeply tanned man looked at her with such disgust, it sliced through the haze of drugs fogging her brain.

She hadn't given much thought to what Ryker's parents would look like, but somehow, she'd pictured them more rustic and down-to-earth. Their matching wedding bands glistened under the fluorescent lights, as if they were brand new or recently cleaned and polished.

Is that a thing? She couldn't recall her parents' bands ever looking that new.

The nurse had broken the ice and introduced her as the sheriff, which wasn't the best way for her to meet them. It was her fault Ryker had been out there that night. Not her job, just her, Rebecca West. He'd come to give her and her team a ride off Little Quell Island and had ended up getting shot in the chest and slamming his head into the steering wheel, which knocked him out cold.

In the front of her mind, Rebecca knew she wasn't at fault

for that. Technically, she wasn't at fault for any of it. But in the back of her mind, where that little whispering voice lived and spoke up so often, it echoed.

What if...?

If only...

This is all your fault.

Rebecca blew out a breath and sat forward. There was one way to make sure nothing like this ever happened again. She had to stop the financiers who kept paying these thugs.

Before her, the coffee table was slathered in paper records. When she hadn't been able to work, reading Wallace's old case files was the only way she could keep herself sane. Every time she picked up or set down a page or a folder, the same thoughts ran through her mind.

The Yacht Club is to blame. If it weren't for them and the illegal activities they're engaged in, people like Wesley Garrett and the drug cartels affiliated with killers like him wouldn't be coming to Shadow Island. I have to chop off the head of the beast, and that's the Yacht Club and its leaders.

Rebecca had people on this island who mattered to her. She knew she would never stay sane if Ryker got shot again. Or if Viviane got hurt. Or if Hoyt never came home.

After the beating she'd taken, no one would blame her for walking away.

Lifting one of the sheets of paper, Rebecca tried to focus on the case at hand. But her mind wasn't done forcing her to relive that night. That trauma was part of her now, along with her newest crop of bruises and broken bones.

She had a sudden vision of two men on the beach collapsing as her shotgun shredded them literally to pieces. Blood and chunks of meat splattered the sand and trees.

I stopped them, all right. So many men.

A sound of fluttering caught her attention. Her hand holding the page was shaking, and she couldn't still it.

Sixteen men. I'm responsible for sixteen deaths in a single night.

Never before had she felt the slightest qualm about killing in self-defense. She still didn't. But knowing she'd ended and helped end so many lives in one night was too much for her to process.

Stop it.

She needed to get over the past and focus on the case in front of her.

Rebecca turned to her laptop and entered the first name from the list of attendees at Amy Washington's retirement party. She planned to look up all the names and check for anything that might've led them to kill the well-loved teacher.

At the end of the day, this was who Rebecca was. The woman who wouldn't stop digging until she found answers. And she loved it. Even now.

That wasn't to say she'd made her decision about whether to stay or leave. Or stay and resign. She picked up her thermos and took a long drink of water. The badge was still hers, and she had a job to get done.

Her future might look different, but for today, she was the sheriff of Shadow Island.

Rebecca rapped on Sebastian Drysdale's apartment door.

It was still fairly early, so she wasn't surprised that it took several minutes before he answered. Especially on a Saturday.

The door swung open. Sebastian looked like he'd just rolled out of a bed made of rocks and brambles, he was so disheveled. He leaned heavily on the door. His watery dark-brown eyes ran over her body, focusing mostly on the badge at her belt. Then they flicked over her shoulder, checking to see if anyone else was with her.

"Sheriff? Something I can do for you?" His voice was dry and hoarse, like he'd spent the night drinking or yelling.

"You could invite me in so we can have a little chat." Rebecca tilted her head, gesturing to the door next to them, which was ajar with a neighbor peeking out.

Drysdale huffed—or it could've been a grunt or a laugh, she wasn't sure—and leaned his shoulder against the door-jamb. He ran his hand through his short salt-and-pepper hair, doing his best to settle it against his head, but the wiry strands stood right back up. "No offense, ma'am, but I'm not dressed for visitors right now. And, considering you're wearing a badge and a gun, I'm guessing this isn't a social visit."

Since he was wearing a pair of sweatpants with the string half tucked in and an undershirt drooping down one shoulder, she could believe the first part. He'd clearly just rolled out of bed and thrown some clothes on. His DMV record indicated he was fifty-two, and he appeared to be someone who kept in shape. Either he worked out regularly or his life-long job as a school janitor was more labor-intensive than she'd presumed.

Rebecca sighed and turned to blatantly look at the snooping neighbor. The door clicked shut. "Amy Washington was found murdered yesterday near the school. Do you know anything about that?"

Drysdale paled, and for a second, she thought he might crumble to the floor. "Damn." He scrubbed his hands over his face and straightened slightly, although the door seemed to be doing most of the work in keeping him upright. "Wait. Maybe I'm not awake yet. Did you say murdered?"

Was this genuine grief she was witnessing or the fear of the killer thinking he was on the verge of being caught?

"I did. Do you know anything about it?" She couldn't watch his expression as he reacted because his hands were still covering his face.

"Know anything? I didn't even know she was dead, let alone murdered." His hands pulled down his face, highlighting wrinkles that hadn't been evident at first. "Was it one of those crazy things that's been happening lately? I know there's been a spike in crime. Was she mugged or something? Amy would have given up her purse. She wasn't a fighter."

That seemed like an intimate trait for him to know about

his coworker. "Not a mugging. All her personal effects were left behind."

Drysdale didn't acknowledge her words, and she wondered if he was still listening. He was frowning and slowly shaking his head. "She was always such a sweet woman. A real angel. She'd help anyone she could. *Give them the shirt off her back* type of person, ya know? If you were sick, she'd bring over soup. Always was the one scheduling birthday celebrations too. She never forgot a birthday."

Rebecca let him ramble on. This was new information to her—though none of it was surprising, considering what she'd already learned about the woman.

"Speaking of celebrations, her retirement party was two days ago. Why weren't you there?"

"Me? I wasn't invited. Retirement parties are done by department. I gave her my gift when she cleaned out her room the first week of break. Unlike the teachers, I work year-round. I..." He snorted and shook his head.

The disdain in his voice had grown with every word. Apparently, Drysdale didn't think much of the teachers at the school. Interdepartmental rivalry, or something more personal?

"A teacher I spoke to seemed to think you had more than a professional relationship with Amy. Can you tell me about that?"

"More than professional? I suppose you could call it that." His shoulders squared, and he pulled back, the grief in his face fading as a touch of anger took its place. "We were actually classmates at the school. Graduated the same year. I was kind of an outcast, but she was always kind to me."

"Did you stay in touch after graduation?"

Drysdale rubbed his five o'clock shadow, apparently fixating on a moment from long ago. "After we graduated, she went off to college, and I took the job as janitor. When she came back to start her teaching career with her brand-new degree, she continued being friendly to me, a lowly janitor. Hard not to be nice to someone you've known nearly your whole life. That's a lot of birthday cakes, ya know? Lots of bowls of soup too."

"Cakes and soup, huh?"

He gave a brief, wistful smile. "I'm sure that's not the kind of juicy gossip you were expecting. Long-term work colleagues and platonic friendships aren't spicy enough for the rumor mill at the school. Those teachers sure do like to talk about things they know nothing about. But then, if they didn't, I guess they couldn't be teachers, eh?"

Oh, yeah, this man definitely did not have a lot of respect for the teachers, other than Amy Washington.

"I wouldn't call them *spicy*, but they were interesting." Rebecca hadn't heard anything of the sort, but she wasn't going to let him know that. At most, they were only suggestive of something inappropriate. "Maybe not something she would want her husband to hear about."

Drysdale rolled his eyes so expressively a teenager would've been impressed. "I'm sure Buzz heard them too. And thought as little about the rumormongers as I do. Hens squawking at nothing, trying to make up something to give their dull lives some thrill."

"So you know Buzz?"

"I do." He shook his head and rubbed his chin. "How's he taking the news? Does he understand what's happened?"

He certainly seemed to know more about the couple than the rest of the island. "What do you know about Buzz Washington's condition?"

"Buzz has early-onset Alzheimer's. It's progressing pretty quickly. That's why Amy retired. So she could move to the mainland with him to get him set up in a home and get proper care. She didn't want to be too far away from him and was going to get a little apartment nearby, so she could still spend her days with him. She was devoted to that man."

"Mr. Washington's health seems to have been a well-guarded secret. Can I ask how you know so much about it?"

"Like I said, Amy and I go way back. I wasn't in her friend circle when we were kids or nothin' like that. But she was always doing nice things for me, and I tried to repay her in whatever small way I could." Drysdale stepped back inside. Rebecca tried to catch a glimpse of what he was doing, briefly worrying he was reaching for a weapon, but he returned with an unframed photo. A tack hole indicated it'd been attached to a corkboard or something inside. He handed it to Rebecca.

The photo was of two men with a woman between them. By the looks of it, it couldn't be more than a few years old. The threesome stood shoulder to shoulder, smiling at the camera with the school in the background.

"That was taken after my thirty-year work anniversary party at the school about four years ago. They give a little party to honor everyone's years of service. Mostly only honorees and their families come. But not Amy. She and Buzz came 'cause my brother couldn't make it. She didn't want me celebrating alone."

When Rebecca handed the photo back, he wiped the dust off before gently placing it on an end table by the door. "Anyway, Amy was pretty upset when they got Buzz's diagnosis. Can't really blame her. And she confided in me because she needed someone to dump it all on. She didn't like to talk about Buzz's declining mental status. She hated the rumor mill as much as I did. That was one of the reasons we got along so well."

"Does that mean she wouldn't have spoken up if something was wrong?"

"Wrong how?" He scowled at her, crossing his arms tight

across his chest. The muscles in his forearms and hands flexed like steel cables under his sunspotted skin, showing his strength.

"Say, if someone was threatening her. Did she worry at all about Buzz becoming violent or tell you of any episodes where he'd lost his temper?"

"Buzz? Hell no. He's gentle as a baby bird. And I've been over there a time or two over the summer and seen his condition getting worse. But never did he even offer a harsh word to Amy. Sometimes, he'd get frustrated, but he never turned that on her, or me."

Rebecca shifted her weight, trying to see farther into the apartment. "What about problems with any of her students or the staff?" She didn't want to think that any of the children at the school could've done this, but she couldn't write them off just because of their ages. Teens were just as capable of violence as any other age group. And Amy had taught both middle and high school English classes.

He shook his head in denial. "No. That kind of thing isn't gossip. If someone was harassing her, she would've spoken up. Most likely to try to get them help. She wasn't a fighter, but she wasn't stupid either. Nice but not a doormat. You know?"

"I get that."

"Besides, she always had a great rapport with her students. She was very understanding, patient, forgiving."

"Forgiving? Was there a lot she had to forgive?"

His left eyebrow twitched, and his arms tightened around his chest even more. "With kids, always. They do dumb shit. Most of the time, they don't mean it. No bad intentions. But it can still be hurtful." He shifted on his feet.

Drysdale might be a decent liar, but he wasn't a great one. He was lying or hiding something. What that something was, Rebecca didn't know yet. She noted his careful word choices

—with kids, most of the time, and *hurtful*. His shifting showed her he wasn't comfortable talking about it, which meant it was something he planned to keep secret.

Chasing down all the theories racing through her mind, Rebecca pondered if one of the kids had done something hurtful to Amy, and she had forgiven them. Perhaps Drysdale knew something and had agreed to keep it secret?

"Can you think of anyone in particular she had to forgive recently?"

His arms relaxed, and he shook his head. "Not recently, no. Who would be mean to such a kind woman? If you ask around, everyone will tell you how much her students loved her."

"Do you know of any reason she would've asked someone to meet her behind the school after her party?"

Drysdale's eyebrows scrunched together. This was why she liked interviewing people early in the morning or late at night. When they were tired, their defenses slowed, and it was harder to make up lies.

"I haven't a clue. She was supposed to go to the party with Buzz. He can't really drive anymore. I mean, Amy was only allowing him to drive short distances if she was with him. She hadn't had the heart to take away his keys, for his pride and all." The janitor rubbed his chin. "But she'd have driven them there, so I don't know who she'd be meeting. I 'spect 'bout everyone she knew was at the party in the gym."

Rebecca was going to have to dig deeper into the note's significance. It surely had some, if it was left on Amy's body after she'd been killed. "You've been very helpful, thank you. One last thing. Since you weren't at the party, can you tell me where you were Thursday evening between nine p.m. and midnight?"

"Nine to midnight? I was out with my brother, Melvin." He straightened, dropping his arms. "We were night fishing."

Rebecca peppered the man with a series of questions about whether they'd run into anyone while they were out and attempted to pin down the exact timeline they were together. "Were you two fishing alone?"

"You're not going to go talk to him to double-check where I was, are you?"

Rebecca tilted her head, holding her notepad with the pen poised to write. He glanced at it and licked his lip nervously.

"Would that be a problem?"

"He…he's had some problems with cops before. I don't want to be the one to send them after him." Rebecca could hear the unspoken *again* in his words.

"What kinds of problems?"

"Just some kid stuff, from back in the day. He's clean now since he got out. Got a stable life. Wife and kid, the whole nine yards. I don't want to mess that up for him."

Clean meant he'd been dealing with or using drugs, probably both. *Out*, of course, implied he'd been in jail or in a gang.

"I'll be very nice to him when I call." Rebecca smiled as she lied. There was no way she would just call him. No, this would require a face-to-face meeting. If Melvin's body language was as telling as Sebastian's, she could learn a great deal just from watching him.

But first, she needed to look up Melvin's criminal record. As weak and sore as she was, she might need to take backup for that meeting.

12

R ebecca lifted a bag of doughnuts and gently shook it, taunting her deputies.

"It's not even Sunday yet, and you still brought in dough-nuts? Aw, you really do spoil us." Viviane grinned, sitting at her new desk in the bullpen—the one that'd been empty, waiting on a new hire, since Rebecca started. No one wanted to sit at Darian's desk. His death was still fresh in their minds and hearts.

Rebecca's smile wilted. "Well, it's your first official weekend on the new job. I wanted to sweeten it up a bit."

Viviane had to have seen the sadness that stole her smile, but she just smiled harder to make up for it. "Or you just have a sweet tooth and wanted to have an excuse for bringing in doughnuts."

"That's also a possibility. A spoonful of sugar helps the medicine go down." Rebecca set the bag on the table next to the coffee pot and pulled out a cream-filled one for herself, then moved out of the way as Viviane joined her.

"You still on meds? I thought you couldn't work or drive while you were taking them." Viviane was sneaking peeks into the bag for the strawberry-topped Danish Rebecca always got for her, but her attention was mostly focused on Rebecca.

"Not painkillers or anything that can slow me down. Just some anti-inflammatories. But it still makes a good excuse for a doughnut in the morning." Rebecca grinned and bit into the pastry. "Where's Hoyt?"

"Getting paper for the machine." His voice came up the hall, and Rebecca turned. He waved a ream of paper at her, but his eyes focused on the bag of treats. "Oh, did you get any maple bacon this time?"

"They were out again. Sorry." Rebecca took a sip of her coffee and motioned at the blank whiteboard now stationed along the back wall of the room. "I don't think Mr. Washington is a viable suspect in his wife's murder. The medical information, combined with the preliminary report his social worker filed, added to our own observations and those of Sebastian Drysdale, all seem to confirm the man has early-onset Alzheimer's."

Hoyt popped a piece of bear claw in his mouth and nodded, then wiped his sticky fingers on his uniform pants before stocking paper in the office printer. "Crappy as that news is, I agree."

With a fresh load of paper, the machine began whirring. Hoyt grabbed the first page, looked it over, and showed it to the two women. "I printed off everything I could find on the internet about the treatments he's receiving. As expected, none of his meds list 'violence' as a possible side effect."

Rebecca appreciated that her team was diving into the case.

"But patients with Alzheimer's can have violent episodes. He might not even remember what he did. And we know he was at the party." Viviane glanced between the two more experienced officers.

Rebecca brightened at her rookie's astute observation. "That's right. But I believe violent behavior, or aggression, is not generally premeditated. Amy Washington's throat was slit in a field, and a note was left in her pocket."

Hoyt's eyes narrowed as he pulled more pages off the printer and moved to affix them to the whiteboard. "I took the liberty of snapping some photos of Buzz Washington when I went to provide notification. This is what he was wearing when I spoke with him. Black trousers, black socks, and a pale-blue button-down shirt."

"Unsurprisingly, that's what he had on when I spoke to him as well." Rebecca moved closer to inspect the images. "Yeah, that's exactly it. Said he'd fallen asleep in his recliner."

Her senior deputy finished at the whiteboard and turned toward Rebecca. "Didn't Marjorie Lamb give you some photos from the party? We can see what he had on that night. I suspect we're going to see they're the same attire."

Viviane moved to the board and leaned closer. "If the clothes he had on at the party are the same as these, there's no way he killed his wife. There's no blood spatter on his clothes and no dirt around the hems of his pants."

Rebecca pulled out her phone and swiped through the photos. She hadn't yet added them to the case file. When she found the best picture with Amy and Buzz, she turned the phone for her deputies to see. "He has on the same clothes. The only difference is they don't look wrinkled."

"Okay, Richard 'Buzz' Washington is off our suspect list, but that doesn't mean we're going to forget about him." Hoyt tapped the whiteboard with a marker.

"Social services is already thereThe report says they've notified Buzz's two sons. Do either of you know them?"

"The oldest boy, Austin, is in his mid-twenties and has a new wife. I can't remember where they live now. And the younger boy, Brandon, he's single and living in New York state, I believe." Viviane turned to her new computer and signed in. "Is there anything you need me to check on them, Boss?"

Rebecca frowned at the whiteboard. "The Washingtons seem like a dead end, so we'll drop digging into them for now."

"Viviane." Hoyt waved the stack of papers in his hands. "You can help me check on all the attendees to narrow down possible suspects and compile alibis."

"Right, go ahead and split them with her." Rebecca grinned as Hoyt dropped half the stack of papers on the desk. It was a given that Viviane would not be going out on her own to do any interviews, but she was safe enough in the office where Frost could overhear her.

Rebecca tapped her rookie's desk. "I have to go run down Sebastian Drysdale's alibi. He said he was with his brother at the time. Do either of you know anything about the man?"

"Melvin?" Hoyt nodded and sat at his desk. "Got arrested once for drug possession. He served twelve months and had to pay a fine. Been clean since then. At least as far as we can tell. I don't know if Wallace would agree."

The thought that Melvin Drysdale could be one of the protected drug runners used by the Yacht Club had crossed Rebecca's mind already. She hadn't yet seen his name in the stacks of unfiled reports Wallace had compiled to work up his RICO case against the crime group, but that didn't mean he wasn't in there somewhere.

"Do you know anything else about him?"

"Married, one kid, a son. They have a place near the marshes. Can't remember her name. I know it's been rocky recently, though. Not unusual for them. They fight pretty often."

"Loudly and in public." Viviane's nostrils flared. "I once saw them get into a screaming match at the movies. Something about how he was in charge of date night but never did enough for her."

Rebecca glanced at Hoyt, who was nodding as well. "Been like that since they started dating. 'Toxic relationship,' Angie says. I always feel bad for the boy, having to hear that crap all the time."

"Me too."

"But never anything more than yelling and screaming?"

"Maybe." Hoyt turned in his chair to give her a knowing look. "But we never had any evidence of abuse. This is a mandatory reporting state, and we'd have filed a report if we'd seen anything."

"I'll check when I run out there. Give me a call if Bailey has any updates. Her assistant said she was going to get started on Amy today. While you two go through the list of attendees at the party, see if you can find out if anyone had a problem with Amy, including any current or former students."

Viviane's eyes widened. "I can't imagine any student wanting to hurt her."

"Don't let your personal bias come into play here. People can keep a lot hidden, no matter how well you think you know them." Rebecca kept her gaze hard on Viviane until she nodded.

That was always one of the worst parts about being a cop, seeing behind the facade that people wore in public. Everyone had secrets they wanted—or needed—to hide.

13

The driveway was empty as Rebecca pulled up to Melvin Drysdale's place. It was a tired-looking bungalow toward the southern end of the island. The houses were cheaper here, with no access to the beach, and close to the marshes. It didn't look like anyone was home.

As she parked on the road in front, Rebecca prepared herself for the potential that Melvin could get violent. Hoyt's subtle warning indicated Melvin might have knocked his wife around and she'd never pressed charges. Glancing at the house and seeing that no one seemed to have noticed her yet, she lifted her laptop onto her lap and pulled up his name.

There was only one record—a charge for possession with intent to sell. That was it. No resisting arrest, fleeing, and nothing in the notes hinted of violence. It meshed with what Hoyt had implied. Domestic abusers were often cowards and bullies who wouldn't fight back against someone stronger than them.

She glanced down at the body armor Bailey Flynn had recommended for her aching ribs. Hopefully, the gun, badge, and SWAT-like appearance would be intimidating enough that Melvin wouldn't try anything with her. In her condition, she wasn't sure how well she could defend herself.

Gingerly climbing out of the SUV, she made sure not to let any of her pain show. Any sign of perceived weakness would be like catnip for an abuser.

No one came out as she walked up the drive to the front door. Nor was there any sign of life as she knocked and waited. Peering in through the single-pane windows was useless, as the curtains were pulled tight against the morning sun.

Glancing around, she stepped off the patio and moved around the side of the house. If anyone was watching her from inside, she was sure her actions would get their attention and bring them out, if for no other reason than to tell her to get off their property.

That never happened. The house stayed silent as she walked around it, looking for a window she could see through. All of them were covered. The house was buttoned up tight. Reaching the back door, she knocked again. The thin, hollow-core aluminum door wobbled under her fist.

Still, no answer came.

Rebecca continued her stroll around the property. Kids toys were scattered in the back and side yards, covered in a fine spattering of aged pollen from the marshlands. A clothesline hung bare. The property gave off every possible indication it was abandoned. Or at least empty.

"Can I help you?" The voice came from the neighboring house. "Sheriff." A man stepped out from under the awning of his patio. He was wearing denim shorts that ran past his knees and no shirt, exposing a colorful American eagle tattoo covering his left shoulder.

"I'm looking for Melvin Drysdale." She tipped her head at the house she'd just been walking around. "Have you seen him?"

"Not this morning, no. Is he in some kind of trouble? Been arguing with his wife again?" The neighbor cast a dour look at the door and sneered. Clearly, they weren't friendly with each other.

"No trouble. Just following up on a line of questioning."

The man grunted and walked over to join her in Melvin's yard. "Excuse me if that's a little hard to believe."

"And what's your name, sir?"

"Bart Welsh." He tossed his head backward to indicate his home. "I'm his neighbor."

"How long have you known Mr. Drysdale?"

"Since they moved in. I'd say about eight years now." He scanned his neighbor's unkempt yard. "You know, he's prolly at work about now."

"And where's that?"

"Mechanic shop. Car mechanic." He added the last bit as if that made it clear. And in a town this small, it did. There was only one shop on the island that worked on cars. All the others worked on boats.

It was the same shop she'd planned to take her truck to when she started having trouble, until Darian Hudson had agreed to work on it for her.

"I got you. No worries. Had a buddy with the same problem after his convoy was ambushed. His was the smell of gasoline. Just don't give me any grief when I have to stop and get sand out of my boots. Okay?"

One day, she knew her memories of Darian would make her smile. Today was not that day, and she had to struggle to shake loose from the pain that accompanied them and focus on what Bart Welsh had to say.

She cleared her throat. "Does he usually work on Saturdays?"

"Pretty much. His lady's always nagging him about his clothes. Though not recently. I think she might've finally left his dumb ass. Been at least a few days since I seen her around."

"Uh, do you know when Mr. Drysdale will be home?" Rebecca twisted slightly.

Welsh was giving her a funny look, letting her know she'd failed to hide her discomfort from her ribs. "I expect he'll be home for lunch. Right around one. That's his normal time, at least."

"Thanks. I'll head down there to talk–"

"No point in heading down there. He says his boss can be a real ass."

"I appreciate the heads-up. I guess I can find that out for myself. If I don't catch up with him there, I'll try back here when he's on his lunch break." Rebecca started to turn away, careful not to aggravate her battered body.

"Wait." He cleared his throat as she turned back. "I'm, uh, sorry to hear about your man. Always a terrible thing when we lose a cop, especially when it's on the job. Glad the rest of you made it back and you're on the job. You're a good one, Sheriff."

Even though his words triggered more painful memories, Rebecca was grateful for his kindness. Forcing a smile, she thanked him and made her way back to her cruiser. The good and bad of small-town life—everyone knew what happened to everyone else.

Maybe that would help her solve this crime.

"YOU REMEMBER WHAT TO DO?" Hoyt glanced down at Viviane as they approached the first residence on the list they'd thinned down by speaking to other party attendees on the phone. They wanted to talk to these folks in person, the last from the gathering to interact with Amy.

"Keep my eyes open. Listen for more than they say. Watch the hands and the background and behind me." She grinned up at him.

"I always said we should have a mom or two on the force. With their eyes in the backs of their heads, they'd get this done no problem."

Viviane was watching him nearly the same way Boomer would when he held one of her tennis balls. It was simultaneously distracting, disturbing, and amusing. And was a dire reminder that he needed to be on his A game. The first few months of a rookie's career would build the habits necessary to survive the job.

And even then, when the cop is one of the best around, they can still be brought down by an unlucky shot.

The idea of sweet, fiery, lovable Viviane being shot nearly had him turning around and getting back in the Explorer. He could lock her in the interrogation room until this murderer was caught.

If he'll kill a harmless schoolteacher, he's just as likely to kill a sweet, young rookie.

"Frost, are you okay? Are we going up?" Viviane cocked a thumb at the house of Cynthia Wells, one of the last teachers to speak with Amy at her party.

"I'm fine. Just wondering if you're ready for this."

If looks could kill, he'd never have to worry about Viviane's safety with the intense glare she turned on him.

"I've passed all my classes. I got better scores on the range than you did. Rebecca, who's FBI-trained may I remind you, approved all my credentials and watched my final drills and practices. I'm ready for this." Her shoulders were ramrod stiff, as was her spine, as she spun away from him. Angry as she was, she didn't walk off. She waited for her backup just like she'd been trained. "I'm not made of porcelain, you know."

"Neither was Hudson." The words were out of Hoyt's mouth before he could stop them, and he winced.

Viviane flinched. When she turned back to him, her glare had softened ever so slightly. "What happened to Hudson was bad. So was what happened to Amy Washington. She was a retired schoolteacher. Death comes for us all, Hoyt. At least now I can shoot back."

Everything she said made sense. He knew. He knew he'd act on it too. When the shit hit the fan, he would treat her like any other officer of the law. But right now, all he could see was Darian's youthful face when he walked him through his first interview six years ago with a drunk tourist who'd witnessed a carjacking.

Hoyt sighed and pulled off his hat so he could run his hand through his hair. "I know, Vi. I really do. And I swear I will always treat you like the badass deputy you are. But right now...right now I'm a sad old man who's lost too many friends and neighbors recently." Stuffing his hat tight onto his head, he nodded. "And now, I'm your superior, Deputy Darby. Make sure you follow my lead."

He took a long stride toward the little house with the green door. Viviane was one step behind him.

"Yes, sir."

God save us old men from the young 'uns who want to make the world a better place.

Reaching the door, Hoyt knocked while Viviane stayed two paces back, watching his six, just like she'd been taught.

"Wait a minute." Hoyt turned on her. "How do you know what my range scores were?"

The cheeky little rookie had the gall to grin at him, looking the picture of innocence. "You'd have to ask our sheriff how I know."

He grumbled and turned back around as the doorknob started to turn.

A middle-aged woman with thick glasses straddling a thin nose poked her head out. "Deputy Frost, can I help you? Is this about Amy?" She leaned over and peered around him. "Viviane Darby, is that you?"

"Yes, ma'am, Miss Wells, it's me."

Hoyt didn't need to turn around to know she was grinning ear to ear. She probably had her chest puffed out to show off her shiny new badge too.

"When did you become a deputy? I'm so proud of you. Come in, come in. Don't just stand in the door and let all the heat in." Cynthia Wells turned around, leaving them to follow her.

Out of habit, Hoyt's eyes shifted left then right as he stepped around the half-open door, checking behind it to make sure no one was waiting to ambush them. It might've been a bit of overkill, but he was going to set the right example and do everything by the book so his friend would live a long and healthy life. Only after he'd cleared the room and nodded to Viviane did she walk in behind him.

The room was small but cozy. Two loveseats were set side by side at an angle facing a giant bookcase crammed with books and one of those little electric fireplaces that couldn't actually hold a fire. He'd never understood why people would give up valuable floor space to have a fake flickering fire.

Hoyt sidestepped, checking the house again as Wells wandered into the kitchen.

"Would you like something to drink? Coffee? Orange juice? I've got some tea bags around here somewhere, if you want."

"No, thank you, ma'am." Viviane stepped around Hoyt, clearing the immediate area as well.

"Deputy Frost?"

"No, ma'am. Just some answers, if you don't mind."

"Of course. That's why you're here. I shouldn't be wasting your time." Mrs. Wells shuffled back into the living room, holding a glass of juice in one hand and a camera in the other. "Smile, Vi! I'm going to add you to my board of children who've surpassed my expectations."

Hoyt glanced over at Viviane as she tilted her head and smiled, hands on her hips, showing off her uniform. The flash went off, and Mrs. Wells glanced at the view screen, beaming with pride.

Viviane caught him looking and dropped her arms, turning a dull red that was barely visible on her brown cheeks.

"Okay, Deputies," Mrs. Wells stressed the S, "what can I answer for you?"

"Where were you around nine p.m. this past Thursday?" Frost followed her to the loveseats and sat on the one across from her. Viviane remained standing near the door, keeping an eye on everything around them.

Dammit. She was good. That scared him. They'd have to do everything they could to keep her from getting a big head. Hubris killed more cops than guns ever did.

"I was at the school, of course. Amy had requested the party be earlier in the evening, so we hadn't expected it to run too late, definitely not past ten, you know? A few people left right after we presented Amy with her big gift basket."

"And what time was that?"

Mrs. Wells scrunched her eyebrows, took her glasses off to leave them to hang around her neck, and pondered his question. "I think it was around seven thirty or so. Principal Hill left right after that too. I think he just wanted to be there for the presentation of the gift and then he disappeared. By nine, the rest of us were collecting our things. Most of us weren't ready to go home yet, but Amy and Buzz were."

"Any idea why Amy wanted to leave her own party?"

"She said she was tired from all the excitement."

"Do you know how many people were still in the gymnasium when the party ended?"

"Well, I certainly didn't count them. Let me think." She closed her eyes, and her fingers twitched as she apparently counted the people she was remembering. When she opened them again, she seemed pleased with herself. "Don't quote me on this, but I'd say there were about ten of us left, me included. Most of the people who weren't as close to Amy had already left by then."

"And where did you go after you left the school?" Hoyt flipped the page of his notepad and continued to write down everything.

"We went over to Pamela Radcliffe's house for some drinks and to let our hair down a little. Principal Hill had put a lot of restrictions on the party, since it was on school grounds, and that kind of threw a wet blanket on things. Did you know he didn't allow any of us to wear sandals or flipflops to the event? Who demands a dress code for a party? You'd never believe he was more than ten years younger than me. Anyway, he's a stick-in-the-mud and can make the best get-togethers feel like work, you know? We were all happy to get away from there. And him."

She nodded at both of them in turn, certain they knew exactly what she was talking about.

"Oh, I remember him," Viviane groused. "He was the worst thing about my school years."

"He still is, dear. Still is."

"He wrote my son up for having torn jeans and sent him home." Hoyt nodded. "It didn't matter that the tear was inches above the cuff and had happened when he fell down the stairs that morning. At the school. Didn't send him home for the scrape or bruise. Just for the tear."

"That's him." Mrs. Wells tapped her fingers rhythmically

on her leg. "Since he'd done his best to suck the fun out of the celebration and Amy wanted to go home, we decided to move the party to Pamela's, where Principal Uptight couldn't tell us what to do. It was sort of a last hurrah before the school year started next week, you know?"

"Amy didn't want to go with you?"

"No. Knowing her, she was probably the last to leave. I think she said something about wanting to 'take a moment' to soak up the memories. But those of us heading to Pamela's went out the front door, since it's closer to the sidewalk, you know. And she went out the side door to the parking lot. Oh, right, I forgot to mention we walked to Pam's. She's just down the street. Didn't make sense to try and fit all those cars in her driveway when we were already parked."

"And what did you do when you got to Mrs. Radcliffe's?"

"We had a few drinks. More than a few, but you don't need to put that in any official report." She waved her hand at his notepad. "We sat in Pam's backyard. Watched the stars. Well, at least a few of us did. Maybe three. Pam's husband has one of those fun little propane fireplaces. With the lava rocks. So pretty. I should get one of those."

A fake fire inside was bad enough, but a fake fire outside? When did people stop burning wood? "And how many people were inside?"

"I'd say just a handful, maybe six or seven. That's where the drinks were, so more people had gravitated to that area." She nodded decisively at that. "I was the second person to leave Pamela's party. Right after Marjorie...Marjorie Lamb. We were tired from organizing it all month. On top of having to get our lesson plans and classrooms ready. It was a hectic day. That was why I needed a drink after. You know?"

Hoyt did know and wished she would stop asking him that. In fact, he might need a drink after this interview. And he still had to talk to a handful of other people, including the infamous Principal Hill.

"Did you return to the school to get your car after you left Pam's house?"

"Well," she glared hard at his notepad until he lifted his pen from the page, "I had more to drink than I should have, so I called my husband, and he came to get me."

Hoyt smiled. "That was the responsible thing to do. Now, can you tell me if you were the one who put together the gift basket?" He pulled up the case file on his tablet, swiping through to the page he was looking for. "This is an inventory of what we collected. Could you look it over and tell us if that looks accurate to you?"

Mrs. Wells took the tablet and held it at arm's length, looking down her nose at it. She glanced around, mumbling about trying to find her glasses.

Viviane's shifting on her feet caught Hoyt's attention, and he looked up to see her grinning at the woman's antics. He had to turn his face away to conceal his amusement when she "found" the glasses hanging around her neck.

That was about the same time he realized he was still using the sheriff's tablet. He'd need to get that back to her before she noticed it missing—otherwise, she might make him keep it. And then he'd be forced to figure out what else it could do other than act as a digital picture viewer.

"No, this isn't right. Obviously, we didn't put the purse in there. That's hers. And the keys and phone weren't from us either." She lowered the tablet and tittered at them.

"Is there anything else different?"

She lifted the device and tapped on it. "There's something missing. I can't remember what, but there's something…" She frowned. "I know there was something else. There's the box that had her necklace in it."

"We found the necklace. She'd been wearing it."

"Yes, we were pleased she liked it so much. But there's still something...oh lord, help me, I can't remember. But there's something. Something else was there." Mrs. Wells moved her hands, mimicking placing things in a container. "I want to say it was a card of some kind. But small, you know?"

That piqued Hoyt's interest, and he noticed Viviane straighten as well. "What kind of card?"

"You know, like one you'd use at a local establishment. We bought her a few different ones. The idea was to give her stuff she could use for their 'bucket list adventure' as she called it. I'm almost positive it was a gift card, I just don't know which one."

Hoyt pressed on. "Can you think of anyone who would want to harm Amy?"

"Oh lord, no. And if I did know anyone, I would have..." She stared at Viviane for a moment before shaking her head. "I would have told the police about it long before now. You'd have to be crazy or on drugs to..." Her eyes slid to the side.

Hoyt seized on the nonverbal tell. "Did you think of something?"

"It's probably nothing. Just a rumor I heard. It happened maybe ten or eleven years ago." She glanced between them with eager, darting eyes, chewing at her lip to keep from being a gossipmonger.

Hoyt decided to put her out of her misery and give her permission to spill the beans. "Mrs. Wells, anything you could tell us would be of great help. Even if you think it's only a rumor."

"Well, I'm not one to gossip, you know?" That was the first provable lie she'd spoken, but he nodded regardless. "I heard there was something between Amy and Sebastian. He's the janitor. Has been for years."

Hoyt tried not to let the disappointment show on his face. That was a rumor they'd already heard and tried to find anything to support. So far, nothing. Rebecca would've mentioned it after her meeting with the man if she'd found anything to substantiate it.

"I heard Amy caught Sebastian," she pinched her fingers together and held them up to her lips, sucking in air, "you know. Smoking the marijuana."

"Smoking marijuana?" That was a new bit of information, but Hoyt didn't see how it could be connected to Amy's death. Nonetheless, he jotted it down, knowing no detail should be overlooked.

"On the job. At the school! She caught him. And she did what a decent woman would do, and she turned him in. To the administration, at least. We can't have people doing things like that around the children, you know? It would be such a bad influence."

"I don't remember anything like that." Hoyt continued to jot everything down in his notepad.

"Oh, well, I know the police were called. That I'm sure of. They talked with Sebastian in the office, then they took him away. He was never charged and came back to his job the next day." She glanced away then back again, fidgeting in her seat. "I just can't imagine that someone could be caught with that stuff and still be allowed around the children."

"Did that make him angry with Amy? Did he react differently around her after that?"

"Well, that's the strangest part. He didn't. Actually, he seemed to be even more friendly with her after. Not anything inappropriate. She's a...she *was* a married woman and wouldn't allow it even if Sebastian wanted to. But I never got that impression of them. Just old friends who knew they could rely on each other. How that fits in with her turning him in for a crime, I could never figure out."

Her take on things seemed to differ from what the others they'd spoken with on the phone had told them about the two staff members. Hoyt underlined *smoking the marijuana* just for kicks. *Darian will find it amusing.*

His heart sank as he remembered, once again, that Darian wouldn't be laughing at anything else with him this side of Heaven.

"Thank you very much, Mrs. Wells. If you remember what else was in the basket, please give us a call."

"I surely will. I kept all the receipts. Or Pam did. I can't remember right now. We used everyone's money to buy those items, so we made sure to keep good records to show how we spent the contributions. It's just…the last few days have been so trying, you know? Having to get everything ready for the new year, trying to make sure the party was good enough, then poor Amy's death."

"I do know, ma'am. Take it easy. But if you could find those receipts, we'd appreciate it."

With a final nod, Hoyt stood up. Viviane preceded him out the door. As they were walking to the cruiser, she turned.

"Are we going to go talk to Pamela next?"

"No, not yet. Let's wait and see if Mrs. Wells can remember what it was first."

"Never let two witnesses know what the other is hiding?"

Hoyt nodded. "Yup. It could be forgetfulness, or it could be malicious intent. Either way, it doesn't help to let them know. Could bias a good witness or warn a false one."

Now the question they needed to figure out was, which kind was Pamela Radcliffe?

14

After a morning of interviewing, Rebecca reconvened with her crew back at the station. Hoyt had loaded all the pictures onto the shared folder and was sorting them.

Melody was at the desk, looking a little glum. It was probably because she was used to working nights and having her days free. The doughnuts were long gone, but it was lunchtime anyway.

"Where's the new guy?"

Rebecca had hired a replacement for Viviane's position, and today was his first official day on the job. He'd train with Melody in the beginning until she was confident he could work the job alone.

Melody nodded toward the front door. "On his lunch break."

Rebecca leaned against the desk. "He doing okay?"

"Absolutely." Melody grinned. "He must have learned some skills from Viviane through osmosis or something."

The replacement was Elliot Ping, Viviane's ex-boyfriend, which seemed a little strange on the surface. But Viviane had been the one to recommend him wholeheartedly. As long as he did his job and fit in with the team, Rebecca didn't care about their previous relationship.

"Glad he's doing well." She headed toward the bullpen. "Let me know if you need anything."

Taking a spot against the wall next to the whiteboard, she twirled her keys around her finger as she faced her team. "How did you do? Find anything new?"

"Cynthia Wells thinks there's something missing from the gift basket. She thought it was a gift card but couldn't remember for sure." Hoyt leaned back in his chair, twisting left and right as he finished off the last pastry.

"Something like a card, she said." Viviane was already typing away at her own computer, writing up the reports.

He nodded at Viviane and sent Rebecca a conspiratorial wink, showing he'd been testing her. "That's right. Like a card."

"She and Pamela Radcliffe were the ones who purchased the gifts and put them together. They kept the receipts and she just needed to find them."

"That'll come in handy if there really is something missing. Have you called Pamela to double-check with her yet?" Rebecca raised an eyebrow at Viviane.

"Not yet. We don't want to bias her memory, so we're going to give Miss Wells some time to remember first. If she can't, we can always go back to Pamela."

"Good plan." Rebecca smirked as Hoyt pointed to himself and nodded, indicating it was his plan all along.

When Viviane finally looked up, Hoyt's face went smooth, not giving anything away as he continued. "We also heard a different rumor about our maybe not-so-lovestruck janitor and teacher. Cynthia, who's a bit of a gossip, heard that those two had something happen between them about a decade ago."

Rebecca straightened. "An affair?"

"Nope. Amy caught Sebastian smoking pot at work and turned him in. Cynthia wasn't sure what the outcome was, but someone from our office, guessing it was Abner or Wallace, had a talk with him. I don't remember anything about drugs at the school, either from my boys or from any official report."

"An incident on school property involving drugs. Any chance you've looked into it more, Darby?" Rebecca stopped flicking her keys and held them in her fist. She hated fidgeting, knowing how distracting it could be in the workplace, but her hands were one of the few things she could move easily.

"Not yet. I'll get on that next."

"Melvin Drysdale wasn't home when I went by earlier but should be soon, according to his neighbor. Melvin is supposed to be Sebastian's alibi for the night of the murder. I'm going to head back over there once we're done here." Rebecca nodded at the sparsely filled whiteboard. "Let's get all their names up so we can see everyone and how they're connected. That way, we can track who heard what and when and figure out what's missing."

"Why can't we just set this up in the file?" Viviane finally lifted her gaze from her computer. "That way, we can post things in there and link them together to follow trails."

"And we'll do that too. But having the board helps us think outside the box and better visualize what's missing. You can't do that on a computer. They're good for a lot of things—"

Hoyt grunted loudly. "Bullshit."

Rebecca ignored him. "But we're limited with our screens. And negative space on a screen doesn't show that it's missing something."

Hoyt grunted again. "Especially when the damn folder

keeps moving things into alphabetical order every time you turn your back."

As Rebecca laughed, Viviane sighed through an explanation. "That's just the default setting, Frost. You can customize how items appear on your computer."

He sat up and frowned at the younger woman, then at his screen. "I can? Since when?"

"About two months ago. When I upgraded the system. There was a walk-through that showed you the new features, but I bet you just clicked your way through." Rebecca straightened, carefully stretching her torso. "Which reminds me, I got us something else too."

Making a quick trip to her office, she came back and handed them each a device.

"Pens. Now we're talking. These, I know how to use. Thanks, Boss." Hoyt clicked the end a few times, then frowned. "Why's it so heavy?"

"Because it's not a pen. It will write, though, in case you need to convince someone. But what you just clicked was the record button."

"You got us spy cameras!" Viviane brightened and started inspecting the pen she'd just been frowning at.

"Pen cams, yup. It was brought to my attention not too long ago that the people who see what we purchase for the office might not have our best interests at heart. Or the interest of anyone else on this island. I special ordered these when I…reordered…" She left the sentence hanging. They all knew they'd had to restock their ammunition after the shoot-out on the island.

"Richmond Vale hasn't poked his nose into things for a while. For right now, no one is looking over our shoulders."

Hoyt spun the pen around and around in his hands. "I get how this can record, but how do we download the footage?"

"Unscrew it and you'll see the hidden USB-C drive." She

patted the one she already had tucked into her pocket. "Keep them with you while you're on duty. Don't drop them in the toilet. And try not to hit the top of them. That turns the recording off."

"So…is mine on or off right now?" Hoyt lifted the camera closer to his face for a better look.

"I'm hoping it's on so we can watch that video later." Viviane giggled and looked at Rebecca.

"If the button's up, it's off. If it's down, it's recording."

Hoyt clicked it a few times, then nodded, satisfied. "This is how we get our body cams without them knowing we've got body cams. I like it."

"Me too." Viviane popped hers into her pocket.

"Me three. We've made good use of hidden recorders already. This will help even more." Rebecca looked at her deputies with their new equipment and knew they'd prove valuable…assuming Hoyt could handle the technology when the time came. The hidden cameras wouldn't stop a bullet, but they could send the men responsible to jail.

"Speaking of equipment." Hoyt leaned forward in his chair, staring at her. "What's with the Kevlar?"

Rebecca shrugged, shifting the stiff body armor around, but didn't offer an explanation.

"You about to go do something dangerous? I can go with you. 'Cause I have to admit, I didn't much like it the last time you went off on your own and we had to send in the search teams to find you." He cleared his throat roughly and sat back, then rocked forward again, shifting in his seat. "Angie would kick my ass if something else happened to you."

"So would Mom." Viviane nodded, concern written on her face.

Knowing she was fine, Rebecca waved them off. "I'm not doing anything more dangerous than what you guys were doing."

Their hard gazes didn't relent.

"I promise. No lie." Rebecca held up her hands. "Bailey Flynn suggested it would help my posture for the next couple of days. And she's right. It's a rib saver." She knocked her knuckles against her Kevlar-reinforced belly.

"Speaking of Bailey," Melody turned around on her stool to face them, "she's on the phone and says she's ready for you, Sheriff."

"Thanks, Melody." After Rebecca went to check on Sebastian's alibi, she could see what Amy's body had to tell them.

15

A sweet tang of orange blossom filled the air as I scrubbed my hands, the abrasive mixture irritating my skin as much as the smell irritated my nose. Though the day was barely halfway done, I was already tired of it. I was tired of them all.

Glancing up, I barely recognized the stranger in the mirror. Where once stood a man of purpose and ambition, now lingered a shell, hollowed out by betrayal.

All because of one day, one mistake. Because of that, everything had turned to ash. My bright future had gone up in smoke. And for such a ridiculous reason too. It wasn't like I'd hurt anyone.

Had that stopped her from destroying my life, ruining everything I'd been working toward and making sure I'd get nowhere? No. It wasn't fair.

"It's not right. What you did to me. You didn't have to do it."

I scrubbed harder, watching the cleaner foam white as it covered my hands. It wasn't enough. I pressed the pump on the bottle and worked the foam into a thick lather.

"It's not. It's not enough. This was all your fault, but it wasn't only your fault." Hitting the knob with the back of my hand, I turned the water on full blast. The heavy spray sluiced through the soap, rinsing it down the drain. The smell of orange still clung to the air.

"She wasn't the only one, you know!" Shaking the water from my hands, I stormed back into the bedroom.

My lazy wife was still lying in bed, growing fatter by the hour. Her stomach pressed out, reminding me of when she'd been pregnant.

"But you took that from me too. Didn't you? It wasn't enough to take my life, my hope, my future, my self-worth! You had to go and take my kid from me too. Why? He needs me in his life to teach him how to be a man. Instead, you've filled his head with emotions and weakness."

I kicked the bed, and her head swung back and forth.

"Don't tell me no! No woman is ever going to tell me no again." I grabbed her hair, forcing her to look at me. Her eyes refused to focus. Yet another act of defiance from her. Even when I twisted her head around, she still refused to see me.

It didn't matter. I could see myself in the white haze coating her pupils. I saw everything she had ruined.

But in that anger, I found clarity. There were those who had taken from me, who had destroyed my life. And now, it was my turn to take back control.

"You did this." I sank down onto the bed beside my dear wife, the place where I'd sat a thousand times before. Back then, she was the one yelling insults and accusations at me. Oh, how the tide had turned.

She rolled away from me to the side of the bed. Froth dribbled from her lips and down her cheek.

"Don't you look away from me! This is your doing, and you need to answer for what you've done. You did this to me. To us!"

I jumped up and glared down at her, but as always, she ignored me and my needs.

"Selfish bitch." I wiped my hands dry on the bedding. She could sleep on wet sheets tonight. I didn't care.

But it wasn't just her fault. Others had played their part.

"No more. I'm not going to let anyone else hurt me. I'm going to determine my own future. And everyone who ever tried to stop me…well, they'll get what they deserve. And then I can finally have the life that was stolen from me."

My mind reeled as I contemplated everyone who had ever crossed me. The sun cast an orange glow through the room as I carefully laid out the photographs of my past.

I studied each one.

Who would be next?

Eeny…meeny…

I smiled at my adversary.

"You."

As I stared at the face I so hated, I couldn't help but wonder, what if? What if he hadn't intervened…just let things run their course? How different would my life be right now?

Clenching my fists, I realized my anger was bubbling up like the froth from my wife's mouth. Only, I was sure my revenge would taste better than the foulness emanating from her.

I knew what I had to do. The path was clear, and I was determined to follow it. The man who had been a roadblock to my happiness needed to be taught a lesson.

And I'm only too happy to provide it.

16

Crossing her arms over her chest wasn't easy to do while wearing a vest. Rebecca wasn't trying to provoke Melvin Drysdale or lead him to think she was afraid of him or expected trouble. After all, she was just here to corroborate an alibi.

She was lifting her arm to knock again when he finally opened the door.

Melvin Drysdale couldn't have looked more different from his older brother. His hair was long and unkempt. Tattoos spotted his arms along with crusty oil, both of which stopped at his wrists, showing clean hands.

"What do you want?" He looked her up and down, focusing on her chest. She was certain he wasn't interested in her vest. More likely, he was trying to gauge her cup size.

Swallowing hard, she wished she'd sent Hoyt to question the man. Not because she was afraid of him. He was thin and sickly looking.

It was the smell.

Used oil with a hint of gasoline that no amount of hand cleaner could erase or cover up emanated from the man. A shudder ran up her stomach as her mind tried to jump back to the parking garage but was staved off as her chest muscles cramped from her labored breathing. Rebecca took a slow, shallow breath through her mouth.

Saved from the old PTSD trigger by the new trauma. What a life I live.

"I'm Sheriff West, here to talk to Melvin Drysdale. Is that you?"

"You're standing on my porch, and you don't even know my name?" He smirked and shook his head, his eyes roving over her like dirty hands. "You got looks, I'll give you that. Too bad you didn't get brains to go with it."

He stepped out, and she stepped back, leaving plenty of room between them for the wind to drag away his smell. Her retreat made him smile, and he stretched up taller so he could look down on her even more.

"You're not getting in my house without a warrant, cop." He spit on the ground, pulled a cigarette from a pack in his pocket, and lit up.

Her face went stony at the childish and rude actions. Being nice wasn't going to get her anywhere. In fact, he'd probably fight her just because of her job or her gender. That was fine. She wasn't in a friendly mood anyway.

"Sheriff, actually. But then, if you could read the side of my cruiser, you'd already know that." Rebecca jerked her thumb over her shoulder. "Maybe it's too far away and you just couldn't see it properly? Not that I think you're so thick you refused to ever learn how to read."

She straightened as much as her ribs and aching side would allow.

His eyes narrowed. "I—"

"And I don't need a warrant. Yet. So far, I only have a few questions. You're Sebastian Drysdale's older brother, right?"

She smiled as he scowled at her. The intentional dig was enough to get him to finally answer a question.

"*Younger* brother. He's three years older than me."

Rebecca ran her eyes over him and hitched her shoulders, showing she didn't care. "A coworker of his died. Amy Washington. I'm sure you've heard about that already."

He took a heavy drag from his cigarette. "That bitch died? Huh. What's that got to do with me or my brother?"

"Well, she worked with your brother."

"And? Lots of people worked with my brother over the last thirty years. Hell, half the town has gone through that building since Seb started working there. Don't mean nothing."

"Not everyone was rumored to have such a..." she paused for a couple of heartbeats to make him uncomfortable as he huffed out his smoke, "complicated history with the victim."

"You cops know all about what went down between her and my brother. Should have her statement too. So why are you out here harassing me about it again?"

Playing on a hunch, she went a different route than she'd originally planned. "And we all know why you don't like her. Why don't you go ahead and tell me where you were Thursday evening between nine and midnight."

As soon as she said the day, he froze, then started shaking his head in denial. "Oh, no, you aren't blaming no murder on me. I got a solid alibi for that night. I was with my buddies, right here, playing poker all night long. We started early and ended late." He slapped the side of the house.

If he was playing poker with his friends, that meant he couldn't have been night fishing with his brother. At least one of the Drysdales no longer had an alibi.

"Was your wife here? Can she confirm that?" Rebecca purposefully leaned to the side into his smoke. It was a nasty habit, but at least it dulled her nose against the smell of burned oil.

Melvin lifted his hand and inspected his pale, spotless fingers. "My wife left last weekend to take my boy up the coast to some art camp."

"And you're sure you were playing poker on Thursday night? Not Friday night."

He glowered at her, mashing the filter of his cigarette between his fingers as he clenched his fists. Sadly, it wasn't enough to put it out. "I'm sure."

"I only ask because most people do that kind of thing on Fridays. You sure it wasn't Friday?"

"I know what damn day of the week it was. It was Thursday night. Fridays can be hectic, but I didn't have any early jobs scheduled the next day, so it stands out in my mind. And my wife wasn't around to nag me, so me and some of my buddies got some beers, got some pizzas, and played poker all night. Or until I took all their money, at least."

Rebecca wondered if he'd won a single round. "I need names of the people you played with." Her pen hovered over a clean page in her notepad.

"Lance, Rod, and B.B."

"Last names?"

"Lance Myer and Bob…ah shit…"

"Bob Ah Shit?"

"I forget." He gestured widely with his hand toward town. "Look, Lance and Bob are always coming into the shop. You can go up there and get their last names. And Lance introduced me to Rod. I don't know how they met. Oh, Rod's last name is Hammond. Or maybe Hamilton."

Rebecca nodded and jotted down the names.

"I guess I'll go learn your good buddies' names then." She couldn't keep the snark out of her voice. *Guy plays poker with his friends and doesn't even know their last names.* Briefly, she pondered if being so clueless was a "guy thing," or if her keen eye for detail came with the job, and civilians just weren't as attentive. *Or he's lying. Dumb lie, though.*

"Anything else?" He took another absentminded drag off his mangled cigarette and shifted on his feet, half turning back to his door.

For a bully, he sure was acting like someone who wanted nothing more than to run away from her. "Actually, yes." She lifted her gaze from her paper and stared him directly in the eyes. "Do you have any plans to leave the island? Because if you do, I suggest you cancel them. I'll be back to talk to you later, after I track down your pals."

"It's a free country! I'll go wherever I want." The words were adamant, but he was already walking inside his house, pushing the door shut behind him.

Rebecca stared at the door. He wasn't anything like what she'd expected. While he had all the manners of a feral cat, he hadn't tried pushing her in the least. Other than looking down on her, he hadn't even tried to intimidate her.

For a man who claimed to clean up at cards, Melvin Drysdale needed a better poker face. He was definitely bluffing about something.

17

"I see you took my advice." Even though she was wearing a surgical mask and standing over a cadaver, Dr. Bailey Flynn's knowing smile crinkled around her eyes.

Rebecca shook her head, pulling on a gown and surgical mask of her own. "You know, you're the only one, besides Frost, who even commented on me wearing a vest. Besides, I've never had any reason not to follow solid, professional advice. And you, more than anyone else, know what I went through."

Bailey had been on the island with the search party and had also been the one to keep Rebecca stabilized while waiting for the evacuation helicopter to take her directly to the hospital on the mainland. If not for her and Justin Drake noticing a second wound that required attention, she'd have succumbed to her injuries on that tiny spit of worthless land.

She'd lost so much blood that it had taken her days, even with medical care, to start to feel whole and to even register how much pain she was truly in.

On the first day in the hospital, it had just been Angie Frost sitting quietly with Rebecca while she wavered in and out of consciousness. Starting on the second day, Rhonda Lettinger, Justin Drake, and Bailey Flynn had all taken turns, stopping by to keep her company and—once she was ready to process what happened—give her updates on everyone else.

She'd initially told herself that Bailey and Justin had only visited her because they worked in the same building. But she had to admit, she considered them friends.

"I probably owe you a thank-you gift. A bottle of wine, bourbon, tequila, whatever you drink."

"For the advice?" Bailey had already turned back to her work.

Tying her protective clothing in place, Rebecca stepped up beside her. This appeared to be a car crash victim, not Amy Washington. "For saving my life. And getting me out of there. I heard you insisted on being part of the search party. If not for that, I'd be dead."

Bailey waved that off with a tiny hand gesture. "I swore an oath, same as you. I take mine just as seriously as you do."

"Your oath doesn't require you to go into an unsecured area to search for the wounded."

Again, the M.E. smiled at her, and it was visible in her eyes. "No, but that's one of the perks of the job. Catching criminals keeps my caseload light. My dream one day is to only work on accidents and natural causes."

That sounded like a pipe dream. A wonderful, hopeful, delirious pipe dream.

"Me too."

"However," Bailey finished up the quick stitches she was using to close up the body, "I won't say no to sharing a bottle of wine with you once your doctor clears you."

"Then I've got good news for you. I'm cleared to drink." Rebecca spotted Amy lying on a table and gestured at her. "After we handle this, we should see about doing that."

"You're on." Bailey set down her instruments in the tray next to her and peeled off her gloves.

Rebecca followed her to the other table as Bailey pulled on a clean pair of gloves.

"Amy Washington, fifty-two, died of exsanguination after having her throat slit. The blade used was incredibly sharp, no jags, no hesitation marks either. Your killer is most likely right-handed." Bailey swung her flattened right hand like a knife over the body, showing how the start of the slash was deeper, then became shallower as her hand angled away. "He knew what he wanted to do and did it efficiently. I doubt he…or maybe she…got lucky with such a clean cut. And the lack of hesitation tells me he's done this before."

"So I'm looking for another body. Fantastic."

Bailey nodded. "I'd say that's a safe assumption. At least one. And despite the state of Mrs. Washington's clothes when you found her, there's no evidence that he defiled her before or after slicing her throat."

That was good news. Anytime Rebecca could cross off sexual assault as a possibility was a good day.

Nodding and taking notes, she remembered she had her own information to share. "I got an update from forensics on the way over. Since you've clearly been working, I'm sure you haven't read it yet. The nail scrapings you took showed only her own DNA and food particles. Potato chips and a sour cream-based dip of some flavor. Chips and dip from the party she never got the chance to wash off."

"And with no defensive wounds on her hands, it appears she didn't fight back." Bailey waved her hand over the body.

"Either she was surprised or didn't think she was in danger." Rebecca looked at the hands, soft and slightly bony. "Or, I suppose, she wasn't any kind of a fighter. She could've simply frozen in fear."

"What about that note you found?" Bailey covered Amy's

face and started removing her personal protective equipment.

Taking the hint that the M.E. was done working in the morgue, Rebecca followed suit and walked to the sinks. "Forensics says that, according to the ink on the note, it was written more than five years ago."

"They can't be more specific?"

"Unfortunately, no. Technology allows them to date when the ink was used, but not if it's older than five years. They also found some aged and degraded prints that couldn't be recovered in any useful way. The next step is to use an electrostatic detection apparatus on the paper to see if they can lift any impressions. It's a long shot, but the hope is that it reveals imprints left behind from other sheets of paper that were on top of it."

"Well, that could prove useful."

"Considering how long Amy Washington was a teacher and how many people she interacted with, it's a pretty big suspect pool. Not just all the students and staff, but all the parents as well. That's the majority of our little town." Despite not having touched anything, Rebecca went ahead and washed up as well. "Some people sit on their anger before they get the courage to act on it. Or something happens and they snap. One final straw that breaks the camel's back."

"Like an abused wife who suddenly kills her husband after years of violence." Drying her hands, Bailey frowned at the third body lying on one of the tables. It was draped in fabric, and Rebecca couldn't tell if there was a man or a woman underneath.

"I didn't want to have to go this route, but it looks like I'll need to do a search of the NCIC to see if there's been any other cases involving a note like this left on a body coupled with a throat slashing."

"You're thinking serial?"

"I don't want to. It'd be nice to have a simple case." Rebecca tossed her paper towels in the trash. "After the summer we've had, it'd be a welcome respite. And we are a tourist destination too. We get people in from all over. I already checked ViCAP, and there's nothing current that matches this, but maybe the pattern hasn't been caught yet. It happens."

Clean and dry now, Bailey made for the door. "But isn't it usually the spouse who snaps in cases like this? Your nearest and dearest are more likely to kill you than anyone else."

"In most cases, yes. In this one, the husband has early-onset Alzheimer's. We're both aware of how people with dementia can have episodes of violence they don't recall. Thankfully, his dementia might actually exonerate him in this case. Because he didn't remember to change his clothes or shoes, we believe he wasn't anywhere near Amy when she was attacked. But due to his cognitive state, we may never know how he managed to get home from the party, which would be quite a walk to their house from the school."

"I'm glad you have the exculpatory evidence of his clothing, but don't forget that a person with dementia wouldn't have planned an attack. The knife and the note sure feel premeditated to me." Bailey rubbed some lotion into her hands.

"I agree Buzz Washington doesn't look good for the murder of his wife."

Eliminating one suspect, especially a cognitively impaired widower, was a tiny step in the right direction. But that left an entire island of suspects who'd had contact with Amy Washington throughout the years.

Looked like Rebecca's hopes for a simple case were dashed again.

18

Rebecca stood by the front desk of the station, chatting with the new dispatcher she'd hired after Viviane's promotion to deputy. Elliot Ping's blond head, surfer tan, and light-brown eyes reminded her of the original reason she'd come to the island at the beginning of the summer. The man exuded relaxation. He'd spent the first part of his shift with Melody, shadowing her before being left solo.

She was glad that Viviane had recommended her ex-boyfriend for the position. They were still friends, and she'd promised Rebecca that, because she knew the job better than nearly anyone, Elliot would do great in the role. He'd passed all his tests with flying colors and had sped through all his initial training.

Today was his first official day on the job, though, so the jury was out on whether he could handle the practical aspects of being the new daytime dispatcher.

So far, so good.

Although she enjoyed getting to know Elliot—he seemed to be a natural at the job—the real reason she was standing by the front desk was because Melvin Drysdale's three poker buddies were on their way in.

Together.

She sighed, wishing she'd thought far enough ahead to schedule them at different times. It wouldn't have stopped them from contacting each other and solidifying their stories, though.

It is what it is.

After leaving Melvin's home earlier, Rebecca had done some digging. A quick phone call to his employer, Island Motors, and its helpful manager, Trey Farmer, and she'd acquired the names of two of the poker buddies. Bob "B.B." Ballinger and Lance Myer. They were indeed "a pair of slackers," according to Farmer, who said they spent too much time chatting with Melvin and keeping him from his work.

Those men, along with Rod Hammond, had been contacted and asked to come in this afternoon. The goal was to find out how airtight Melvin's alibi was for the night of Amy Washington's murder. She wasn't sure if they'd carpooled, but the three men walked through the front door of the sheriff's station together.

They approached the dispatch desk with an air of confidence only seen by those who believed there was safety in numbers.

"Hello, gentlemen. I'm Sheriff Rebecca West. And you are…?"

A stocky middle-aged man wearing a stained t-shirt, Hawaiian-print shorts, and flip-flops stepped forward. Sweat glistened on his scalp through his closely cropped sandy-brown hair. "I'm Bob Ballinger. My friends call me B.B." He extended his hand, and Rebecca shook it, before he stepped to the side for his friends.

The second man sported a black concert t-shirt for a band she'd never heard of and a pair of jean shorts. His thin, clean-shaven face paired with his tiny hands and feet made him seem androgynous. "Hey, I'm Rod Hammond." Inexplicably, he winked at Rebecca, and she had to stop herself from rolling her eyes.

"Guess that leaves me. I'm Lance Myer."

Rebecca guessed the man was in his early thirties. He was the best dressed in the group, sporting a collared knit shirt and cotton shorts that hadn't been ironed, possibly ever.

"Thank you for coming in, gentlemen. This shouldn't take long."

Elliot released the lock on the half door, and it buzzed as it swung open. Rebecca led the trio back to the interrogation room, motioning for Hoyt to join them. She'd briefed him on the purpose of their visit, and he was more than happy to sit shotgun in the meeting.

Hoyt and Rebecca took seats opposite the three men who'd chosen to all sit on the same side of the long table. The senior deputy took out his notepad and nodded to her that he was ready.

At Rebecca's prompting, each man recited his name, age, and current address. Once Hoyt had jotted everything down, she posed the million-dollar question. What she hadn't expected was how profoundly Melvin Drysdale's alibi had crumbled.

Taking in the eclectic group assembled across the table, Rebecca wondered how they'd come to spend time together. B.B. had admitted that Melvin was a horrible poker player, and they hung out with him because they could line their pockets with his cash.

Lance added that Melvin also had a fridge full of beer and never stopped them from helping themselves. "What's better than easy money and free beer? Besides, it's not like we don't like the guy. But his gruff personality goes down better after a few cold ones."

The men admitted to having played poker at Melvin's home on Thursday night, but the game broke up earlier than usual. Myer got a call from his boss at Mi Caretta, the Mexican restaurant near the sheriff's station, asking him to fill in for someone who went home sick mid-shift. Since Myer had given Ballinger a ride, they left together. That was around seven thirty. They hadn't seen Melvin since that night.

Hammond said he stuck around for another hand or two but grew bored with the small pots and added that "two-person poker sucks," and he left around eight, leaving Melvin alone. At least, to their knowledge.

After a few follow-up questions, the men were excused, and Myer and Ballinger quickly departed. But Hammond leaned back in his chair as if he had more to say. And Rebecca was never one to turn away a potential witness. Perhaps there was something he wanted to share away from his friends.

"Is there more you wanted to add to your official statement, Mr. Hammond?"

He beamed from ear to ear like he was going to spin the greatest tale ever told. "You know, I usually only play poker with the guys during the summer. That's when my wife and son go visit my mother-in-law. My wife can be pretty strict about our finances and spending too much time away from her. She's sweet on me like that."

Hoyt snorted.

Realizing she might get more out of the man if she dismissed her senior deputy, Rebecca asked him to check the case file for any updates. Hoyt wasted no time in exiting the interrogation room.

Rebecca pushed her chair out with a loud screech across the tile floor, drawing out the action to give Hammond time to respond. It was possible his wife's departure had left the man few people to talk to, and she hoped the lonely man might decide to get chatty.

The million-watt smile was back. "You know, I spend a lot of time with those guys. And Melvin does a lot of sharing when he's had too much to drink, which is pretty much every time we play poker."

Perfect. Now you have my interest.

"What kind of things does he share?"

"Look, it's none of my business. But he's said stuff about his brother, money trouble, women trouble. I can't remember half of it."

"Did Amy Washington's name come up in his women troubles? Or his brother's troubles?"

Hammond shook his head, his million-watt smile still fully in place. "Couldn't tell you." Rebecca got the distinct impression he was lying, but she couldn't puzzle out a reason.

Yet another Shadow's mystery she couldn't explain.

Maybe he wanted personal attention. Maybe he thought talking with a cop gave him some kind of street cred. Maybe he just didn't like Melvin and wanted to get him in trouble.

Whatever his reason, she was pretty sure he was wasting her time.

As she came around the table, Hammond also stood, and she instinctively moved her hand toward her holster.

Rebecca scanned the hallway for her senior deputy, but he'd made himself scarce once she'd sent him on the fake task.

As she walked toward the bullpen, Rebecca probed one last time for more details. "You can't remember anything Melvin may have said?"

"I suppose it's kinda sad, in light of what happened to the Washington woman, but did you know he had a big ole crush on her? Yup. She was a few years ahead of him in school, and he was really head over heels. But she didn't feel the same way. Melvin's brother, now…he was closer to Washington, if you know what I mean."

After another wink, he held her gaze as they arrived in the desolate bullpen. A clattering of a locker door closing indicated where her deputy had gone. Hopefully Rod Hammond didn't realize Frost couldn't check the case file in the locker room.

"I wouldn't want to assume anything. Can you clarify what you mean? Did Melvin say his brother had an affair with Amy Washington?"

Hammond waved at the air. "Naw, he never said it outright. He'd just start ranting about how his older brother was always better than him at everything. Like, Melvin flunked some classes and barely made it out of high school, but Sebastian had pretty decent grades. He also had a job with great benefits from the county. Even girlfriends who were both pretty and smart. Once, he mentioned how his older brother managed to skate on drug charges awhile back, but Melvin ended up doing time."

Shaking his head, Hammond stretched his arms up high. He was way too at ease in the middle of the sheriff's station. *Maybe it's because this place is suddenly a ghost town.* Rebecca's thoughts were cut short as Hammond continued to unwittingly throw his poker buddy under the proverbial bus.

"You know, it's tough to get a good job when you have a felony on your record. One night, when Melvin was drunker than usual because he'd had a fight with his wife that afternoon, he was talking about his time in prison. I'm not gonna lie. What he said was kinda scary. He talked about how dangerous it is 'on the inside' and how you have to learn to fight or you'll be picked on all the time. He said no one ever picked on him. I guess that means he learned how to fight, huh, Sheriff?"

Rod Hammond was a strange man with unusual idiosyncrasies. That didn't make him, or anyone like him, a killer. He'd offered some helpful insights into Melvin Drysdale that deserved follow-up, after all.

But until the killer was found, everyone was a suspect.

19

The buffer skipped and slid across the tiles of the classroom floor. After removal of generations of sneakers scuffs, the surface had been worn thin and the edges didn't always meet up perfectly. That was why he put so much time and attention into keeping the tiles waxed and smooth. No child was going to take a fall and skin their chin because of the uneven flooring. Not while Sebastian Drysdale was on the job, at least.

Most years, this was his favorite day. The final Saturday walk-through after summer when the building was all his. When he could relax into his work and make sure it was perfect.

This time, it was just sad and lonely.

There'd only been a few years of Seb's life when he hadn't shared this building with Amy Washington. Of course, she hadn't been a Washington when she'd been Seb's classmate. The four years when she was off getting her teaching degree had left a hole in his heart.

Not in the way everyone around here liked to gossip. He'd never been *in love* with her. She'd been like a big sister to him, always looking out for him, despite her being one month younger.

Each section of hallway and room he finished, he left dark and locked, much like how his heart felt now without Amy in his life. There'd been no funeral yet, what with her death being a crime. No real chance to say goodbye. No closure.

The floors were nearly done...just one last corridor to finish. With the sun still up, the building wasn't completely dark—just dim and a bit shadowy—but the halls echoed like a tomb. Seb pondered if the loneliness had more to do with his best friend's death than the deserted corridors of his second home. Maybe he should retire. Amy had tried to do that and never even gotten a chance to enjoy her golden years.

I'm not going to let that happen to me.

Pulling the heavy machine from the most recent room, he paused for a moment. This wasn't the room Amy had always taught in. But it had been her last. She'd moved around the facility as much as all the other teachers, never knowing for sure where she'd end up next as the needs of the children changed year by year.

Sebastian reached into his pocket, lifting out the tiny one-hitter pipe he'd already loaded up. It shouldn't have been like this. He flicked his lighter and took a deep drag, holding the smoke. Knowing his dear friend would disapprove, he couldn't even enjoy the escape he sought.

He'd acknowledged for more than a year that this day would come—when he would be working at the school without his closest friend. But knowing she was gone, not just from the school but also from his life forever, magnified the ache in his chest.

Sebastian had helped when and where he could, but Amy had still been overwhelmed by her husband's progressing illness. He'd patted her shoulder the day he found her crying the first time her husband had looked at her and not known who she was.

If he could've done more, he would have. But dealing with emotions was never something he'd been good at. He wasn't a cold man, or at least, that was what Amy had told him. There'd just never been a chance for him to learn how to feel or express his emotions. That was why he liked this job so much.

He could stay behind the scenes. No one bothered him or even really saw him. He could do his work, clean things up nice for everyone else, and go home, knowing he'd made the world a better place, even if it was just one building's worth of shiny floors and sparkling toilets.

Amy always saw him, though. She was the only teacher who called him by name. She'd thank him for emptying her garbage can. Even lift it up and hand it to him. Then she'd ask how his day had been.

Her acts of kindness, something she probably did hundreds of times a day, had meant the world to Sebastian. Still, he'd never said anything like that to her. Instead, he'd made sure her room was always the cleanest and freshest and that her desk was always polished. And she'd noticed.

He'd promised to visit her. That they would get coffee or go on walks with Buzz, his second friend, around the facility grounds.

Now that would never happen.

Amy was gone, and he'd never see her again.

Sebastian blew out the smoke, then turned off the light and closed the door. Maybe he could still visit Buzz up at his new place. They could still take walks together. And he could help Amy's husband remember the amazing woman he'd married.

That would be nice. A tiny act of kindness would be his

way of repaying Amy for the unconditional friendship she'd given him his whole life. She'd once called him her hero. That was silly. It had been just the opposite. She'd been *his* hero.

Back then, he'd been prone to making poor choices. Why he'd ever brought that joint to work, he'd never know. And when the principal had snatched it up and flown into a rage, he was sure he'd be canned.

But when Hill asked Amy to tell the police what she'd seen that morning, she claimed she hadn't seen the joint. And because the principal was so concerned about a tiny bit of marijuana being on school grounds, he'd flushed the only evidence he had in a crazed huff.

Seb inhaled deeply from the pipe and closed his eyes. Was marijuana on campus, again, his most brilliant idea? No, but given the circumstances, he felt secure no one would show up to witness him using his one and only coping mechanism.

A squeak down the hall jerked him out of his memories, and he turned to look. *Dammit!* That noise was the distinctive squeak the old crank windows in the classrooms made. He'd been opening the windows to speed up the drying time of the wax and must've forgotten to close one. If the wind outside blew hard enough, some of the weaker cranks would turn from the pressure exerted on them.

The lit hallway was empty, with all the doors closed and nothing moving. Shaking his head at his stupidity, Sebastian pocketed his little vice, backed the buffer to the center of the floor and started it again. He'd take another pass when he was done and make sure all the windows were closed.

When the squeak came again, he paused, shutting off the loud machine. If he could hear a noise over the powerful motor, it wasn't created by something small. He heard the *thunk* of a classroom door swinging closed. It'd come from the other wing, where the elementary students studied these days.

It had to be another group of teenagers. For some reason, they thought it was hilarious to break into the school and rearrange the furniture in the younger students' rooms. Sometimes, they even went so far as to sneak adult books into the little libraries set up in the reading corners.

Sebastian went to track them down before they could make a mess of his perfectly organized and cleaned rooms.

Turning down the dark corridor, he immediately clocked which room the teens had infiltrated. Light filtered out from under the door, marking it clearly.

"If you kids clean up any messes you made, I won't tell the principal on you." Sebastian stepped heavily down the tiles, letting them hear how close he was getting as a warning. "And if you're gone out the window before I open the door, I won't even call your parents."

Their juvenile sense of humor might annoy him, but it did make sense. After all, they were adolescents. He'd been a stupid teenager once and knew how easy it was to be talked into doing stupid things. Hell, he'd even turned into a stupid adult.

Reaching the door, he flung it open but paused, giving the boys—because it was always boys—a final chance to run out the other door and not be seen.

The room was empty as far as he could tell, but he stepped forward to crane his head and be sure.

A person in a hoodie reached out from behind the door. Silver glinted as a knife slashed forward.

Seb jerked to a halt. Kids had thrown punches at him a few times, but they'd never pulled a knife! That was a whole new low. This kid must've been doing something much worse than fiddling with some books.

He grabbed the kid's arm as he swung again, but his mind

short-circuited as he realized the person trying to attack him was actually a grown man.

Before Seb had any time to recover, Hoodie spun around from where he'd been hiding beside the door. His fist plowed into Sebastian's nose, the cartilage crunching as it broke.

Seb's eyes squeezed closed reflexively.

That was a bad move. Bad move! He had to open his eyes. This guy was going for the throat, and if he didn't fight back, he was going to die. He couldn't fight if he couldn't see.

His eyes snapped open. Amy had been killed nearby by someone who'd slit her throat. Now a man was attacking him with a knife, trying to kill him the same way.

"Killing the kindest woman I ever knew was cowardly, you bastard. You'll fry for what you did to Amy." Screaming primally, Seb twisted the man's arm, making him drop the knife. It clattered on the tiles, and Sebastian hit the hilt with his heel, sending the blade spinning down the hall.

Hoodie pulled back his fist to punch him again.

Sebastian ducked under the swing and pushed hard against the back of his arm, slamming the man into the door-frame. He wanted to beat the crap out of the guy who'd killed his best friend.

Undeterred, Hoodie pushed back.

Sebastian's shoes, covered in splattered wax from working, slipped on the floors, and he went down hard, his pipe clattering out of his pocket. His head bounced off the floor, and he was momentarily stunned.

Hoodie made the best of the situation, taking off down the hall after the knife.

Rolling to his knees, Sebastian tried to get up and go after him. His feet slipped on the floor, and he fell again. The world spun like a broken whirligig, wobbling chaotically. It didn't matter how fit he was. At this point, he was going to keep losing if he couldn't stay upright.

Losing was a death sentence.

After pulling himself up using the wall, he took off after Hoodie, who was running toward the knife. Which also happened to be by the nearest exit.

Having toiled all morning in the school, Sebastian knew the lobby door was also the only one with the chains removed, as he'd unlocked it earlier. He needed to rush past Hoodie and out the front door. Once outside, he might be able to get help or, at the very least, gain some traction in the parking lot.

Hoodie scooped up the knife, blocking Seb's escape as he spun to face him.

Instincts taking over, Sebastian lowered and charged his attacker, desperate and determined. The hand holding the knife moved in a lightning arc, slashing deep into his arm. Blood sprayed in a horrific fountain, painting his perfectly polished tiles in shades of terror. His shoes slid on the slick surface, but his momentum carried him into the lobby.

The door was only a few yards away, the red exit light a beacon of hope. Clutching his wounded arm to his chest, Sebastian sped toward freedom. He slammed into the crash bar. The latch, notched and worn from decades of abuse, resisted for a terrifying heartbeat before yielding.

A hand landed on his shoulder like claws of impending doom. Knowing what was coming, Sebastian tried to block the knife, to grab it, but the original cut made him too slow, too damaged. The glint of the blade caught his eye before its edge sliced past his hands into his neck.

He was going to see Amy sooner than he thought.

But…who would go for walks with Buzz?

20

Two dead bodies on the school grounds, and both of them were longtime staff.

But this one had been much more violent.

Just as the witness had said, there was most definitely blood everywhere. Rebecca examined Sebastian Drysdale's body. The camera in her hand wasn't being utilized just yet. She wanted to observe every detail first.

He'd gone down fighting. Perhaps the scene was bloodier because the killer was escalating. Rebecca also had to consider that the victim was a man who was stronger and could put up a fight. If Amy had fought back, her death might've been equally brutal.

There was a drip mark line down a long hallway leading up to the victim. The line ended in a large arterial spray by the door, where someone had sliced the janitor's throat. She could tell, even without the techs there, that the perpetrator had caught Sebastian from behind right as he reached the lobby door.

He'd been trying to get away after surviving an earlier attack, where he'd probably gotten the broken nose and the defensive wounds across his arm and hands, creating a bloody connect-the-dots. If her theory was correct, Drysdale had been pulled back from the door and flipped onto his back.

The timeline of events was written out in the trail of drops, the spray across the door, walls, and inside the jamb, and the streaks where his body slid through the rest. Once the techs arrived, she was sure they'd confirm her hypothesis. This scene reminded her of those old learning-to-dance kits that laid out the steps to follow on the floor. Even a rookie could look at this mess and know what happened.

And her newest deputy had done just that before leaving to take witness statements. Viviane was outside with Principal Steve Hill and Pamela Radcliffe. School would have to be put on hold at least until they could get the scene processed.

"This wasn't done this morning."

"Hmm?" Hoyt looked up from where he'd been taking measurements and recording them.

"The blood is old. I'd say this happened yesterday. Look how much of it has seeped into his clothes from the puddles on the floor. Rigor and lividity also indicate this happened more than ten hours ago."

Hoyt nodded and went back to measuring. "Seems about right. Bailey will weigh in time of death when she gets here."

"You know, I looked for him yesterday. I drove by his home and the school. Needed to talk to him about his alibi since Melvin didn't corroborate it. None of the lights were on here." Guilt did its best to overtake Rebecca, but she was too tired to deal with that. And this new layer couldn't really compete with the one she'd been buried under for the last two weeks.

Sleeping had never been easy for her, but now it was nearly impossible. She kept waking up unable to take a full breath. Last night, it wasn't because of the dreams, or rather, not solely because of them. Lying down made her ribs hurt more. When they started aching, she would reflexively take smaller and shallower breaths, trying to avoid the pain. Then she'd wake up because she felt like she was suffocating, and she'd gasp. Which made the pain worse.

A vicious cycle.

And that dark part in the back of her mind, the one that blamed her for surviving when Darian didn't, told her she deserved it. Locke had been injured too. And Ryker? His uncertain prognosis stoked the flames of her nightmares. This was karma for failing, and she deserved every bit of pain that came with it.

And more. So much more.

"Can't see the lights back here from the street." Hoyt waved his pen around them, bringing Rebecca out of her self-pitying funk. "With the way the wings were added on, this one is blocked in by all the others. That's why they decided to move the younger kids here this year. Since it's easier for the young ones to be closer to the hunker points for hurricanes and whatnot."

"Hunker points? Is that what you guys call them?" Rebecca carefully crouched down, keeping her back straight. She still had a job to do, regardless of how much pain she was experiencing. Forensics would be here in the next half hour. If her team could get this all done first, it would make the job easier.

"Yeah, the center or most structurally stable part of the building. That's where you go when a tornado or hurricane is coming. For us, it's usually hurricanes. Hunker points." Hoyt looked at her to see if she understood.

She nodded, grateful for the reminder. "Right. I got familiar with those when I read the hurricane manual Greg gave me. I just didn't realize that was what they were called."

"Well, they are." Hoyt jotted down some numbers, grinning at the paper. "Because I named them."

Rebecca snorted and had to catch herself on the wall as a vicious cramp went through her chest. Hoyt started to reach out for her, but she ignored him and rebalanced herself so she could take pictures. "It's a good name. Makes perfect sense."

His gaze dropped to his notepad, and he gave a slight shrug. "I thought so."

Moving her feet carefully, Rebecca took pictures of the body, the blood trail, and the wavering lines of blood on the janitor's cotton coveralls.

"I'm going to have to open the door to get the rest of the pictures." Rebecca nodded at the doorway.

Hoyt straightened. He'd already walked the length of the blood trail twice. Pointing back to where it started, he tucked his notepad into his breast pocket. "So far, I've only cleared the rooms. I'm going to do a full walk-through and see if I can find any more evidence."

"See if you can find the janitor's office too. I saw a floor buffer sitting in the next wing over. He was clearly working before he was killed."

"On it, Boss."

As he left to search the building, Rebecca pushed open the door with her hip. They'd already taken pictures of the door and crash bar on their way into the scene. All she had to do now was photograph the rest of the blood.

She stepped through the doorway, taking more pictures from the outside.

Once she was done with that, Rebecca tucked the camera into her pocket and stripped off the gloves and booties she'd been wearing. She walked around the side of the building to the parking lot where Viviane was taking Principal Hill's statement while trying to soothe Pamela Radcliffe.

From what Rebecca had been told, Pamela hadn't gotten close to the crime scene, but the woman was shaking and crying as she paced between the lines of an empty parking spot.

Or was she just a very good actress?

A chill ran down Rebecca's spine as she considered the possibility. Could the teacher's distress be a performance? Was she hiding something?

She was connected closely to both cases, after all.

Rebecca's mind raced with the implications, but she forced herself to stay calm. Now was not the time for accusations without evidence.

Maybe I'm going crazy, seeing and feeling things that aren't there.

With a deep sigh, Rebecca knew that she would have to dig deeper, reexamine every piece of evidence, every witness statement, every person's behavior. She couldn't risk making a mistake, not again.

I won't let you down, Darian. I won't miss anything.

Lives were at stake, and she would leave no stone unturned.

Not this time.

21

"I can't delay the opening of school. Surely, you understand that, hun."

As Viviane was formulating a response, Sheriff West strode up to join them. She appeared upset, and Vi wondered if she'd failed to follow a procedure.

"It's *Deputy* Darby, Principal Hill," Rebecca interjected as sternly as any administrator ever could. "She's not one of your students anymore."

Aw, she's defending me.

"What? Well, of course she's not. I'm well aware of that." Hill glanced nervously between the sheriff and Viviane.

"Good. Deputy Darby, please continue your interview."

Principal Steve Hill's blond hair was darkened by a thick layer of gelled product holding each lock firmly in place. His perfectly straight teeth made Viviane wonder whether anything was allowed to be out of place with this man. He was dressed in a crisp, white, long-sleeved, button-down shirt with a solid navy-blue tie cinched tightly around his neck. His tie was held firmly in place by an American flag tie bar. The creases on his blue trousers looked sharp enough to slice bread.

Before Vi could go on, her childhood principal threw up his hands. "It doesn't matter to me which one of you gets that body out of here. It just has to go."

"Sir, you're talking about one of your employees. He's worked here as long as I've been alive. Don't you want to help us find who did this?"

"Of course I do. Are you questioning my actions as the leader of this school?"

Now, that sounded an awful lot like an administrator admonishing a student. She had to prove to the sheriff she could handle difficult interviews.

"No, sir. I'm trying to educate you about the realities of the situation and to learn from you what you saw and heard when you arrived today. There have been two murders around this school in the past seventy-two hours. As principal, I'm certain you want the school board and the parents to know you've cooperated fully with authorities and are doing whatever you can to bring justice to our community."

The principal's mouth gaped, and he looked to the sheriff for relief.

Rebecca wore her emotions on her face. The smile she was fighting to hold back let Vi know her boss approved.

"Principal Hill, it's only going to get hotter as the sun climbs higher, and we're both overdressed for these conditions." Vi waved her hand between the well-dressed man and her own neatly pressed uniform with the shiny badge.

She wasn't fibbing. Although it was still early morning, it had to be close to eighty degrees. Even though her uniform had short sleeves, it was too hot to be standing in the asphalt parking lot. Of course, the school was a crime scene, so going inside wasn't an option. At least she'd steered them both into the shade of the building before beginning her questioning.

"Now, please tell me what time you arrived here today."

"It was just before eight a.m. I always unlock the building the day before classes begin so the teachers can wrap up any work they left for the last minute. They wouldn't need to come in if they didn't laze about all summer."

The man who'd been Vi's principal for her high school years had a reputation for being a stickler for the rules. But calling the amazing teachers who worked there lazy was a side of the man she didn't know. She wondered if he'd always been this way.

Jotting down his response, she set aside her own opinions to avoid biasing the interview. "And what did you do when you arrived?"

"I parked in the employee lot and walked up to the doors. When I noticed the glass panes were dirty, I worried Drysdale hadn't shown up for work and the place wouldn't be clean."

"What did you do next?"

"I'd planned to unlock the building, on schedule. When I broke out my keys, I noticed the door wasn't even chained, and I could see a blob on the floor through window. When I pressed my face up to the glass to see what it was, I realized it was a dead body. That, or a terrible prank."

Viviane glanced at Rebecca after hearing the man had pressed his face to the glass. She made a note to tell Justin Drake that he might find transfer DNA from the principal on the door's glass. "Did you notice anyone suspicious around the building? Any cars in the lot you didn't recognize?" She guessed the principal knew the make and model of every car permitted on school grounds.

"Other than the dead body and an unlocked door, everything else was normal. Is that all? Can you clear the building now?"

Ignoring his whining tone, Viviane mentally ran down

the rest of the questions the team would need to know. "What time had Mr. Drysdale been scheduled to work?"

"He prefers to work in the evening, after the teachers have cleared out of the building. He was scheduled to wax and buff the floors, giving them time to dry overnight. He opens the windows to help the wax dry more quickly. Today, the staff is supposed to come put the chairs down and set up their students' desks."

"You mean the lazy teachers who leave everything until the last minute? They're expected to come in on a Sunday to set up their classrooms after Mr. Drysdale's finished with the floors?"

When the man's face flushed, Viviane mused that he was turning into a walking American flag. She wondered if he'd be flattered by the comparison to his tie bar.

"The time, sir? What time did he do the floors?"

"He was supposed to arrive at five p.m. yesterday evening and leave when they were finished."

Rebecca stepped forward but hesitated, staring at her. It took Viviane a minute to realize she was waiting for her approval to insert herself into the interview. She nodded at her boss.

"Deputy Darby and I appreciate your time and cooperation. As she said, I'm sure the school board and parents will be appreciative of your efforts to bring the investigation to a speedy conclusion. So in that vein, we just need you to provide a sample of your DNA."

"What? You can't think I—"

Viviane jumped in, holding up her hand to stop the tirade. "If we don't get your DNA, we can't release the scene. You pressed your face against the glass and may very well have come in contact with the killer's DNA."

And there it was. After being unfazed by a dead body and

bloody doors, Principal Hill finally cringed over the reality of the situation. Or maybe he was just a germaphobe.

Rebecca called over one of the forensic techs—who'd just arrived and begun processing the outside of the building—and had him swab the principal's cheek before thanking Hill for his cooperation.

As the man walked briskly to his car, Viviane turned to find Pamela Radcliffe sitting on a concrete parking block a few spaces away. She, too, had managed to find some relief from the sun's rays.

Pamela looked up at her as she and Rebecca approached the teacher. "Hi, Vi, Sheriff. Is Sebastian Drysdale really dead?"

"Yes, Miss Radcliffe. I'm afraid he is."

"He was such a sweet man. A real teddy bear. Why would anyone do something like this? Does it have something to do with Amy? Is some psychopath hunting down the sweetest, kindest people who work here?" Pamela's voice was hoarse from crying and wobbled as she struggled to get the words out.

"We don't know that yet."

She pointed a shaky hand vaguely toward the building. "Poor Sebastian. I just can't believe he's dead. I was just here last night, finishing up tasks in my classroom. I was running behind and he had to wait on me." Her voice started to get higher. "I didn't even say goodbye to him when I left or apologize for getting in his way." Radcliffe's mouth dropped open as her eyes grew wide. "Do you think the killer was in the building when I was here too?"

Viviane wrapped her arm around the woman's shoulders as she started to shake. "I didn't see Sebastian's car. Did you?" She dodged the question, directing the woman down a different line of thinking.

"No, he doesn't own one. He likes to walk everywhere, including to work."

Knowing how fit Sebastian was, that made perfect sense to Viviane. "Why don't you go home, Miss Radcliffe? Do you need us to call someone to give you a ride?"

"No. No need. I'm going to walk. I think the fresh air and exercise will do me good." The teacher turned, and Viviane shot a worried look at the sheriff.

Rebecca shook her head slightly, signaling Viviane to let her go on her own. If Rebecca wasn't worried for the teacher's safety, Viviane would have to put her concerns aside. She was a deputy now, not a dispatcher.

"Hey, Boss, you got your ears on?" Hoyt's voice cut through their radios, and Rebecca picked up.

"What you got, Frost?"

With Rebecca motioning for Viviane to join her, they followed the sidewalk back inside.

Hoyt's report echoed through their radios as they skirted the forensic team in the lobby. "Found one of those single-hit pipes, a one-hitter, with fresh ashes and some resin. It was down the hall, inside a room, in a section that was already cleaned and locked up too."

"And we've been told Sebastian was a user in his past." Viviane followed Rebecca down the corridor to where Hoyt was waiting for them. Once they got close enough, the sheriff and senior deputy dropped using their mics.

"Also, I found where the killer most likely came in. There's a classroom next to the new playground. One of the windows was open so I took a closer look. There's mulch, like the stuff used on the playground, on the floor under the window."

Even though the building had been cleared, and the three of them were alone, Viviane felt like the person who'd killed Sebastian was nearby. Somewhere on the streets, lurking outside, there was a killer with a grudge against people who worked at this school.

Her school.

Lifting her chin, she glanced around. *I may be new, but watch out, asshole. I'm not letting you hurt anyone else.*

22

Hoyt had found Sebastian's janitorial office door unlocked and open, and he'd been ready to conduct a thorough search. But when the forensic team and the M.E. showed up, Rebecca sent him back to the office.

She'd told him to make sure everything was running smoothly with the new guy, who was working on the weekend to get a feel for the role. She also wanted him to go through Wallace's files to find out why Sebastian didn't have a criminal record if he'd been caught red-handed with drugs on the school grounds.

Or maybe it was just to get him out of the way again.

Hoyt felt petty thinking like that. Except it didn't make any sense for her to send him away. He was a good investigator, and he knew it. And he knew she knew it. Rebecca wasn't one to use her resources poorly either.

Still, he mulled it over on the drive back. Angie would've said he was stewing on it, or brooding, but he wasn't. He was trying to figure out Rebecca's motives, like the trained professional he was.

He checked in with Viviane's ex-high school sweetheart—

also known as the new daytime dispatcher—Elliot Ping, to make sure he was doing okay. From what Hoyt could tell so far, he was going to be a good addition to the team.

It didn't dawn on him until he returned to the office that they couldn't access the files on Sebastian or his brother in the field because Wallace hadn't digitized them, all in an effort to keep them safe from prying eyes. Instead, he'd have to sort through the papers by hand to find the information.

If he found something relevant, he could add it to the case file. He was being overly sensitive and second-guessing Rebecca. It had to be from overworking and not getting enough sleep. Well, that was what he told himself.

Following a hunch, he ignored Wallace's secret stash of files and went for the more accessible ones stored in the sheriff's office. Sure enough, he found a folder for Drysdale right where it should've been.

But when he pulled it out, Sebastian's name wasn't on it. Melvin's was. It made sense they had a file for Melvin. He'd been to jail on drug charges in the past. But there wasn't a file on Sebastian at all. Nor was he mentioned in Melvin's except as next of kin.

Hoyt skimmed through the papers, finding that Melvin's drug arrest occurred near the time of Sebastian's incident at the school. But there was no mention of Sebastian, Amy Washington, or the school. Flipping back to the first page, he checked the name of the arresting officer.

"That makes it easy." Hoyt plopped down into what had become his favorite seat and leaned over to use the phone on the sheriff's desk.

"Hey, West, you need me?" Greg Abner's deep voice answered.

"It's me, Abner." Hoyt leaned back, propping his feet up on the case of paper he kept there for that exact reason. Why

Rebecca let him get away with it, he didn't know, but he wasn't going to ask and bring it to her attention.

"Frost, you back in the captain's seat again? Where's the boss lady? Is she okay?"

The simple words transported Hoyt back to the last time he'd captained a boat. Pulling away from Rebecca struggling in neck-deep water, he'd left her behind to get shot and nearly beaten to death.

"West, no!"

Rebecca shoved the boat away from her, pushing them out into the current. He struggled to keep his feet, leaning over Ryker's unconscious body, getting a smear of thick blood on his uniform as the younger man's head fell to the side. For a second, he desperately prayed it was just blood and not brains on his clothing.

"Go! That's an order."

"Rebecca! Damn you!"

Impotent rage poured out of Hoyt as he watched his boss slip under the waves kicked up by the boat. But, as always, she managed to pull herself back up again. Just to be hit in the face by another wavelet as he once again tried to reach out to help her. The boat was so low in the water, every move he made sent more water slapping up against her, making her struggle harder until the current pulled them farther away. Then she smiled at him.

She fucking smiled. His blood ran cold as sweat poured down his back.

He was the only one moving on the boat. Locke and Darian were in the bow, both so hurt and tired they just lay there, splattered in blood. Everyone was bleeding profusely except him.

Maybe it was because he felt his senior's heavy gaze on him, but Darian struggled and managed to push himself up, just a little. Bloody bubbles suddenly erupted from Darian's mouth.

Hoyt knew what that meant. The man's lung had been punctured. He was dying. Their eyes met, and they knew just how bad this all was.

Their only hope of surviving was the boat, and the boat wouldn't hold everyone. That meant leaving someone behind. And they both rejected that option.

That moment of silence stretched on forever, until Rebecca's voice broke it, calling him back to the island where everything had gone so very wrong.

She took the choice away from him.

"Sorry, Hoyt. Get them home."

It was all up to him now. The bubble burst, trickling pink saliva down Darian's cheek and chin.

The stench of blood filled Hoyt's nose, and he jerked, pulling his lip free from the teeth in his suddenly dry mouth. He was back in the office, in his boss's comfortable chair but no longer in charge. Suddenly, everything Darian had tried to tell him about triggers and flashbacks made sense. He needed to get a better handle on this shit.

"Frost, you there?" Greg's voice softened in concern. "Everything okay?"

"She's fine." Hoyt pulled himself upright and took a deep breath while running his tongue over his teeth to spread some moisture around his mouth. "Boss is fine, and so am I. In fact, she's working a scene, and we think it might be tied to a case you had back in 2010. I was here then but don't remember the incident. You were the responding officer, so I'm calling you. I'm using West's phone because it was one of our paper files."

There was a small stretch of silence, and Hoyt spent that time rethinking everything he said, his tone, his inflection.

How the hell did Rebecca and Darian deal with this crap all the time?

"Okay, what's the case?" Greg's tone was all business.

Maybe Hoyt had been overthinking things and the man was just getting himself situated before answering. Or working a crossword puzzle or just yawning. "Drysdale drug charges, possession with intent to distribute."

"Oh, yeah. I know that one. Janitor was caught smoking pot on school grounds. His boss called us in."

Hoyt looked at the file and the two different handwriting styles. "Wallace worked with you on it?"

"Yup. Sure did."

"That explains why there isn't a lot of information on this one." Hoyt tried to ignore the bitterness he felt.

"Don't be like that. That idiot principal had already tossed the evidence before he even called us. Said drugs weren't allowed on his campus and flushed it. All we had was his word to go on that anything had happened. You can't make a case on that, and writing a report for it's a waste of time."

Rustling paper echoed through the line, and Hoyt surmised his guess about Greg doing a crossword had been correct.

"There was another witness, but she refused to testify. Kept insisting the janitor was a good guy. We had to bluff and threaten the janitor to even get the information we got, and that was tracking the seller all the way back to the grower. This was after the smoke bans went into effect in our great state. No one was supposed to be smoking anywhere, certainly not in a school, and definitely not any type of drugs."

He chuckled at the thought. "It's crazy how much things have changed since the aughts. Now plenty of places have made pot legal and smoking in a restaurant illegal. Back then, we wanted to get the bastards smoking pot and nail them to the wall. Another thing to know, we did it by the book. Well, the way the books were written then. You know, before they passed that smoking ban, we could smoke cigarettes during interrogations. I had an ashtray, big heavy glass one, on my desk."

"Can't believe doctors actually prescribed that shit years ago."

Greg sighed gustily. "Anyway, we got the janitor to roll on his brother after the principal mentioned he'd seen Melvin hanging around after hours while Sebastian was working. He'd been there that morning, too, but left before we showed up. Using that, Melvin rolled on his dealer. Ended up being a big deal, but that was out of the county by then. The staties took down a few more people and Melvin got a slap on the wrist in exchange for his testimony. Twelve months and a fine, if I remember it right."

Hoyt couldn't believe what he was hearing. "Times have definitely changed. Twelve months for selling pot to his brother seems excessive for a slap on the wrist."

"Oh, no, it was way more than just the pot charges. Sebastian was only caught smoking pot, but he tested positive for a lot more. Heroin and X, if I remember right. That let us know we had a dealer on the island. Sebastian didn't have a car, so someone had to be bringing it to him. Since we knew Melvin was stopping by to see him frequently, we figured he had to be the dealer. We used that information to convince Sebastian we were already going after his brother and had evidence on him."

"I already dug through the file. I'm reading it now, in fact. There's no mention of either heroin or ecstasy in it." Hoyt rifled through the pages, checking to see if he missed anything.

Greg grunted. "Commonwealth's Attorney made a deal with him. None of that was added to the report. It's in my notes, though. After the bust, he was offered the deal. The bust wouldn't go on his record if he flipped. And he flipped. Melvin, that is."

"That other teacher, do you remember her name?" He was pretty sure where this was going.

"Amy Washington. The woman who was murdered the other day."

Hoyt sighed and leaned back in his chair again. "Actually, our most recent victim is Sebastian. That's as of this morning."

"Melvin's kid brother who turned him in?" He sounded shocked.

"The same one."

Greg went into a short cursing tirade that Hoyt waited out. "In order to get Melvin to confess, we might've bent the truth a little with him. We told him that a teacher at the school was friends with Sebastian and knew Melvin was trafficking drugs around the school."

Knowing how prone to gossiping the teachers at the school were, Hoyt was dead certain that Melvin would've had an easy time figuring out who else had been there when Sebastian was caught. And who his "teacher friend" was.

If they're still gossiping about it now, it had to be the talk of the teacher's lounge back then.

Hoyt closed the file and slapped it down on Rebecca's desk. "Well, now both people involved in his arrest are dead. That's not looking too good."

"I'll find my notes and bring them in. I remember Melvin had an extreme reaction to the news, but I can't remember what it was. Let me gather my things. See you in ten."

23

Rebecca maneuvered away from the corpse still sprawled out in the school's lobby to provide the medical examiner the space she needed while she narrated her findings.

"Well, I see this one put up a fight." Bailey stepped around Sebastian Drysdale's head, keeping clear of the blood on the floor. "Broken nose, banged-up knuckles, sliced arm. Looks like the nasty gash on his arm made that blood trail." She squatted down on the balls of her feet.

"Not sure if you saw or not, but he also had a cut from shaving yesterday." Rebecca tapped her throat.

Bailey leaned back and widened her eyes. "Hey, would you look at that! You're right. Good eye, Rebecca. Keep it up, and you'll take my job one day."

Rebecca nodded sagely while Bailey chuckled and continued her inspection of the corpse. "I do have a keen eye and familiarity with human anatomy."

"But you missed this bump on his skull."

"Think the killer hit him over the head?" She took notes as Bailey moved along.

"Can't say one way or the other. But I can tell you he was moved. In case you missed that."

Rebecca did a slow turn, taking in the drag marks and streaks of blood she'd been avoiding all morning. "Huh. I think you might be right about that. You know, if you keep practicing, you might take my job one day."

The techs moving around them ignored their banter for the most part except for the occasional smile. Viviane was standing nearby like the eager student she was. Which didn't stop her from turning away when Bailey pulled out her thermometers and prepared to get a liver temperature.

"Door is self-closing and was closed when we got here."

Bailey nodded, paused to take the readings, and did some quick math. "Based on the level of rigor, lividity, and liver temp, preliminary time of death was most likely," she looked at her watch, "twelve to eighteen hours ago. I should've been here sooner, but it's been a rough day. Two fatalities already this morning."

"You got here soon enough." Rebecca watched as Bailey patted the body down. "I was guessing his death was more recent than that." She motioned to the not-completely-dry blood pools around the body.

"Floor was freshly waxed and still damp in spots." Justin Drake, the CSI tech, held up a small dish with a scraping inside. "That slowed down the dry time and made these rings here." He tapped the floor.

Rebecca tried to lean over and see what he was pointing out but had to stop when her ribs protested. "I'll take your word for it."

Viviane, on the other hand, happily squatted down, hunkering low to see what he'd been talking about. Rebecca knew her newest deputy was more comfortable with blood than with bodies. That was a good sign, and she made a mental note to encourage Viviane to take some blood spatter courses.

"Got something for you." Bailey showed Justin a laminated strip of paper that looked like a bookmark. "A pencil-shaped hall pass? That's a bit unique. Think he picked it up while cleaning?"

Justin snapped a few pictures before carefully flipping it over as Rebecca watched and Viviane photographed.

"It's got Miss Washington's name on the back." Viviane reached forward, which made Justin shy away with the evidence, so she dropped her hand. "Sorry. I wasn't going to touch it, I swear."

Justin placed the evidence in a bag. "I've learned I can't be too careful."

"That definitely links this to Amy's murder. It's unlikely he'd have found this in the school after her room was emptied at the beginning of summer. We need to know if these souvenirs left on the victims are meant for the targets or for us." Rebecca turned to Bailey. "Did you find anything else on him?"

"Not a thing." The M.E. didn't bother looking up from her work as she continued her inspection of the body.

"Hmm." Rebecca tapped her pen on her pad.

"You expected me to?"

"We found indications that he might have been smoking right before he was killed. We'll need to test what we found for DNA, but we're working under the assumption that what we found belonged to Drysdale. And he was waxing the floors, which is a time-sensitive project." Rebecca raised a questioning eyebrow at Viviane.

Deputy Darby frowned in concentration. "Then what did he use to smoke? He needed a lighter, matches, something."

"Exactly." Rebecca nodded in approval. "His pockets were

empty when I checked them. Go do another lap, search everywhere. We need to find what he used."

"Is it that important?" Bailey was flipping through the pictures she'd taken.

"If it isn't here, that means the killer might've taken it. And he might've taken other things. Both bodies were found with only what the killer left on them."

"Hey, Boss, got an update for you." Hoyt pushed through the exterior door, returning from completing his research back at the station.

"Boss is sending me to make sure you didn't miss anything when you searched the school earlier." Viviane gave him a teasing grin.

"Good idea. Should always double- and triple-check a crime scene." He waved away her teasing, his gaze focused on Rebecca.

"And the techs will go behind and check you too. That's what we do at crime scenes." Rebecca shooed Viviane on. "Frost, what've you got for me?"

"Couple things. First, I found Melvin's arrest record. Sebastian didn't have one. Amy never gave a statement against him, and there was no evidence. Just the principal's word. So they, Abner and Wallace, pushed and made Melvin think Amy had accused him of trying to sell drugs to kids in order to get him to turn on his supplier."

Rebecca glanced down at Sebastian. "Which means two of the three people responsible for Melvin's arrest are now dead."

"Leaving just the principal." Hoyt's lips thinned. "Hey, did you have time to check out the mulch I told you about?"

Shit. She'd forgotten about that. "Show me where?"

"Justin, would you care to join us?" Hoyt asked loudly.

The forensic tech looked up, startled. "What?"

"Frost alerted us to another scene we need to process." Rebecca gestured to his kit.

After checking with his coworkers, Justin joined them. "Lead the way."

Hoyt did, through the elementary wing and halfway down the next. He stopped at the last classroom on the right and led them inside, where he pointed at the floor under an open window. "There's fresh black mulch from recycled tire pieces on the new playground. This looks like it came from there. And it's on top of the wax and polish."

"You got this, Justin?"

"On it, Sheriff." The tech dropped, pulling out his camera.

Rebecca cued her mic. "Darby, leave off checking Frost's work and head outside. Frost, let's check out the playground."

Her hand hovered momentarily over her holster as her gaze swept the room, a gesture not lost on those present. Her instincts were on high alert, but she recognized the need for restraint. Unsnapping her weapon now might set off a chain reaction of anxiety among her deputies.

Instead, she straightened her shoulders and projected a calm assurance. "Let's remain vigilant. Keep your eyes peeled but remember we're in control here."

Her words settled the room, but the underlying tension remained. Everyone sensed something was amiss, and Rebecca knew her composure only served to underline the seriousness of their situation.

Now every step had to be measured, every decision weighed carefully. But they had a job to do. Leadership wasn't just about acting on instinct. It was about knowing when to keep those instincts in check.

Keep it together. Being reckless costs lives. Don't let it happen again.

24

Rebecca and her small group came up empty at the school playground. There was nothing to be found—at least not without a microscope—other than a few scuff marks showing someone had walked through the mulch.

Leaving Viviane with Bailey and the techs, Rebecca and Hoyt rode over to Melvin Drysdale's house. Even if he was a suspect, he was still next of kin and had to be informed of his brother's death.

It was just after noon when Melvin answered the door on the first knock. He was holding a cigarette between his fingers and glared at them as he pulled a lighter from his pocket.

"Now what do you want? You still trying to pretend this is all about my brother and you're not here to harass me? I see you brought backup this time." He smirked at Hoyt, eyeing him up and down.

To his credit, Hoyt kept a neutral face and didn't respond.

"This is about your brother, Mr. Drysdale." Rebecca motioned to the door he was blocking. "Do you mind if we come in?"

"I sure do mind." He stepped out, forcing them to give way and make room. "You want to talk, we can do it out here."

Rebecca nodded, clasping one wrist in front of her body. "Mr. Drysdale, we regret to inform you that we found your brother's body this morning. It appears he was killed at the school last night while finishing up his shift."

Melvin's face went slack, then he nearly grinned, his lips twisting and straightening in rapid succession. "You're shitting me." He glanced at Hoyt's blank face and all attempts at a smile faded away. Shaking his head, he stepped sideways to get away from them, going slightly pale. "You've got to be. This isn't funny, man."

"No, sir, it's not. We would never joke about something so serious."

"No." He jerked away, bumping into the side of his house. "No. That can't be. Why would someone kill Seb? He was just a janitor, for god's sake. He never did no one no wrong. Just cleaned up their messes."

"He did you wrong." Hoyt shrugged as the bereft man stared at him in confusion. "He's the one who sent the cops after you ten years ago. The reason you ended up doing time."

"Cops? Me? Man, don't try to put that on my brother." Melvin's color came back with a flush of anger. "You guys tricked him into giving me up. He was scared, and you took advantage of him. I get it. Not really his fault. And I know that principal fingered me, too, way before you confused Seb with your lies. My brother told me all about it." Melvin took several long drags of his cigarette through trembling fingers.

"When was the last time you talked to your brother, Mr. Drysdale?" Rebecca watched him, trying to gauge his reaction.

If she didn't know anything else about this man, she

would've said his reaction was wrought with true loss and sorrow. Melvin was shaken. Because of his brother's death? Or because they were here so quickly afterward? If Pamela and Principal Hill hadn't gone in today, no one would've known about Sebastian 'til tomorrow when the school opened.

Countless kids would've been traumatized by a bloody crime scene with a bloated corpse.

"Thursday. When we played poker."

"I thought you said you were playing poker with friends." She shook her head, not believing a word he was saying.

"I was! Never said my brother wasn't my friend. You never asked if he was with me. Ask my buddies I told you about. They'll tell you." He took a long drag, stared at the lighter in his hand with a frown, then tucked it away in his pocket.

"We did. That poker game broke up early. Plenty of time to get over to the school and kill Amy Washington."

Hoyt glared at the man. "Your alibi doesn't hold up. Sebastian told us you two had gone night fishing. Never said a word about playing poker with you and your pals."

A look of sudden realization crossed Melvin's face. "That explains his voicemails."

"His voicemails?" Rebecca was confused.

"Yeah, some shit about fishing. I didn't really listen." Melvin looked momentarily distracted by his thoughts, then shook himself back into the present. "That's just like my bro." He glanced at Hoyt. "Seb was trying to protect me. He doesn't want my parole officer to know I gamble. It's not a high-stakes game, nothing bad. But he's always looking out for me. He's a good guy. Was. Who would want to kill my brother?"

"So you're saying it wasn't you?" Rebecca still wasn't

buying his story, but the pieces weren't falling neatly into place. She was missing something.

"Of course it wasn't me! That's my big bro you're talking about. I'd never hurt him. He's my family. The only one I got."

Rebecca wrote that down. It didn't say good things for his wife and child if he thought his brother was his only family. "But you gave him drugs."

"Well, sure." He threw up his hands. "But that's back when I didn't know how bad it could fuck him up. And he needed the pick-me-up, working all those long shifts at the school. He was doing the job of two people."

"But now you know better?"

"I went to prison, lady. I saw what those drugs were doing to people on the inside. What it looked like when addicts couldn't get their fixes. What they would do for just one more hit. I never would've done that to my brother if I'd known how bad it could be for him."

Rebecca tried to keep her skepticism in check. A rehabilitated drug dealer wasn't a statistical impossibility. But all the dealers seemed reformed when talking to the cops. "Are you trying to say you hold no resentment toward Sebastian for what he did? Or for Amy Washington for turning you both in and destroying your lives?" She took a step closer.

Melvin reared back as if she'd struck him, staring at her. "Hell, no. That was probably one of the best things to ever happen to us. Both of us. And Amy didn't turn us in. Her boss did. Principal Stick Up His Ass."

Hoyt snorted. "Right."

"Amy was just someone doing her best to help people who she thought were fucking up." Real fear flashed in Melvin's eyes as the words flew from his mouth with growing intensity. "Never blamed us. Or me. Just tried to help as best she could. Hell, she visited me in jail and even brought me soup when I got out on bail."

His sudden change didn't make any sense to Rebecca. Was he lying before or lying now? And why? "Then why did you seem so pissed when I told you about her yesterday afternoon?"

He took another deep drag on his cigarette. "I've got a reputation to maintain, don't I? Besides, talking to cops never did me no good. What good would it do to tell you how much it meant that some schoolteacher came to see me in prison and drove my brother up to visit too? You'd have thought I was some kind of pansy. I'm not a pansy. I deal with my shit on my own."

Hoyt, who'd been standing silently behind her, leaned forward. "Well, maybe if you did talk to us every now and then, we could actually help you. Like now, when we're trying to find out who killed your brother. When you've lost all your family to violence."

Rebecca kept her gaze on Melvin, who was looking more like a trapped animal by the moment. There was a depth to Hoyt's words that made it clear he knew more about the Drysdale family than she did. Not surprising, considering the men had both lived here their whole lives.

Melvin only had eyes for Hoyt now. "And make my life even worse? I think not. I gotta do what I gotta do to protect myself." He waved them away and reached for his door. "Now get off my property before things get even worse."

Hoyt clenched his jaw, barely holding back whatever was on his tongue.

While tapping her deputy on the arm, Rebecca lifted an eyebrow at Melvin. "Worse? Is that a threat?"

Melvin shrank before her eyes. "N-no. I'm just upset."

She took a step closer to him. "And that's the only reason

I'm not hauling you into my interrogation room this instant. But hear me right now, Mr. Drysdale..." She waited until he met her gaze. "We'll be back."

25

After leaving the crime scene, Viviane had been drawn to Pamela Radcliffe's house. She was worried about the woman and wanted to make sure she'd gotten home safely.

Just as she raised her hand to knock on the door, a thought struck her. Crap. She was supposed to always have her training officer with her. And did she?

How am I ever going to remember all these new rules?

She was just about to key her radio to call for her training officer when the door opened, Marjorie Lamb standing on the other side.

"Vi, can I help you?" At Marjorie's mention of her name, Pamela Radcliffe got up from the couch and joined them at the door.

Viviane shook her head, glancing between the two women. For a moment, a flurry of worry swirled in her. She was alone, about to walk into a house with two people connected to a murder investigation. Frost was supposed to be here, and, more importantly, no one knew where she was.

This wasn't a good idea.

"Nope." Despite the door being open, Viviane ignored her manners in favor of her training. "Just wanted to make sure Miss Radcliffe got home safe, is all. Pardon my saying, but she didn't look too good when she left."

"Oh, thank you, Viviane. You're so kind. I made it home fine. The fresh air helped clear my head. Would you like to come in?"

"No, thank you, ma'am. I'm still on duty. In fact, the sheriff's going to come check in on me soon. I'm still a rookie, always being watched by someone." She rolled her eyes and flashed her million-watt smile, which always drew people in.

Both women laughed. "Oh, we understand." Pamela Radcliffe nodded at her friend and colleague. "I've been at the school eight years now, and they still watch me like a hawk."

"Miss Lamb, is that why you're here? Checking in on Miss Radcliffe? Do you need medical assistance? I can call the paramedics if you feel you need it."

"Oh, my goodness, no. That won't be necessary. I'm doing better now. In fact, Marjorie was talking me into going out for lunch. Get my mind off things. We don't need to worry about going to work tomorrow, right?" Pamela Radcliffe paled. "You're going to keep the school closed until it's all cleaned up."

"Yes, ma'am. The school is considered a crime scene. Until we believe we've collected all the evidence we can, and we've documented the whole area, the school is off-limits to civilians."

Lamb shuddered. "That's why we're going to go to a nice restaurant. With a bar. And spend the next few hours relaxing. I think we deserve it after the last couple of days we've had."

Pamela Radcliffe's jaw dropped open, and she clutched

her friend's arm. Both Viviane and Marjorie Lamb reached out, ready to catch her.

"The restaurant. Relaxing. That's it!" Pamela Radcliffe twisted about, looking for something. "Where's my phone. I need to call Cynthia. Cynthia Wells."

"Here, I'll get it. You left it on the table." Marjorie Lamb pulled her arm free and rushed into the house.

"Viviane, do you have a copy of the inventory list? From the gift basket. Remember you and Deputy Frost asked me if anything was missing and I wasn't sure. I think I just remembered."

"Of course." Viviane pulled out her work phone and opened the file needed. She turned it so Pamela Radcliffe could read it.

"That's it. We're missing one of the cards." When Marjorie Lamb returned and handed Pamela's phone to her, Pamela immediately dialed a number. "Cynthia, it's Pam. I'm with Deputy Darby, and I just remembered something. Didn't we decide to buy a gift card to that fancy fondue place for Amy to take her husband to? She'd always wanted to go but couldn't afford it."

Viviane could hear the excited squeal even on the other side of the doorway.

"Yes, it's not on the list. You were right. Yes, I'll tell her right now. Thank you." Hanging up the phone, Pamela nodded decisively. "There should've been a gift card to The Dip and Dine, the fondue place. But it's not on your list. Do you think the killer took it? Cynthia has the receipt. She's going to send Deputy Frost a picture of it with the card number."

Proud of herself for gathering this important piece of information, Viviane shot a quick message to Frost, letting him know about the gift card.

"That's incredibly helpful, thank you. By the way, since I

have you both here, would you look at this hall pass? It has Amy Washington's name on it, and we need to know anything you can tell us about it."

Finding the picture of the evidence, Viviane showed both women.

Marjorie Lamb nodded rapidly. "Oh, yes, that's hers."

Viviane tried not to show her excitement. "Do you know what year Miss Washington used this design?"

"I'm sorry, dear, but I don't. When Principal Hill was hired, he implemented a rule that we were required to change our design every year. Those things went missing all the time, so he was trying to prevent kids from having a 'free pass' to roam the halls, or so he said. Have you checked with the office or Principal Hill? Maybe they kept records of each teacher's passes."

Taking back her phone, Viviane smiled and tipped her hat to them. "Hopefully, we can get to the bottom of this little mystery. Thank you, ladies. I appreciate your time."

Pamela Radcliffe returned Viviane's smile. "Of course. You're a great addition to our sheriff's department. I hope your boss knows that."

Keeping her smile until she turned away, Viviane hoped the same, since there was no way she could hide the fact that she'd gone off on her own to interview witnesses now. Her blood ran cold, and she looked down. The button on the pen cam in her breast pocket was up, indicating she'd forgotten to turn that on as well.

As she slid into her cruiser, her mind was a whirl of thoughts and emotions. Was her eagerness to prove herself clouding her judgment? The image of her former teacher had lulled her into a sense of familiarity, a comfort zone that made her forget the very basics of her training.

The inside of the car seemed to close in around her as she gripped the steering wheel, a cold sweat forming on her brow. Her mistake gnawed at her, not only for the potential danger she'd put herself in but for the trust she might have broken with Rebecca and Hoyt.

She started the car, the engine's hum a distant noise as her thoughts spun. What if something had gone wrong? What if Pam was their killer, and she'd walked into a trap? She shook her head, forcing those thoughts away.

Viviane glanced at her reflection in the rearview mirror, eyes filled with determination yet shadowed by doubt. She knew she had to face her team, admit her mistake, and grow from it. It was the only way to prove to herself and to them that she was cut out for this job.

With a deep breath, she put the car into drive. "You've got this, Viviane," she whispered to herself. But the nagging doubt lingered, a lesson learned the hard way, one she knew would stay with her. And, in all honesty, that wasn't a bad thing. It would help shape her into the deputy she aspired to be.

As she drove away, the weight of the badge on her chest felt a little heavier, a reminder of the responsibility she carried. She wouldn't forget this day. It had taught her more about being a law enforcement officer than any class or training session ever could—it had taught her about herself.

She had a lot left to learn.

26

Even though Rebecca offered to have a state trooper go down to babysit the scene, Viviane had volunteered to stay at the school until the techs were done. Rebecca was impressed at her newest deputy's dedication to her responsibilities. Her senior deputy sat with her in the bullpen, staring at the murder board while they ate a late lunch.

Hoyt seemed to be chewing on more than just his food. He kept looking over at her but then looking away before saying anything. Rebecca left him to it, knowing he'd talk about whatever was bothering him when he was ready.

Leaning back carefully, Rebecca raised her legs one at a time to rest in the empty chair in front of her. "We've got two missing items. Since we didn't find any spent matches at the school, we're assuming Sebastian Drysdale used a lighter when he was smoking. M.E. should be able to confirm that once they run tests on his hands for trace elements from a lighter."

When she caught herself pausing in her rundown, she realized she was waiting for a joke from Darian. This was the moment in these meetings when he would've thrown in a funny quip. Or a sharp observation, even. But the silence of his absence rang in her ears.

Wallace's death never haunted me like this.

Rebecca mentally shook herself. No time for letting her mind wander. "That's the second item. The first is the gift card Amy Washington received in her retirement basket. We also have two messages of sorts, the invitation to meet after school and the hall pass. What do those two sets of items have in common?"

Hoyt sat at his desk, leaning on his elbow with his fist under his chin, glancing between the board and her tablet again and again. Maybe he'd *actually* get that tablet back to her one day. "The invitation could be for a tryst or an innocent meeting between student and teacher. *Hall pass* is also a phrase that means cheating on your partner with their permission. We've been told Amy and Sebastian had a relationship. What if they were having an affair and the killer wanted to punish them? Maybe he's a moral enforcer."

"But if he wanted to send a message, why were they tucked away?"

"Because…" Hoyt rubbed his chin, "it wasn't about sending a message, only stopping them?"

Rebecca nodded, rocking her chair slightly, then reminded herself not to do that again. Stopping the painkillers might not have been her best idea, but a hefty dose of acetaminophen would've been great for her back right about now.

Hoyt twisted his head, watching her intently out of the corner of his eye. A trick he'd learned from her. Again, she ignored him, going on with their brainstorming.

"That only makes sense if the killer is her husband. And we've ruled him out as a suspect. Forensics tested his clothes and shoes from that night, and they were completely absent of any traces from Amy's crime scene. Bailey already suspects both deaths were by the same person. The slashes to the throats were nearly identical. And almost since the day we found Amy, someone has been with Buzz Washington twenty-four seven. He couldn't have killed Sebastian Drysdale."

Rebecca pondered Buzz's circumstances. There wasn't anything she could change, so she didn't want to dwell on it. She had a living will, and that was as much as she could do about such a possibility for herself.

"Melvin Drysdale's date of arrest was in 2010, right?"

"Right. He was charged in early 2010, went to jail later that same year. We know from forensics that the ink and paper from the invitation left with Amy is more than five years old, and 2010 is definitely more than five years ago."

"Amy's car was towed. Could you make sure forensics prints the car along with the basket? Including the center console."

If the killer took the gift card out of the basket, why didn't he take more items?

Hoyt began tapping away at his computer, sending off the message she'd dictated.

"Do you think there's any significance to the specific restaurant that gift card was for? Maybe the killer met Amy there?"

"I don't think that could be right." He glanced up from his monitor. "I asked that same question to Cynthia Wells when she called to let us know about the gift card, and she told me that all the gifts in that basket were all on Amy's bucket list. That'd mean The Dip and Dine fondue place was somewhere Amy had never been but wanted to try."

True.

"So let's examine the supposed affair angle. Rumors have it being active in 2010. Melvin was jealous of whatever relationship Amy and Sebastian had, at least according to Rod Hammond."

"Did Melvin confess his love for Amy at these poker games?" Hoyt rocked in his office chair as if he were on a porch gossiping about the neighbors. The image made Rebecca smile.

"Hammond said when Melvin Drysdale drinks, he tends to have loose lips. And Melvin apparently has some deep jealousy when it comes to his big brother. Grades, relationships, even has a better pension than Melvin."

"Interesting. But how much stock do you put in Hammond's account?" Clearly, Hoyt was skeptical. He stopped rocking.

"Let's throw it on the board with the rest of the rumors and conjecture. Maybe there's a pattern in all that, and we just aren't seeing it."

After adding the information, Hoyt stepped back and focused on a board that still showed way too much white space. "The only people who definitely know the nature of the relationship between Amy and Sebastian are dead."

Tapping her short nails on the desktop at her side, Rebecca went back over her conversation with Sebastian. At the time, he'd specifically indicated he and Amy were just close friends. He'd seemed genuine, but how much truth had he been telling? She wished she could interview him again, but that was an impossibility now.

"Both of them worked at the school. They'd been classmates since kindergarten. After going through the most recent five years of employee records, we have a list of the people whose work history overlapped with Amy and Sebastian's. The good news is that the school must be a great place to work, because there isn't much turnover. That keeps the pool of people we need to talk to on the smaller side. And I think we can prioritize who we speak to first."

Flipping through some papers on his desk, Hoyt tapped one of them. "There's one person on the island who worked at the school forever and seems to know everyone's business."

He'd lived on the island his whole life, and his familiarity with its residents was an invaluable resource.

"Yeah? Who?"

"There's a librarian who used to work at the school. I guess she wasn't enjoying retirement and works at the Shadow Island Public Library now. Not full-time, but even when she's not working, you can usually find her there."

"I'd like to talk with her. Is the library open on Sundays?"

"It is for special events. Today is a children's story hour. She's probably there setting it up. Did you know librarians hear everything that happens around them?"

"They do?"

"Of course. Their ears are trained for the slightest sounds of conversations." Hoyt hunched down, his eyes shifting side to side. "And then they pounce on you, even though you were certain you'd been quiet enough."

"That's a motive we hadn't thought about. Both victims were, in fact, loud talkers, and the librarian finally had enough." Rebecca cracked a smile. "We need to get down there and interrogate her, perhaps add a little waterboarding for fun."

"If she's not at work, I know where she lives." Hoyt pushed out of his chair with a comically grim face. "That little librarian won't get away from us!"

27

H oyt eased the cruiser through traffic. They'd taken Rebecca's SUV, and at every turn, someone seemed to spot them, wave, and give a salute. For her part, Rebecca mostly just smiled and waved back.

This was something Hoyt had gotten used to with Alden. Everyone in town had loved the grandfatherly old sheriff. But Alden had lived there his whole life and had known nearly every resident. Hoyt doubted Rebecca knew a single person who waved. That was how much she'd impressed the townsfolk since she'd started working for them.

"You finally going to spit out whatever's been bothering you all day, or do you need another night to sleep on it?"

Her words jerked him out of his reverie, and he glanced over.

She was sitting stiffly in the passenger seat, but it was because of her vest and her ribs. Her face, the most honest part about her, was completely at ease.

He opened his mouth to lie, to say he didn't know what she was talking about, but she lifted an eyebrow as if to say, *Try hiding it.*

Hoyt sighed. He wasn't going to get away with it. Rebecca was too good at reading people.

"I might need another night to think on it."

Rebecca nodded and went back to waving at people out the window. For some reason, that got his feathers ruffled. The way she could just so easily accept this shit pissed him off more than he could hold in.

"Don't ever pull any shit like what you did back on Little Quell Island again." The words came out angrier than he'd meant. They held every bit of fury and resentment he'd tried telling himself he didn't hold against her.

Her draw dropped. Before she could say anything, maybe reprimand him for insubordination or being hurtful, he pushed on, letting it all out.

"I mean it, Rebecca. I'm not playing around. Don't do that shit ever again." His hands drummed on the wheel as he fidgeted in his seat. "I can't go through that again. I'm too fucking old. Wallace dying made sense, kind of. He was an old man, and he'd put in a lot of years on the job. He'd lived his life. It hurt...still hurts, but it made sense in a tragic way."

When a red light caught them, he hoped no one could see through the tinted windows how angry he must look.

"But dammit, you guys are younger than me. You're barely older than my kids. Fucking Darian could've been my kid. Same with you and Ryker. I'm the one who's supposed to die first. Not you guys. I thought you knew better than to go doing reckless shit that would put you in danger like that. You abandoned me. I don't think you can understand how awful that made me feel."

Rebecca stared at him, her face turning blotchy, and he waited for her to blow up. To tell him off, call him a misogynist, anything. Instead, a long sigh was followed up with a damn chuckle, which pissed him off even more. Then, to his utter amazement, she straight up laughed. Loudly.

He almost yelled at her before grasping how bitter the sound was. There was no mirth to it, no amusement or joy. It held the edge of tears.

A quick glance confirmed his suspicions. Tears glittered in the corners of her eyes. He knew it wasn't from her busted ribs. This was a much deeper pain. One he'd been struggling with as well.

"I didn't want to do it, Hoyt. I was scared to death." She turned her face away from him. "I almost didn't. I was so close to giving in to my fear."

He suddenly remembered when he'd had to confess to her on their drive to Coastal Ridge. He'd stared out the glass, too, so she couldn't see the shame on his face. Opening his mouth, he tried to think of a response. She wasn't done, though.

"Pushing that boat away was the hardest thing I've ever done in my life. And I hope it always will be. Because I know what you had to do was even harder. You had to drive away. Leaving me there. It felt like giving up, which I don't do. It's not who I am."

She was right. That day, he would've happily traded positions with her and been the one left behind. Hell, he'd thought the same thing so many times since then. How he should've boosted her into the boat first, and then she would've been the one taking the others to safety. And maybe they all could've fit onto the boat that way.

He'd stared at the boat and the pictures from the report, seeing so many ways they all could've fit and gotten away. It was useless and stupid and he couldn't stop himself from playing the "what if" game.

Rebecca scrubbed her hand on her knee. She was silent for so long, he glanced over to make sure she wasn't crying. He had no idea what he would do if she was but had to check anyway. There were no tears, just a faraway look, as if she were seeing something that wasn't there. The thousand-yard stare.

"I couldn't get in the boat." Her voice was thick, gravelly, and she paused to drag her hand down her chin.

If she was wiping away tears, he hadn't seen them. He widened his own eyes—crying with his wife was one thing, crying with his boss was something altogether different. Crying while driving was also a bad idea.

"I'm not sure if you could see it, but as soon as I put my weight on the edge, the rim went below the surface of the water. It would've capsized. We were too heavy. Where would that have left any of us? Stuck, that's where. Back where we'd been before Ryker showed up and got shot for trying to help us. And even if I'd tried, I would've had to literally crawl over the bodies of my men, *my wounded men*, to get in there. I couldn't risk everyone else's lives like that."

He glanced over again, wishing to have not started this conversation while they were driving, and saw her fist clenching tight, pressing against her thigh.

"That damn boat was white. Not just white, but glowing white. Bright, reflective, with a fresh coat of paint. Ryker had just finished fixing it up. And the moon was full. It was a perfect target for anyone still on that island. I don't know much about boats, but I do know that the more weight you put in them, the slower they go. Like a plane, they have weight limits."

She was right. A loaded-down boat had more drag, less speed and maneuverability. In all his hours of playing human Tetris while staring at the boat pictures, he hadn't considered the weight limit on a boat that size. Especially one riddled with bullet holes.

"We would've all been sitting ducks out there, just waiting for someone to put another bullet in us, or in the hull. And I knew there was at least one more guy behind us. I'd heard him in the trees, making his way closer."

Rebecca gave a little wave and a tiny smile. Hoyt didn't see who she was responding to this time.

"If I'd jumped in that boat, we would've all died. All of us. I'm certain of it. The rest of those guys would've stood on the shore and filled us with holes. I think there were six more total. I can't really remember much after the boat. We couldn't have dodged it, though. There wasn't even any room for us to crouch down and get cover. And what if they had something more than just their guns? They could've tossed a grenade in the boat."

Again, she was right.

His fingers clenched the steering wheel. He hated to admit it, but it would've been so much worse if they'd taken fire while crammed together like sardines. Only by someone staying behind to defend them could they have gotten away. Not that it had done much for Darian in the long run. Except for allowing his wife the chance to say goodbye. Which Hoyt knew meant a lot.

"I really didn't want to be Rambo. I didn't even want to be Gandalf." She laughed her bitter, tear-filled laugh again. "I didn't think about it at the time, but right after the wizard says, 'You shall not pass,' he falls with the Balrog. I guess Wesley Garrett was my Balrog."

Hoyt thought that through, then couldn't help but laugh with her. His laughter was even more bitter than hers. "That's gotta be the nerdiest thing I've ever heard you say."

Thankfully, she laughed with him, this time with a hint of amusement.

"I guess it's a good thing you didn't come back with white hair like Gandalf did after his epic battle."

Rebecca smiled and nodded, but her expression was still

pained. Their light joking didn't erase the weight of their discussion, or what they'd carried away that night.

"But I did get a lot of grays out of it." She finally faced him. "If you tell anyone, I'll deny it, and you know what a good liar I am. But I actually ended up with some gray hair afterward, much like Robert Leigh's hair changed color after Cassie's death. One of the first things I did once I got out of the hospital was hit the salon. I had them dye my hair back to my natural blond."

Even though he knew better, Hoyt still peered at her head. The shoulder-length hair was pulled back in her normal ponytail for when she was working. Then he jerked away as she slapped at him.

"It's a good dye job. Don't you dare try to look." The tension in the SUV eased, and Rebecca even wore a real smile instead of just stretched lips. "I can't promise you I won't do it again, though." Her voice was low and husky, her eyes staring into the distance. "It wasn't just you guys in the boat, don't forget. Ryker was too. He might hate me now for what I did, but at least he's alive to hate me."

"Hate you?" Hoyt pulled the Explorer into the parking lot of the library. That didn't sound at all like the man he knew. People might change after a traumatic incident, but not that much, surely. "What are you talking about?"

She sighed and shook her head. "I don't know. You know he was in a coma for the first three days."

He turned the SUV off but neither of them got out. "Yeah. We went to visit him a few times. He was having memory problems for a while too. I spoke to his parents."

"Yeah, so did I." She took her time unbuckling her seat belt. "And I'm fairly certain they hate me. I didn't even know they'd moved him to a different room 'til I went to see him again and he wasn't there."

"Moving him is a positive sign...means he was good enough not to need all those machines and specialists."

"I know. And I hope he makes a full recovery. If he doesn't..."

"Hell, Rebecca, you know as well as I do that healing from something like what he went through takes a lot of time and energy. I can tell you I haven't seen him out and about, but I've seen a lot more of Larry Trotta, Ryker's old boss. So he must still be covering for Ryker."

"You think so?" The hope that entered her voice touched something in Hoyt. She was presenting tough, but she had to be missing Ryker.

"Yup. We don't know what his prognosis was, remember. At least, I don't. Do you know?"

She rubbed her temples. "No."

"There you go. Don't go jumping to conclusions until you've got all the facts."

Rebecca pinched her lips together, nodded, and took a deep breath. "Good point. And with that in mind, let's get inside and find out what this librarian knows."

28

H oyt climbed out, meeting her at the door, and pulled it open for her. "You know, it's funny how the tables have turned. Me being the one driving and opening all the doors for you."

"Shh!" The vicious hiss came from a checkout booth next to the door. A thin, older woman with tightly curled white hair scowled at them. "Hoyt Lloyd Frost, how many times do I have to tell you to be quiet in the library?"

Hoyt's cheeks heated as the woman used his full name. "I'm sorry, ma'am. Carol Krieg, this is Sheriff West, we're here—"

She scowled at him again and held her finger over her lips.

Rebecca, smirking, held her badge up.

Not relenting in the slightest, the woman only pointed at a large sign that read *QUIET*. And then, with a regal nod, Carol slid a *Be Back Soon* placard to the middle of the desk and stepped down from her stool. She was barely taller than the counter, and it took her awhile to walk all the way around it to join them.

Hoyt held the door open for both women as they went outside to speak.

"What can I do for you, Sheriff West?" Carol totally ignored Hoyt's presence.

"You used to work at Shadow School?"

"I did. For thirty-five years. After I retired, my husband died. I gained some grandkids, then got bored sitting around the house all day and came back to work here part-time for the past five years. What's this about?"

Her demeanor was very birdlike in the way she peered up at them both through her glasses. But more heron, less song-bird. As if she were waiting for the wrong movement before she snapped and bit their heads off.

Or maybe Hoyt just felt that way because he'd known her most of his life.

"It's about two of your old coworkers. Sebastian Drysdale and Amy Washington."

Carol put her palm against her chest. "What about them? I heard the terrible news yesterday that Amy had been killed."

"And Sebastian was found this morning."

"Oh no, that's awful. Both of them are gone now?"

"Yes, ma'am, and their deaths seem to be connected. Have you heard any rumors about them possibly being linked in the past?"

Carol sighed and folded her hands primly, looking around. "I heard things, yes, but most of the rumors about them weren't true."

Rebecca motioned for Hoyt to take notes, and he retrieved his worn notepad from his pocket. At the last second, he remembered the function of his pen and clicked the button down to turn it on. His boss gave him the slightest nod of approval before addressing their witness. "Can you tell us the rumors and the truths as you know them?"

"I hate spreading rumors, but since it's the police asking…" Once again, the elderly woman looked around. "All the rumors, and their derivations, about Amy catching Sebastian doing, buying, or selling drugs…those are lies. So are the ones that claim she turned him in."

Rebecca nodded. "What can you tell us about that day?"

"Amy was walking with the principal, Mr. Hill, on their way in one morning. A joint fell out of Sebastian's pocket when he went to unlock the door for them. Mr. Hill flew into a rage, snatched it up, flushed it down the toilet, then called the police. Amy always claimed she saw nothing on the ground."

"Who told you that?" Rebecca asked.

"That comes from Sebastian and Amy directly, not gossip." Her fingers tightened around each other, and she narrowed her eyes at Hoyt. "I know this because people seem to think that if they stand in the bookcases, no one can hear them. But I assure you, these ears have been through rigorous training."

Hoyt tried not to think of all the conversations he might've had like that over the years and just kept writing.

"Anything else?"

"The other rumors, the ones about an affair or other inappropriate relation between Amy and Sebastian are also false. There was nothing of the sort between them, in my firm opinion. Amy was devoted to her husband. Sebastian was a staunch friend to them both. Also, I do not believe he was interested in women."

Hoyt had never heard such a rumor, and Rebecca must've been equally surprised, as she pressed the librarian for clarification. "Do you mean he might have been gay?"

"No, I don't mean gay." Carol waved a dismissive hand. "I mean the man was so conditioned to being used and hurt, he no longer believed in love. He barely believed in kindness.

It's something I've seen repeatedly in children with terribly abusive mothers. They either grow to hate women, marry a woman like their mother, or they simply cannot ever trust them. His brother seemed to hate women, and Melvin chose to marry someone like his mother. And Sebastian, well, he never seemed to trust ladies."

"Except Amy?"

Carol shrugged her thin shoulders and bobbed her head. "Yes, I suppose Sebastian did love Amy. It was the way someone might love a younger sibling, or even a rainbow. Something he could not connect with, but enjoyed from afar, nonetheless."

Hoyt noted her despair as the petite woman shook her head and wrung her hands together.

"Anything else you can tell us about them?" Rebecca prompted.

"I know of another incident that happened between them." Carol rubbed a spot between her eyebrows. "The problem is that this is all secondhand information. From the bits of the story I overheard, I couldn't tell you if they were discussing a recent event or rehashing ancient history, so make of it what you will."

That piqued Hoyt's interest. What she'd said about Sebastian and Amy already made a lot more sense than anything else he'd heard.

Carol checked around them again, but they were still the only ones on the sidewalk. "One of Amy's senior students, someone she was tutoring, tried to take advantage of her. He got quite aggressive."

As Rebecca stiffened, Hoyt's jaw dropped. He'd never heard of anything like that happening.

"Who?"

"I don't know the boy's name. And like I said, I couldn't

tell if this was something recent or from their past. Sebastian heard the commotion and broke it up. He also put the boy in his place. Amy knew it would've ruined the student's life if it got out, and Sebastian had managed to put a stop to it. By no longer tutoring him, she wouldn't have to be alone with him. It sounded like Sebastian took on the role of Amy's protector after that."

Rebecca rolled her shoulders. "Why do you say that?"

"He hovered around Amy's room like a mother hen. They both felt the threat ended when the boy graduated, but Sebastian continued to lurk near her classroom, mindful of any danger that might come Amy's way."

"And that didn't feel suspicious to you?" Rebecca asked gently.

"No." Carol finally relaxed her hands and her shoulders visibly drooped. "If you ask me, it was the fact that Sebastian was trying to protect Amy that made folks gossip about something more to their relationship."

"Do you have any idea what happened to the student?" Rebecca's question shook Hoyt loose from the spell Carol's tale had woven around him, and he had to quickly write down everything.

"I heard her lament that the boy had failed her class. He didn't bother getting a different tutor and never did the extra credit she offered. But he did manage to graduate."

"But you don't know his name?"

"I don't. They never said his name, and I never saw him either. For all I know, he could've been long graduated from the school when they were still commiserating over the horrible incident. All I know was that he was a student, male obviously, and failed her class. Oh, also that he was eighteen at the time of the incident."

A young adult, who might've faced adult charges if she

had reported him. Was it possible that Amy Washington had paid for a kind and benevolent deed she'd done years ago with her life?

No good deed...

29

R ebecca sank down in her office chair with a weary sigh and started to lean back. The muscles in her back cramped, letting her know that was a bad idea, and she stopped.

"Frost, we need Mrs. Washington's class rosters, starting in 2015 and going back to at least 2000."

He'd been heading for his chair across from her but stopped. "Why those dates?"

"The ink analysis tells us the note found with Amy was written at least five years ago. So we'll start there and work our way backward."

"Only the senior classes, right?"

"Right." She opened the directory with their templates and pulled up the one she needed.

"I doubt Principal Hill will cooperate without the legal nudge to do so."

Rebecca was already nodding, knowing where he was going and agreeing with him. "I know. That's why I'm preparing a request for a warrant. Now that we've somewhat narrowed our scope of suspects, there's no point in wasting time with Hill's penchant for filing in triplicate. We know we need to be searching for a male student, eighteen years old, failed her class, and barely graduated."

"This is why you're the boss." Hoyt left her office.

Rebecca rose to follow him as she heard someone enter the lobby.

"How's the new dispatcher working out?" Viviane's eyes were sparkling as she walked into the bullpen, and she spoke loud enough for Elliot behind her to hear. She wasn't the type of person to talk about her friends behind their backs, but she would tease them to their faces.

Elliot's loud snort told Rebecca she'd succeeded.

"He's not broken anything yet. That's all we can ask for with a newbie." Frost grunted, leaning over his desk as he stared at the printer. "But he's also not been tested yet. Right now, it seems he's fairly well settled in. I made sure to put a sick bucket over there again, in case he turns out to be like our last newbie dispatcher."

Viviane wasn't the only one prone to teasing.

Rebecca moved over to Viviane's desk, where Viviane was making it a point to actively ignore her training officer. "Did forensics find anything new at the scene?"

Viviane glanced at the murder board on the wall of the bullpen. "So far, we haven't heard anything from forensics. They're running behind at the lab." She dropped her gaze to her wringing hands.

Concern stirred inside Rebecca. "What's wrong?"

"I did talk with Pamela Radcliffe again." Viviane blew out a long breath. "And Marjorie Lamb remembered the gift card to The Dip and Dine fondue place, like I texted Frost. Cynthia Wells is looking for the receipt, along with the copy of the gift card number, and will send those over when she finds them." She raised her head. "I need—"

"Cynthia called to say she found it and will be bringing in the receipt." Hoyt tapped his notepad.

Viviane dropped her gaze to her hands again. "That's good. I—"

"Yes, that's very good." Rebecca couldn't worry about Viviane right now. She faced the murder board and began writing their to-do list. "We need to follow up on that with the restaurant as soon as the receipt is in our hands. We're also trying to get records for Amy Washington's students. After talking with the librarian, Carol Krieg, we managed to narrow the suspect pool somewhat."

She leaned against the wall, tired from all the sitting she'd done today. It was probably a good workout for her—sitting down, getting up, sitting down—but it was tiring, and she wanted a moment to just relax. Once again, she debated if it had been a wise decision to come back to work already.

"Frost, I uploaded the warrant request to the case file. Will you go ahead and send that in?"

"Sheriff." Elliot spun around to face them, then snapped back as the cord on his headset pulled taut.

Rebecca fought to keep a smile from her lips. "Everything okay?"

The new dispatcher untangled himself from his equipment, looking flustered. "Got a visitor. Says she has something for you on Miss Washington's case."

"That must be Miss Wells. Send her back." Viviane dug through her desk and pulled out an evidence bag while Rebecca covered up the murder board.

Cynthia Wells walked back, looking around with the awe that most people wore on their faces the first time they walked into the working section of a police station.

"Sheriff West, good to meet you in person. Um, Pamela Radcliffe called and said you needed this. It's the receipt from when I bought the gift card for Amy. It has the gift card number on it, you know."

"I do know. Thank you very much, ma'am."

Cynthia nodded and dropped the receipt into the bag Viviane had handed to Rebecca. The woman continued to inspect the bullpen. "I just knew I had to bring it over right away. Pam said Vi had come by her house earlier and that was when she remembered it. Soon as she called me, it triggered my memory too. Just so much going on right now, you know. It's so easy to forget the small things."

Viviane went to her house? That explains the wringing hands.

A chill of irritation slithered between Rebecca's shoulder blades, and she looked pointedly at Viviane when responding. "And we're going to go follow up on this right now. Thank you so much for bringing this to my attention, Mrs. Wells."

"Always happy to help the police."

"Deputy Frost, give Deputy Darby the keys to the cruiser so we can follow up on this piece of evidence, please."

Taking the keys from her senior deputy, Viviane slipped past Rebecca and out the door with her tail between her legs.

Rebecca followed her, evidence bag in hand.

She waited until they were driving to the restaurant so she'd have time to think about what she was going to say. "So you left the scene where you were assigned, and went over to a person of interest's house, alone, without calling it in."

Viviane's fingers gripped the steering wheel. "I did. I'm sorry, Boss. I didn't even think about it. I wanted to make sure Miss Richa...um, Pamela Radcliffe was feeling okay."

"Without notifying dispatch, your senior deputy, or the sheriff, me." Rebecca kept her voice calm and level, even though her guts were roiling with anger and fear. Viviane could not be allowed to be this lax with her personal safety.

This time, she hadn't gotten hurt. That didn't mean it would never happen.

"I know, and I'm awfully sorry for that. I realized that after I got there. No one knew where I was, there were two people in the house, and both witnesses in the crimes, which does not rule them out as suspects." Viviane twisted her fingers on the steering wheel. "That's why I stayed outside, well back from the door too."

Rebecca glared at Viviane, who'd started to sweat. "You knew you'd put yourself in a possibly dangerous situation, yet you still didn't call dispatch to inform them of your location, call for backup, or call your trainer, who you're supposed to have on scene with you when dealing with other people."

"I know." A bead of sweat trickled down Viviane's temple. "It won't happen again."

"It better not!" Rebecca's yell echoed in the cabin of the SUV, making Viviane flinch. She pinched the bridge of her nose. She needed to pull her shit together. "This job is dangerous, Viviane. You can end up dead."

"I know! I'm sorry. I wasn't thinking about that. I've known Miss Radcliffe most of my life and—"

Rebecca wasn't having it. "No, you haven't. Not like this. You only knew Miss Radcliffe, the teacher. You've never known Pamela Radcliffe, the person. That's your bias talking, and you need to set that aside. Ignoring all that, what if Pamela Radcliffe was the next intended victim? What if the killer had been at her house? That's why rookies have training officers. To teach them all the ways a scene can change and what they need to look out for."

"I'm sorry."

Rebecca let out an angry breath, tears burning the backs of her eyes. "Then you could've been hurt, and we wouldn't have known where you were. Did you stop to think about how long it would take us to find you if something went wrong? Or how dangerous it would be for the rest of us if we had to charge in to pull you out of a bad situation?"

When Viviane went ashen, that was answer enough for Rebecca.

"I'm really sorry."

A huge part of Rebecca wanted to reach across the console and squeeze Viviane's arm. She was her friend. But the biggest part of her demanded she make sure her friend stayed alive. She needed to make this a lesson Viviane would never, ever forget.

"It's not just yourself that you put at risk when you do things like that, it's your backup too. You're not dispatch any longer, Deputy Darby. When you wear that badge, your actions affect the rest of us. Because you know we will go through hell to save your ass. Think about that next time. Before you put your neck on the line, remember the rest of us will be joining you."

Viviane's fingertips touched her shiny badge, but she kept her gaze straight forward. "Yes, ma'am."

"Think of us as brothers- and sisters-in-arms." Rebecca fisted her hands in her lap to stop them from reaching out to comfort Viviane. "And as your boss, I will rip you a new one and make you wish you'd never been deputized if you ever do something that stupid again."

Viviane swallowed hard, blinking the wetness in her eyes away. "Yes, Sheriff. I'm sorry. Really, I am." She pulled the cruiser into the parking lot of the restaurant.

"Sorry doesn't bring back the dead, Viviane. Or unbreak bones." Regret tiptoed through Rebecca, trying to gain hold again. "And it doesn't do an ounce of good against the guilt you'll carry for the rest of your life if you screw up and get someone killed."

Putting the vehicle into park, Viviane turned to her,

concern written across her features. But Rebecca couldn't have that discussion right then.

Getting out of the passenger seat, she headed straight for the door. She might have gone a little too far in her chastisement, but Darian Hudson's death was an enormous weight on her shoulder.

"Welcome to The Dip and Dine. Do you have a reservation?" The man who opened the door wore black trousers and a matching vest over a snow-white shirt, and she was betting he was the person in charge.

"Next best thing." Rebecca pulled out her badge, showing it to him. "I need to speak with a manager."

"That would be me. I'm Ibrahim Chase. What can I do for you, Sheriff?" Smiling wide enough to make his mustache twitch, he looked at Rebecca, then over her shoulder as Viviane walked up behind her.

"I have a gift card number, and I need to know if it's been used."

"I can certainly look that up for you. Let's take this to the register." He gestured, and Rebecca and Viviane followed him to the nearest point-of-sale terminal. "What's that number?"

Viviane read it off, and he tapped it into the machine.

"As a matter of fact, that was used last night, at this location."

Excitement stirred in Rebecca's gut. "Can you tell me anything about the person who used it?"

"Only what was ordered." He paused, his finger running down the screen. "However, the server who served him can tell you more, and she's working right now. Let me go and fetch her for you."

Ibrahim left, and they stood in tension-filled silence until he came back with a server, probably in her late teens, whose brown hair was pulled back in a loose bun. She brandished a fake smile upon seeing them.

"Julia, can you tell the sheriff about whoever used the gift card last night?"

"Yeah, I remember this guy." She nodded, her bun bobbing. "It was weird, though, because he mentioned he had to use it before it expired. But our gift cards don't have expiration dates. But I saw the little envelope, and today's date was written on it."

Rebecca made a mental note of that as Viviane wrote it down. "Anything else you remember about him?"

"He was kind of rude. And he dined alone. I asked if anyone would be joining him, and he just kind of growled at me. Oh, and he ordered drinks. But alcohol isn't covered by gift cards, so I had to put the drinks on a different ticket. He wasn't too, um, happy about that, paying for those with his credit card."

I got you, you bastard.

"Which means you can tell me his name?"

The manager and server went back to the register, and he quickly typed on the pad. She pointed out an order, and he nodded.

"The customer was Melvin Drysdale."

30

The Drysdale bungalow looked just as run-down and lifeless as it had the last two times Rebecca had visited. Melvin answered her knocking within moments.

"Oh, it's you again. Of course it is." He swayed and came to rest against the doorframe. A cigarette dangled from one hand. The other held a beer bottle.

"Are you drunk?"

Rebecca glared at Viviane, making her clamp her lips closed.

"My brother's dead. Of course I'm drunk. What's it to you?" He lifted the bottle to his lips, pouring the rest of the liquid down his throat, then chucked the bottle behind him, where it thumped into something but didn't break. "I was over at the funeral home, making arrangements for Sebastian. Didn't even know those places were open on Sundays. Guess death waits for no one."

His head drooped, and he stumbled out the door, leaving it open. "What do you want, Sheriff? Haven't you done enough to screw up my life already? Why do you have to keep coming around like a nagging wife?" When he flung his hand up, Viviane flinched. He smirked as he finished raising his cigarette to his lips and took a long drag.

"You went to The Dip and Dine yesterday, alone."

"Yeah, so? What? You think that just because I'm a dirty mechanic I shouldn't be allowed to have a nice dinner?" He swayed forward and back, tapping against the side of his home while trying to stay upright.

"I have no problem with your choice of restaurant. I have a problem with you using a dead woman's gift card to do so."

His head wobbled on his neck as he attempted to focus on her. "Must be why it had an expiration date."

His words made absolutely no sense. But it aligned with what the server had said.

"Those gift cards don't expire." Rebecca watched his hands and his eyes, waiting for his reaction.

Melvin shrugged. "Okay...whatever. Well, mine did." He frowned as her words finally made their way through the beer foam soaking his brain, and he paled. "What dead woman?"

"Amy Washington. She was given that particular card on the night of her retirement party. The same night she was murdered. It went missing shortly after. Care to explain that?"

"I didn't have anything to do with that." He fell against the siding before trying to push himself upright again. It wasn't a successful attempt, and he slumped back instead. "I won that fair and square. Came by it honest."

"Who did you win it from?"

"Well, now, I'm not exactly sure. The guys and I played poker again on Friday. One of 'em threw the gift card into the pot instead of cash 'cause they were tapped out."

Was he lying? He was so drunk, Rebecca couldn't tell.

"You play for gift cards?"

He snorted. "It's not like we're playing for city hall, so we all agreed. You'd be surprised how often we toss in stuff besides cash. When you've got great cards, you've got to play them to the end. I won that hand, and when I was raking in my winnings, I noticed the envelope had an expiration date."

Is he covering for himself or for whoever gave him that card?

"So you went for a solo dinner?"

Melvin hiccupped, then grumbled under his breath. "I didn't commit any crime by using my poker winnings to have a nice dinner." The cigarette fell from his hand, sparking as it bounced off his bare foot.

"Do you still have the envelope?" Rebecca glanced down at his foot. The cigarette was still burning against the porch, but he was so drunk, he didn't seem to notice.

"'Course not. I threw it away. Or the restaurant did. Hell, I don't remember." He gestured to the run-down patch of grass between them and the road. "The hits just keep coming. All the good things in my life end up causing me pain."

"Well, for right now, we're going to have to take you in." Rebecca crushed the burning end of the cigarette beneath her boot. No need for a fire to start with no one home to put it out.

"For what?" Melvin finally managed to right himself, and he glared down at her.

"Possession of stolen property." Rebecca took hold of his wrist. He noticed her no more than he'd noticed the cigarette butt. "We'll figure out the rest of it down at the station."

Viviane stepped up and helped handcuff Melvin. Oddly, he didn't resist.

Something was off, too straightforward. Rebecca didn't like it at all. Still, taking Melvin Drysdale in seemed like the best idea. If he wasn't the killer, he'd certainly attracted the killer's attention.

One way or the other, staying at the station would be the safest place for him.

31

Rebecca hip-checked the half door, the fob in her pocket unlocking it, while Elliot stared at them, trying and failing to look uninterested as the two women dragged the inebriated man through the station. "Deputy Frost, can you escort our guest back to the interrogation room, please?"

"Sure, Boss." Hoyt met them in the hallway, frowning as he took in the stumbling man. He had to damn near hold him up by one arm as he walked back with Viviane to the interrogation room.

Rebecca, glad to be rid of the burden and doubly glad to have others who could carry Drysdale for her and save her aching ribs, swung over to the coffee pot, wondering how long it would take the man to sober up.

As sloppy as Melvin had been at the scene, he was only getting worse. He must've been drinking hard and fast to be in as bad a shape as he was now. Or he was acting. Either way, he could sit in the interrogation room for a while until he sobered up.

Fortified with hot caffeine, she went back to her office to

see if the request she'd made on the way out had been approved.

Hoyt joined her soon after with a knock on her open door. "He's all tucked in, with an empty wastebasket in case he decides to hurl."

Rebecca plucked a document off her printer, which doubled as a fax machine, and read it over. "Thanks. Have a seat while I write up his paperwork."

He sank down into his chair as Viviane joined them.

"Vi, why don't you give Hoyt a rundown of what we learned?" Rebecca kept an ear on their conversation, making sure nothing was left out.

By the end of it, Hoyt was shaking his head. "You really think we have enough to hold him?"

"For murder?" Rebecca turned away from her monitor, caught up on her work as well. "No. And I'm not certain he killed either one of them. But we have plenty for possession of stolen goods, the gift card, which he admitted to using."

Hoyt scraped a thumb across the five o'clock stubble peppering his chin. "So he says he won it off one of his friends at a poker game Friday night. After he won it, he saw there was an expiration date written on the envelope. The server at the restaurant said he told her the same thing last night, that he used it because he thought it was going to expire. But the restaurant cards don't expire. Right?"

Viviane shifted in her seat, clearly thrilled at being part of this process as she watched them, like they were playing tennis instead of just talking about a case. "She even said she saw the envelope it came in, which had today's date written on it. Meaning he thought he had to use it no later than yesterday, the day of his brother's murder."

A dubious scowl crossed Hoyt's face at that. "You think the killer gave him the card and tricked him into using it, knowing it would incriminate him?"

"That seems far-fetched, but not impossible. And Melvin Drysdale doesn't strike me as the creative type who could come up with a story like that." Rebecca picked up her phone and started texting. "If it's true, that means one of Melvin's friends wanted to frame him for his brother's and Amy's murders. I didn't get a chance to ask Melvin if someone has a grudge against him, but given his attitude, I wouldn't be surprised. Did you find anything while we were gone?"

Hoyt waved his empty hands out flat. "Not a report, a call, or anything about Amy Washington being assaulted, at work or elsewhere. Nothing about a sexual assault on campus. A few regular assaults, but none that involved staff or adults at all, just kids fighting. Those were all handled with no criminal charges being pressed."

Rebecca didn't like the idea that this had been planned out and on a timeline. Or that they might be following the trail the killer wanted them to see. Melvin could be a distraction, an easy scapegoat.

She tucked her phone back into her pocket. "If Amy Washington didn't want the kid to get in trouble, she might not have told anyone, leaving the only other person who knew about it to be Sebastian, since he witnessed the assault."

"Well, it also leaves Carol Krieg, the librarian. But since she only overheard conversations between Amy and Sebastian, the killer wouldn't know that."

"That should keep her safe, at least. How's Elliot doing?"

Hoyt side-eyed Viviane. "Our new guy doesn't seem to need any help on the phones. He might actually be useful and a good fit."

"Good, that's what I like to hear."

Viviane grinned as Rebecca's printer began to hum. "Of course he is. I picked him, didn't I?"

Rebecca held up the latest document she'd pulled from the printer. "Well, I got my warrant for Melvin's house based on his confession to using stolen goods. How about you? Did the one I asked you to send go through yet?"

Hoyt lifted himself out of his chair and went to check. He came back holding the warrant moments later. "Looks like you greased the wheels. We now have access to the school records."

Rebecca stood from her chair. "Good. I've got Locke coming to pick me up. We'll go check Melvin's residence and then swing by and check the school records. It's still our scene, so we may as well use it. You two stay here and keep an eye on Melvin. If he starts talking, Frost, you take lead but let Viviane sit in. She's a great actress. Use that to your advantage if you can."

Hoyt nodded, sizing Viviane up. "Will do, Sheriff. Until then, Deputy Darby can explain to me what she thought she was doing going out and conducting an interview on her own instead of staying on the scene like she was ordered to."

Viviane turned ashen again, her liveliness disappearing as Hoyt leaned back and made himself comfortable.

"I'll just shut the door on my way out, then." Rebecca might have already chewed Viviane out for her carelessness, but at the end of the day, Hoyt was her training officer. It was up to him to make sure she did a good job. Besides, she had a different deputy she needed to keep on the straight and narrow.

And he was all she could handle right now.

32

"The door's unlocked."

Rebecca glared at Deputy Trent Locke's back as his hand rested on Melvin Drysdale's doorknob. She knew smacking him upside the head would be unprofessional, but it was so tempting. He'd raced out of the cruiser like a toddler reaching grandma's house, never checking for any signs of danger.

With the search warrant for Melvin Drysdale's residence in one hand, she unsnapped her holster with the other as she met Locke at the door. "I know. And do you remember when I said that *the killer* might be trying to frame Melvin by planting evidence in *his house?*"

The remedial deputy scowled, trying to work through what she was getting at. His hand dropped from the knob to rest on his own gun as his eyes widened and he finally thought to take in his surroundings. "There could be a killer waiting inside."

Ding. Ding. Ding.

She waved the paper at him. "Also, the warrant hasn't been presented yet, so you aren't legally allowed to go inside.

Don't forget, his wife and ten-year-old son live here too. We do this by the book. We always do it by the book. The rules were written to keep us and innocent civilians safe."

He stepped away from the door, standing to the side. Finally, he was waiting for her the way he was supposed to after making himself a target for the last two minutes.

"Show me how it's done." Rebecca handed him the warrant. Abner and Hoyt had been working with Locke for the last few weeks, retraining him and going over standard operating procedures.

After several long chats at work, she'd realized he'd been rushed through his private training paid for by his über-rich friends who were all members of, or associated with, the Yacht Club. Always scoring high marks and passing every course, he came away with barely more than rudimentary skills other than being a semi-decent shot. Considering how expensive those courses had been, and who'd covered the cost, she was certain the instructors had been paid off.

And his Yacht Club buddies, who'd "helped him" start his career with those free classes, had been there the entire way. They listened to him talking about his job, built him up, and created the perfect inside man on the force who didn't even know he'd been corrupted from the start. He still wouldn't if he hadn't had a crisis of conscience after seeing one too many murders.

The case that had started his change of heart hadn't even been related to the Yacht Club. That didn't stop them from lashing out when he didn't want to talk about it. They hadn't counted on him eventually caving to Rebecca's questions about his new bruises and oddly shaved face. Or that she would help him work through it all and get him properly trained.

One of the first lessons Abner and Hoyt had drilled into him had been to keep his damn mouth shut about active cases. The second had been all the standard operating procedures he'd been screwing up for years. Now it was time to see how well those lessons had stuck. So far, she wasn't impressed.

I'll give him a few months, then he's out if he doesn't get better.

Rebecca stood at his back, ready to cover for him if anything went wrong. At her nod, he pounded on the door.

"Shadow Island Sheriff, we have a warrant, open up." He waited fifteen seconds before repeating himself a bit louder.

With no answer forthcoming, he took the warrant and pressed it against the door, posting it for all to see. Then he pulled his gun. "Shadow Island Sheriff, we're entering the premises." He pushed the door open, then started to step inside.

"Open it all the way. Make sure no one's behind it." Rebecca kept her voice low as she pulled her weapon. This was when they were most likely to be attacked, anytime they walked through an entryway.

Locke pushed the door the rest of the way open until it was flush against the wall. With Rebecca at his back, they entered the house. She looked around the filthy home, eyeing the takeout boxes, overflowing garbage cans, and ashtrays that looked like nicotine volcanoes had spewed ash over every surface.

They had to step high just to make it around the coffee table. Clothes, men's and women's, were strewn everywhere, ready to catch a careless foot. They were embedded with layers of refuse and created an uneven surface. The furniture was broken and sat at crazy angles, making it even harder to clear a path through.

"Hallway." The words whispered from between Rebecca's lips as she delicately sniffed the air. There was such a heavy blanket of tobacco stink, she couldn't even smell the box of rotting pizza that squelched as she pushed it aside with her foot.

Locke gave a short nod and headed for the hallway.

They had to pass through the kitchen first. Rebecca's shoes slid in the slick of oily build-up on the cracked linoleum even under the carpeting of clothes and discarded junk. Her hip knocked against one of the dining room chairs held together with duct tape and screws. It slid across the floor without a sound but elicited a flurry of skittering feet she couldn't see.

Rebecca knew that sound was the horrifying staccato of disturbed cockroaches leaving their nest. There was even a snow shovel leaning against the wall as she turned into the hallway. Everything about the place spoke of either neglect or depression.

"Door." Locke waved his left hand, indicating where it was—even though she could see it—like he was supposed to.

With Locke doing better after such a rough start, her shoulders relaxed a bit. If he kept this up, he might survive visits like this in the future. That was the main goal in all the training Abner'd been going over with him. Stepping closer, she covered him as he turned into the room.

"Clear."

She froze. That was way too fast. Even if the room was small, he shouldn't have been able to clear it that quickly. Locke stepped back into the hallway and continued as Rebecca paused and investigated the first room.

Immediately, she could tell it was empty. A single mattress and box spring sat on the floor. What once was the closet had been dismantled, showing the discolored lines on the ceiling and carpet where the walls had been removed. Children's clothes were folded and stacked neatly in that area. Nothing else was in the room. The bed didn't even have sheets on it.

She turned her attention back to Locke and to clearing the rest of the house. So far, he was doing a great job, and she was pleased the training was sinking in.

He called out another doorway and stepped through it. Rebecca glanced in as she caught up. Locke was completing his turn, glancing out the window of the back door he'd found in the utility room. The floor was taken up by boxes of dirty clothing staged in front of the washing machine.

But the clean top of the dryer held more stacks of folded laundry. Even a set of brand-new sheets for a boy's bed was neatly stored there.

Someone had been doing a serious cleanup job. So far, the rooms they'd cleared had been an odd mix of organized and clean and filthy and cluttered. In the laundry room, the smell of pine cleaner wrestled with the perfume coming from the dollar store box of dryer sheets.

Rebecca stepped past the second door, taking the lead as Locke finished clearing the room.

There was a bathroom next, right beside a closed door at the end of the hallway, which was most likely the master bedroom. Rebecca signaled Locke to clear the bathroom while she waited in the hallway, gun trained on the only closed door in the house. The clatter of the curtain rings as Locke yanked the shower curtain aside made her twitch.

Where were Mrs. Drysdale and their son really? The front of the house could've belonged to a bunch of college frat boys, while the back looked like it'd been professionally cleaned. Maybe Melvin had been alone for longer than he'd claimed. What was he trying to hide? Or was he getting rid of something?

Rebecca waited until Locke was at her back again. "Shadow Sheriff. We have a warrant. If anyone is in there, put your hands up. We're coming in." It didn't hurt to call out one more time, and it could save a life if there was a child in there.

With her left hand, Rebecca took hold of the knob, twisted, and pushed the door open.

Shock flitted through her as she took in the room and the mess on the bed. A large stack of women's clothing took up one side. Stepping in, she twisted right while Locke went left behind her. The closet was in front of her. It had one of those sliding mirror doors, so she could watch Locke as he stepped around the bed. The door was open, allowing her to see the half-empty rod and the plethora of empty clothes hangers too.

Someone had taken all of Mrs. Drysdale's clothes out of her closet and laid them out on the bed. But why? Checking to make sure there was no hiding space first, Rebecca turned away to examine the lumpy pile.

Reaching out again with her left hand, she pushed and pulled the clothing, making sure no one was hiding under it.

"Clear." Locke straightened after checking under the bed. Unlike in the child's room, this bed was sitting on a cheap wooden frame.

"Clear." Rebecca tucked her gun into her holster and secured it. "What the hell is going on in here?" She looked at her deputy.

Locke was staring around the room too. "I'm no expert on women, but I think if I had a wife and made a mess like this, she'd kick my ass."

"Unless she's in no condition to complain about it anymore." Rebecca studied the nightstands. One was empty except for a blue bottle of hand lotion. The other was spilling over with books, scraps of paper, a full ashtray, and a tangled mess of jewelry. "Or she's the messy one. And when she left, Melvin started cleaning things up." She gestured to the stack of women's clothing.

"Maybe." Locke holstered his gun, donned a pair of gloves, then started poking through the nightstand. Rebecca was impressed she didn't need to remind him of this all-important step.

"I'm going to check the front room." Leaving him to deal with the bedroom, Rebecca pulled on her gloves and went to the other end of the house. It was even stranger walking back through. The mess seemed to end at the hallway, as if an imaginary line divided the two areas.

Right next to the shovel leaning on the wall.

Rebecca took the time to inspect it. The tool was brand-new, the sticker on the handle not even worn off yet. But the plastic scoop was covered in what looked like bug guts, dirt, and other streaks of black. Checking the floor, she saw the marks. Someone had used the shovel to clean the house.

Why?

Walking into the boy's room, she saw no such streaks. The floor had already been scrubbed. Turning around, she noticed that the hallway and bedroom had been too. Everything was clean except the kitchen and the front room.

He started in his bedroom and worked his way out. But where is his wife, and why are her clothes laid on the bed like that?

Just one more question to ask Melvin once he sobered up enough to chat with her. Which would go better if she had pictures to show him.

"I'm going to the cruiser to get the camera."

"Yes, Sheriff." Locke's shuffling echoed down the hallway as he thoroughly inspected the room.

When Rebecca stepped into the front room again, she caught a faint breath of fresh air. They'd left the door open, but it wasn't coming from that direction. A curtain swayed in the breeze. Pausing, she lifted the thin fabric. Behind it, the window was open halfway. Probably for this very reason, to let fresh air in while Melvin chain-smoked in the front room.

As she let it fall, something silver caught her attention. Sitting on the table, across the room from the ashtray, was an engraved Zippo. Picking it up, she tilted it to read the inscription.

In large, looping cursive were two letters. *SD.*

Sebastian Drysdale.

Could this be his missing lighter? The one he'd used right before being killed at the school. If so, how had it ended up here? One brother having the other brother's lighter at his house wasn't conclusive evidence, but it was another strike against Melvin that he was going to need to explain.

This was only one warrant served. The one that would allow them to follow a different line of thinking was next up. Time to go through the school's records and see if they could find the name of the mysterious attacker from so long ago.

33

I watched as the last of the kids left the library, chattering to their parents about the special event the library had hosted. Happy families with happy kids and happy husbands and wives.

Happy, happy, happy.

Those wives weren't screaming at their husbands about how worthless they were. None of those children were slackers. I knew, because they were reading when school hadn't even started yet.

Perfect families.

I tried to have that, but nothing was ever good enough for Crystal. And my son was soft. A weak little boy who'd never grow into a man if I didn't beat a little toughness into him. That was a father's responsibility. Crystal never understood that. She was the reason the boy was so soft. He'd been babied, and now he was practically a girl. He'd never amount to anything.

I could smile about it now. Crystal had done me a favor when she'd shipped the little sissy off to her mom's house. He wasn't my concern anymore, and I could wash my hands of him.

Sitting in the adjoining parking lot, I was far enough away to not be seen while I kept an eye on the families leaving. One little girl seemed to be putting up a fight, not wanting to put her book down long enough for her exasperated father to get her strapped into her booster seat.

Maybe some of the families weren't as perfect as they appeared. I could show that dad how to discipline that child, and she'd never disagree with him again. Women, even little girls, needed a firm hand and strong direction. Otherwise, they'd embarrass their fathers. Ridicule their husbands. The worst ones even tricked men into thinking they loved them.

Once my mission was done and everything was cleaned up, I would be a free man. With nothing holding me back anymore, I could finally succeed.

Melvin wasn't a bad man necessarily, but he'd take the fall for me just the same. I was starting a new life while he had nothing to live for. His slob of a wife had even left him. A man like that, who didn't have the balls to stand up to his wife like I did, deserved to rot in jail for the rest of his life. I didn't.

That was why I'd felt no compunction about tricking him into using that gift card. I'd been clever in my deception, pretending I was broke and using the stolen gift card instead of chips. He'd believed me, of course, because I had a great poker face.

And he sucked at poker. When Melvin drank too much, he held his cards loosely. Everyone at the table knew what was in his hand, except maybe Melvin, based on how rarely he won. I'd brought joy to his whole day when I "lost" that gift card to him.

Once I added something from the old-bat librarian to the

lighter I'd left at Melvin's house, I could begin my new life. What kind of idiot left their windows open all the time anyway? The kind who smoked so much his walls were yellow. The same idiot I'd watched open the windows night after night at all those poker games. Then he'd be too drunk and pass out before he closed them. It was like he was inviting me to go into his house.

The cops were already looking at Melvin—just as easy to manipulate as I thought they'd be. I'd watched them go to his house a few times. Hell, I'd even marched right into the lion's den and pointed the finger at old Melvin. I was right under their noses, and they never suspected a thing.

When Melvin shared with our little poker group how he'd been visited by the cops and how he had an alibi for the first murder, it'd been too perfect! First, the cops were following the bread crumbs I was leaving right to Melvin's doorstep. But how lucky could a guy get? Melvin's alibi had been the next target on my list. So many times, I'd tried and failed to get my revenge on that nosy janitor. Then, like a sign from above, Melvin had delivered him on a silver platter. I'd killed two birds with one knife in the lobby of that school.

Melvin had no alibi for Amy's murder. I'd made sure of that. I'd truly outdone myself with that stunt. The timing had to be perfect when I gave Lance's coworker a case of food poisoning. He was a sap, so I knew he'd go in when his boss called him to cover the shift, taking B.B. with him, since the man made a career out of bumming rides.

All the evidence pointed to Melvin.

A car door slammed, and my gaze drifted back to the library. The father was finally getting into the driver's seat. There was only one car left in the parking lot.

Picking up a book in its yellowed plastic dust jacket with its Dewey decimal sticker, I got out of my car. I couldn't help but grin. It was the perfect camouflage. Just a man walking into a library to return a book. I jogged across the street, squeezing the cover and pages around the knife I'd tucked within so it wouldn't slip out.

Old Lady Krieg had been the one to suggest I tell Amy how I felt. And I'd tried. But that started a whirlpool of shit I hadn't been able to break free of.

From that fateful moment, everything went down the drain. The woman I loved rejected me, while the woman I didn't love got pregnant and tricked me into marrying her. And she did nothing but nag and criticize. Nothing was good enough.

Until the night I finally felt the sweet release of freedom. And silence. I knew my actions had fucked up my life. Sure, some of that was from my wife. But when I saw Amy's retirement party announcement, I saw red.

Amy told the newspaper about her "bucket list adventure" and how amazing retirement was going to be. Just her and Buzz living their best lives. Why the hell should she be happy when she destroyed *my* happiness, *my* hope, *my* whole world? Her smiling face mocked me from the third page.

I tore her face from that page and mounted it above my bed. The bed she should have shared with me. She'd been the one who got away, rejected me, humiliated me.

The lights were off inside the library, and, for a moment, I thought I'd taken too long. Glancing around, I made sure no one was nearby and put my hand on the door lever. It swung open easily.

Of course it did. Now that I was the one in control, everything was working out perfectly. Turning, I reached for the dead bolt to lock the door. Nothing met my searching fingers. Looking down, I realized this was a double-sided dead bolt. I'd need a key to lock it.

No problem. I'd get the key from her. Then I could drop that off at Melvin's house too.

"Did you forget something?"

The short crone was smiling as she stepped around the counter. She stopped when she saw me. I wasn't a kid. Not anymore. I held the book up. My smile felt crazed, even to me. I went with it. This was going to be good.

"I have something for you, Miss Krieg."

34

"What the hell?" Rebecca attempted to lean forward in her seat but was stopped by her vest.

"Did you call crime scene cleanup already?" Locke pulled the SUV into the employee parking lot of the school. There were three cars and one large truck. That last one belonged to the remediation techs their department used.

"I did not." Rebecca gritted her teeth as they pulled up next to the truck. She had no idea who'd done such an idiotic thing, but she'd roll heads if her scene had been disturbed without her consent. Considering how much of a stickler for the rules the principal was, she was pretty certain of who'd gone over her head.

Sal, a man with muscles under the thick layer of fat that covered his body, was holding a large sprayer, which he used to wave at them. He started talking as soon as she opened the passenger door, already going on the defensive. "Hey, Sheriff, are you here to sign off on the release form?"

"I most certainly am not, Sal." Rebecca lifted herself out of the passenger seat. "We haven't released the scene yet."

Sal's lips pressed into a grim line. "Yeah, I thought something was hinky. Considering it was that asshole Vale who called us, I thought it'd be best to take my time when I didn't see any of you out here after not getting the proper paperwork."

As she had suspected. Vale still seemed to think he was a one-man power structure and that the rules applied to everyone else but never him. Not on her watch.

"Thanks."

He shrugged. "I know the school's supposed to open tomorrow, but I'm not committing a felony over it. Or risking my livelihood." His white bodysuit swooshed as he slung a tank filled with industrial cleaner over his shoulder. "And don't worry, we haven't touched a thing. Just had Tammy staging equipment outside the tape for now. The plan was if you didn't show up by the time we were staged, I'd give you a call. I get paid for every callout, whether I'm allowed to clean it up or not."

Slightly appeased, since no evidence had been tampered with, Rebecca was also a smidge disgruntled at the realization she couldn't go down to Vale's house and bring him up on charges. "Can you forward me the request you received? For our records."

Sal's eyes lit up with devilish glee. "Of course. I'd want you to have a copy for your records anyway. And if it gets that man off the board, that'll suit me fine. I've never liked dealing with him."

They were interrupted by the crackle of the radio. "Sheriff, ten thirty-nine?"

Surprised and amused by Elliot's by the book call, Rebecca grabbed her handheld. "Yes, I'm available, Dispatch. What do you need?" There was a long pause, and she could practically hear him flipping through the radio code booklet, trying to figure out what he wanted to say. She mouthed the words *new guy* at Sal, and he gave a nod of understanding. "Just use English, Dispatch."

Locke snorted and leaned against the hood of the SUV, waiting to see what was going to happen.

"Uh, Sheriff, I got a call from Select Board Chairman Vale declaring that the crime scene was going to be released. But Viviane, er, Deputy Darby said that was something you had to do since it's a murder case."

Anger seethed through Rebecca's brain. That little cretin thought he could call her and tell her how a scene would be handled? Yet he didn't even have the balls to call her directly —instead he used intermediaries like Sal and Elliot.

"Deputy Darby is correct, Dispatch. I'm on scene now. If Vale calls again, send him to me. Do not engage with him more than that. He's not your boss. I am."

Sal gestured as if to say, *There you go*, then shrugged, jostling the tank on his shoulder. "What do you want me to do, Sheriff?"

Rebecca debated the options. It was true she hadn't released the scene yet, and she hadn't planned to either. But while she was here with an extra set of hands, she could finish clearing it and let the school get back to normal business. If nothing else, this would be a good lesson for Locke. "Follow me."

"You're the boss." He grinned as Rebecca scowled. Too many people were picking up Hoyt's habit of calling her that. She'd never wanted to be anyone's boss, just good at her job.

As the two men trailed behind her up the sidewalk of the school, she realized she didn't actually mind the nickname too much anymore. The scowl had mostly been out of habit. Being a leader was something she was good at and had never shied away from. Yeah, she'd taken classes on how to lead effectively while she was in the FBI, but it also came naturally to her. A boss was a leader who also had to do the paperwork.

Tammy, Sal's much smaller coworker, was fiddling with equipment they'd kept more than six feet away from the blocked-off area. She looked up at their approach but didn't say anything.

Rebecca frowned as Locke jogged ahead of her, but he stopped at the yellow tape, lifting it up for her. Realizing she probably wouldn't have been able to easily duck under it, she nodded her thanks before walking through.

"Sal, wait here. We'll do the last pass, then let you know."

"Right."

The *thunk* of Sal's metal tank hitting the ground echoed off the door as Rebecca pulled it open. Without a set of keys of their own, the scene had remained unlocked so it would be accessible to all the necessary personnel.

A state trooper who'd been babysitting the scene glanced over, then tipped his hat to her. He didn't say a word, but he pointed with his eyes at the cleanup crew outside.

"Yeah, I know. Someone tried to jump the gun here. Has anyone gone inside?" Nothing seemed to have been touched, and the trooper looked bored.

"No, ma'am. A teacher came to the door, but I sent her away. That was a few hours ago."

"Has the principal or Richmond Vale been by?"

"No, ma'am. I haven't heard anyone else in the building, let alone had to check IDs." He glanced up and down the halls, taking in the dried blood. "Things like this should never happen in a school. Why can't the crazies at least keep it away from the kids? I hope you find the bastard who did this."

"So do we." Locke stared at the walls, his gaze constantly returning to one section of lockers.

She wondered if his locker had been there. He was a local

and would've gone to school here more than twenty years ago. "Okay, Deputy Locke, walk me through the final pass of the scene. What do we do?"

Straightening his shoulders, Locke's eyes narrowed. Not in anger, but in concentration as he recited the procedures. Rebecca followed him as he made his rounds, double-checking all his work. He didn't miss a single thing when they hit the end of the sectioned-off area.

With a clap on his back, she nodded. "Well done. Go ahead and release the state trooper. Then let Sal know I'll sign off on the paperwork. I'm going to head to the school office."

"Ma'am." He nodded and jogged off.

Rebecca watched him. He'd been injured at the same time she had. A gunshot wound to the back of the thigh. Yet there he was, jogging up and down sidewalks and corridors, while she was barely limping along. And he was older than her.

She glanced at her right bicep and the fresh scar she knew was under the short sleeve. That had been clean through and through and hadn't really bothered her at all after the first week. Maybe she wasn't getting old and broken ribs really just sucked that much.

Yeah, that had to be it. She scanned the walls until she found the small sign directing her to the school's main office.

Walking down the long hallway illuminated by daylight glinting in through the windows of the classroom doors, she struggled against feelings of nostalgia. One doorway was dark, and when she reached it, she knew why. It was the girls' bathroom for this wing of the building.

Blood on the linoleum...

She picked up the pace until she reached an intersecting hallway. Although it was dark, as she'd expected, she spied the office. The trooper had done a good job of keeping the staff and any lookie-loos away.

Her shoes didn't make a whisper of sound on the freshly buffed floors as she approached the closed office door. She tried the lever. Locked.

With the precision of a military formation, a lone pair of footsteps echoed closer to her. "Sheriff West."

"Principal Hill, thank you for meeting me down here. As you saw when you arrived, I've officially released the school, and it's no longer a crime scene."

"Yes, I saw that the trooper guarding the door wasn't out there anymore."

"Sir, did you call the remediation team?"

He lifted his chin. "No, but I did call Richmond Vale and ask him what he could do to get things back to normal around here."

"Principal Hill, I respect that you're a man who appreciates rules and the order they bring to society. As someone who has sworn to uphold those rules, I think we share a healthy respect for procedures."

Hill nodded at her like a bobblehead. "I agree."

"So you can appreciate how upset I was that a civilian decided to neither follow procedures nor respect the chain of command."

Hill squirmed and tried his best to appear offended.

Rebecca wasn't buying it. If he was going to live by the book, she would use that to her advantage.

"Until only a very short time ago, this whole building was my crime scene. Not your school. Mine. And I can quote the statute that gives me that authority, if you're interested. Further, by contacting Mr. Vale, you thought you were going over my head. Except Mr. Vale has no authority over a crime scene. Though that doesn't seem to stop him from trying."

"Now, listen here. I—"

"Another reason *I* decided to release the crime scene is because I brought you a present." Rebecca reached into her pocket and pulled out the warrant. "Because I know you appreciate doing everything by the book." She slapped the paper into his outstretched hand.

Hill stared at the warrant like it would bite him before unfolding it. "What's this?"

"That document details the files I need access to. Deputy Locke is on the premises and will be helping me go through the records."

Finally finding his voice, he cleared his throat. "Yes, I appreciate that you got the appropriate authorization. Our files are all digitized, but if you need any help navigating the system, I'm happy to assist you."

Pulling one singular key from his breast pocket, Hill unlocked the office and flicked on the lights.

As he set about powering up two computer workstations and turning on more lights, as well as the massive office printer, Locke appeared in the doorway.

Rebecca pulled out a hard plastic chair and waited for the computer monitor to prompt her. She tapped the chair next to her. "Take a load off, Locke."

After a brief tutorial, covering where on the server the records were stored and how to use filters to create more effective searches, the principal plopped down in the secretary's chair behind her desk. "If you find anything useful, I see that your warrant allows you to print out the records. Our printer takes about ten minutes to warm up, but then I can show you how to access it on the LAN."

"Thank you. I appreciate your help."

Locke's screen lit up, and he began rapidly tapping on his keyboard. Suddenly, a long list of Amy Washington's students began scrolling across his screen.

"They really do keep permanent records."

"Yes, we really do. But if you want to see an impressive collection of files and other school memorabilia, you should check out Amy Washington's. I haven't seen it myself, but it's the stuff of legends. I'm told she's kept every grade book from every class she taught over her thirty-year career. Honestly, I don't know where she stores it all."

Oh yeah, I very much want to see this impressive collection.

"Okay, Locke, you seem pretty adept at this. Here's a list of the filters we need to put on the search, if at all possible."

A few more clicks and the list repopulated with fewer names. Each time he clicked on various column headings, the list grew a little shorter. In less than thirty minutes, Rebecca and Locke left the Shadow Island school with a warm piece of printer paper containing exactly fourteen names.

35

Austin Washington patted his father's shoulder, rousing him from his enjoyment of the local weather forecast. A man who looked more like an English teacher than a TV personality was gesturing to a forecast with a row of smiling suns.

"Dad, Sheriff West and Deputy Locke have come by to see you." It'd only been a few days since Rebecca had seen Buzz Washington, but Alzheimer's appeared to be aging him in triple time. Recognition flickered in his tired brown eyes, though, when he focused on Rebecca.

"Sheriff West. Hello." His words came out as if great thought went into choosing each one.

Rebecca returned his smile. "Mr. Washington, it's nice to see you. It must be great having your son, Austin, visiting." She'd learned in a training class at Quantico that some ways of speaking to a person with dementia were more effective than others.

"Are you here to see Amy?" The reverence he expressed when he mentioned his deceased wife's name was something dementia had not yet stripped away.

She'd also learned not to intentionally traumatize them either. "Actually, I'm here to see your son."

Austin bent down next to his dad's recliner. "Dad, Mom died. We're having her funeral this week, once Brandon can get here."

Buzz's shoulders shook as grief overcame him. "Oh, Amy. My Amy. No."

Apparently all too familiar with the patterns of dementia, Austin smiled weakly at his father and stood. "Hey, Dad, it's dinnertime. Let me get you something to eat."

"Dinner. Okay. Thank you."

As Austin moved toward the kitchen, he jerked his head to Rebecca, silently asking her to follow him. "Sorry about that."

"Please, don't apologize. How are you holding up?"

"I'm okay. Caregivers come and help me, but Dad seems pretty confused when they're here. I'm hoping when Brandon and my wife come down next week that he'll have some good moments."

They arrived at a side door leading off the kitchen.

Austin's shoulders rose as he sucked in a large breath before slowly blowing it out. "Do you really think there's something useful in all that crap out in Dad's garage? It would be a little ironic if, after all these years of begging Mom to declutter, her killer's identity could be hiding in the boxes in the garage."

AMY WASHINGTON genuinely loved her students.

Rebecca could tell that much from the notes she'd kept in her grade books. Each dip in grades was highlighted as a concern. They were almost always followed by lines for extra credit and additional assignments, which brought scores up.

There were even erased grades on tests where it was clear she gave her students a second chance as the new grade was always higher. Sometimes, the low number was erased and rewritten a few times.

There were also notes in the margins. Once Rebecca figured out the shorthand, it was clear what Amy was doing. Different symbols indicated meetings, conversations about higher education, tutoring, check-ins with families, and meetings with guidance counselors. This was a teacher who wanted her students to succeed.

Each senior also had at least one "college checks" planned. Some were then followed up with a notation of "trades" and had various names attached. It appeared Amy had set up internships, apprenticeships, or interviews for her students before they graduated.

It was a wonderful thing to see. A teacher who cared for her students as much as most parents, perhaps even more than some.

The more grade books Rebecca read, as Locke dug them out and passed them to her, the harder it was for her to believe that someone would want to kill this living treasure. After being an agent for so long, she'd grown used to finding plenty of skeletons in the closets of victims. But Amy's worst deed so far was that she refused to testify to a misdemeanor possession charge of a coworker.

Which made sense, considering all this evidence of how willing she had been to give second and even third chances.

If what Carol Krieg had heard was true, Amy had even given the student who had assaulted her a second chance. Which begged the question—would Amy have that in her notes as well?

Rebecca kept reading, getting caught up in the quaint codes Amy left. One student even managed to get an exclamation mark on every test grade, even though the classwork portion was consistently low. Curious, Rebecca checked the name.

She had to cover her mouth with her hand to keep from laughing when she saw V. Darby. The year matched Viviane's age as well. Deciding to keep that little tidbit of information to herself, Rebecca set the book aside without remark.

Then she found the outlier. A section of the book had been filled with slots for extra credit assignments, but the last few months of the year had been crossed out instead of being filled in with grades. It also had the indicator for higher learning but no mark indicating there'd ever been a meeting about college or trade school.

Everything extra Amy had been doing for this student stopped overnight. The student's recorded grades continued to fall dramatically, and Amy hadn't done anything about it.

"Rod Hammond, 2010."

Locke stopped, still holding the next box he was pulling down. "Boss?"

"Dammit. Just like I mentioned on the way over. This guy's been under our nose the whole time. And I think Drunk Melvin was covering for him. No way he didn't know who threw in the gift card. Why would he do that?"

"Guy code...?" Locke shrugged before digging through a box of yearbooks as Rebecca connected all the dots.

"Rod Hammond graduated in 2010. He was doing poorly in class, but with Amy's tutoring, he was getting better. Then she stopped all her efforts. Carol Krieg said Amy was assaulted and Sebastian intervened. If Rod was the one who assaulted Amy, it would explain why such a devoted teacher would stop helping a struggling student."

Locke began flipping through the pages of one of the yearbooks. "Wouldn't that also explain why he killed Sebastian Drysdale?"

Rebecca was pleased Locke was sorting through the

different pieces of the case. "Right. Though I'm not sure why he left a hall pass with Sebastian's body."

"Hall pass? Dang. I noticed a shoebox labeled 'Hall Passes.' Hang on." He set down the yearbook and shuffled some items over, lifting a shoe box decorated with wrapping paper around its lid and base. He handed it to Rebecca.

It didn't take long to sift through the box of hall passes from over the years before two of them matching the one left on Drysdale's body surfaced. And Amy had marked each one with the year they were used. The note on the pencil-shaped passes also indicated 2010.

Rebecca set down the shoe box and moved to a stack of file boxes she'd already been through.

"Boss, what are you looking for?"

"Mrs. Washington kept detailed notes on students. Stuff a guidance counselor might track. Now that I have a name, I can see if she kept similar notes on Hammond."

Locke resumed flipping through the yearbook, purposefully scanning the pages.

It didn't take long for Rebecca to find the folder, and it was huge. Having to use both hands to pull it out, she set the folder on top of another box and started skimming through Rod's school years.

Kindergarten and first grade, things were fine. After that were years of notes detailing how Rod was bullied. There were even references to nurse visits after Rod came to school already bruised.

It was a heartbreaking look into the life of a troubled child. Amy had copies of notes from the guidance counselor, who'd suspected abuse in the home but had no evidence. Rod never spoke up or named names.

Instead, there were things like falls down stairs, bike accidents, or tripping in the marsh. All those excuses were in quotation marks, as if the counselor didn't believe a word of it.

There was also a notation about Rod possibly being the victim of bullying at school. Amy had added a note of her own that she'd tried to watch out for such behaviors.

Year after year, it was the same, until the end of middle school. There was a single incident where Rod fought back. After that, the bullying stopped for about a year.

Then the bullying continued again in his sophomore year, with a twist. Teen Rod was written up and disciplined for bullying younger students.

"And the cycle continues," Rebecca whispered to herself, flipping through the last of the pages of notes. She read how Rod was eager to start his college career, popping in often to ask about scholarships and tuition and to pick up pamphlets for several prestigious universities. It seemed that Rod had once aspired to be a professor.

But as with Amy's grade books, there were no further entries in the last months of his time at the school. Something had happened during the spring of 2010 that threw Rod Hammond off course. By now, the answer was obvious.

It all made a terrible kind of sense. An emotionally vulnerable young man bullied and struggling, who mistook his teacher's compassion for something more. And when he became a bully himself, he felt overconfident enough to finally do something about it. It was textbook.

"Boss, I think you're going to want to see this."

Rebecca twisted toward her deputy, then froze as her ribs screamed in protest.

"You really shouldn't be moving like that." Locke dropped the yearbook onto the box in front of her and reached out toward her, stopping short of touching her.

"Yeah. That's pretty obvious now." She blew out a slow breath, trying to convince her muscles to stop spasming, then shifted her feet so she was facing Locke. "What did you find?"

Locke tapped the page of the open yearbook. "This is Hammond's senior picture. I'm guessing that quote means something."

Rebecca examined the youthful Rod Hammond. His intense stare into the camera contrasted with the image of the winking, socially awkward creep who'd sat across the interrogation table from Rebecca. In his senior photo, his shoulders were rolled forward in a juvenile, wannabe threatening pose.

Below the photo was a quote each student could share for others to remember them by. *RH & AW Always Remember.*

"Rod Hammond and Amy Washington." Rebecca grimaced, already reaching for her radio. "Dispatch, I need a 10-29A on Rodney Hammond."

"Copy that."

She started gathering all the information they'd compiled. "Locke, as soon as Elliot gets back to me with the outstanding warrant information, we're going to ride out and have a little talk with Hammond."

36

"You can't hide forever, you crazy old bitch." I slammed my hand against the solid steel gate. The ancient crone had been much faster on her feet and more cunning than I'd imagined. And this damn old library still had a reference section that was kept under literal lock and key.

The librarian had managed to get herself into that room and locked the gate behind her, keeping me out. It didn't matter. No one else was in the library. It was Sunday. No one in this sleepy little town, where everyone always looked the other way, would even think of coming in until tomorrow at the earliest.

I had all the time, and she had no food, water, or a bathroom. I could wait her out. Except I'd already waited years too long to get back at her for what she'd done to me. Closure was one more slit throat away, and I wanted it settled tonight.

"Get your worthless ass out here! You know you deserve this."

Carol Krieg stood in the middle of the room next to the

reading tables, staring at me like I was some kind of animal as I paced back and forth in front of the bars.

"I know nothing of the kind. Never once have I done anything to you that would warrant my death."

She sounded so sure of herself. Of course she did. She, like everyone else, thought they could get away with treating me like shit. It made me laugh, long and hard.

"Nothing? Nothing! You're the one who told me to be bold. 'Faint heart never won fair lady,' you said! You told me to show my crush what she meant to me. But when I tried to show Miss Washington how I felt, she rejected me."

"*Amy Washington* was your crush?" She reared back, holding a finger to her lips. "She was your teacher! And a married woman more than twice your age."

"And the only woman who ever showed any interest in me! But when I expressed my love to her, she swatted me away like some household pest."

"You're the student who assaulted poor Amy!"

The worthless woman backed away, clutching at her blouse as if she were afraid I'd rip it open. As if. Amy had been special. The only woman I ever really cared about.

Remembering that horrible incident pissed me off as much as it had back then. I grabbed the *Restricted for study inside the library* sign and ripped it off the wall. "I gave her what she wanted!"

I shoved the sign through the bars and flung it at Old Lady Krieg. She gave a little squeak and dodged, even though my aim was off and it came nowhere near her.

"She knew how I felt about her. Why else would she have kept meeting with me after school hours? Leaving her husband waiting at home while she was with me?"

"Because you were her student!" The old lady clenched her fists 'til her arms shook. "She did that for all her students. You weren't that special!"

"I. Was. Special!" I pounded the hilt of my knife on the bars. As useless and stupid as that was, I couldn't help myself. "She told me I was special! She said she would help me be the man I wanted to be. But when I tried to be that man, her man, she rejected me! Then that lumbering oaf janitor came in and beat me. Threw me out of the school. And Amy acted like she didn't want me around after that."

My eyes raced around, trying to find some way in. Talking about all this old shit was making me angrier. I needed to finish this. There had to be some way into the old bird's cage.

She snorted derisively at me. "I heard her cry so many times, thinking no one else could hear her. You hurt her so much, she nearly quit her job. I'll never understand why she didn't turn you in to the police."

"So she could hold it over my head!" I beat my fists into the wall. Pounding out my frustration. "That damn janitor followed me around every moment of the day. They held it against me. I didn't get into a good college because of it! My life turned to shit because I listened to you!"

"You said you had a crush on a girl in your class."

"I was in her class!" My anger got the best of me again. Like it did on that first night when everything finally started changing for the better.

The drywall cracked as my fist smashed through the Sheetrock. I stopped. Then I laughed. It was so obvious.

"Fine, don't come out. I'll come in instead." Using the knife, I started digging so I could create a hole large enough to get to the librarian who'd ruined my life.

37

R ebecca kept her attention on opening the passenger door and climbing in, her ribs still freshly tender from twisting suddenly in the Washingtons' garage.

Locke, keys in hand, gripped the steering wheel as he waited for her to settle into the passenger seat.

The radio chirped, then went silent, then chirped again. "Uh, Sheriff, 10-39."

Rebecca and Locke moved at the same time to turn down their personal radios, then Locke took the cruiser radio and passed it to her.

"Dispatch, this is the sheriff and I'm available. Do you have that warrant check for me?" Rebecca leaned back in her seat, waiting for the address.

"I…maybe? Um, sheriff, I might have screwed up."

Locke rested both wrists on the steering wheel and snorted. "FNG."

Rebecca mouthed, *Really?* and cued the microphone. "What happened, Dispatch?"

"I tried to look up the name you gave me. And I don't

know if I typed it wrong, or looked in the wrong place, or what, but I got something." There was the tiniest waver in Elliot's voice. First-week jitters could get really bad when you were dealing with the legal and criminal side of things. And so could screwups. It would be best for everyone to get this settled as soon as possible.

Holding back a sigh, she hit the button again. "What did you get, Dispatch?"

"I got a report. A brand-new one." There was a pause. "I think. I'm pretty sure."

"What kind of report?"

"It's a wellness check. But it's not for Rodney Hammond. It's for Crystal Hammond. I looked into it a bit more, because I got confused. She's Rodney's wife."

Rebecca gestured for Locke to start the engine, but he was already turning the key. "Where?"

"1697 Bellend Drive, Coastal Ridge, Virginia."

The SUV lurched forward. "Brace yourself, Boss." Locke tore out of the school parking lot. "That's just over the bridge." His head whipped back and forth, checking traffic as he pulled onto the road.

"Who called it in?" Rebecca asked, fingers tight on her shoulder belt, keeping herself upright as the SUV jounced around.

"Um…" Rebecca tried to wait patiently as Elliot read the report. "Her boss called it in. Chloe Frame. Said she hasn't heard from Crystal since last Tuesday. She did speak to her husband, Rodney Hammond. That must've been how this came up in my search."

"Dispatch, reach out to Coastal Ridge PD and let them know one of the residents at that address is now a suspect in two homicide investigations. Considered armed and dangerous." Rebecca let go of the mic. "Locke, get us there quick.

These guys don't know they might be walking into a bad situation. Hit the lights and siren."

Locke nodded, easily shifting through the sparse traffic at the same time as he hit the proper switches.

Cars, blessedly, started moving out of their way. That was something Rebecca was still trying to get used to around there. Even the cars with out-of-state plates pulled to the side and let them through. Motorists on the island seemed more in tune with their surroundings, and she'd yet to encounter anyone who seemed oblivious to an approaching emergency vehicle.

Rebecca's work phone rang, and she answered on speaker. "This is Sheriff West."

"Sheriff West, this is Officer Blane of Coastal Ridge PD. My dispatch said you might know something about the wellness check I'm answering."

"Yes, Officer. Are you going to 1697 Bellend Drive to check on a Crystal Hammond?"

"Yes, ma'am."

"We're heading to the same location to talk to her husband, Rodney, about two homicide victims here on Shadow Island. They both had their throats slashed. Our evidence is compelling."

"Well," he chuckled, "I'm damn glad you called when you did. I'm about three minutes out. I think I'll wait for backup instead of going alone."

"We're about," she glanced at Locke, and he held up fingers, "ten minutes out. If he's got his wife in there, don't wait on us."

"The caller said they have a young son as well."

The engine revved as Locke pushed the pedal even harder.

"Do what feels right, Officer Blane. But he's suspected of slashing the throat of a woman he claimed to love and the man who saved her from him. I'm not going to say he wouldn't attack his own son or wife."

There was a long pause. "Will do, Sheriff. Backup is en route now."

"We'll be there as soon as we can."

Rebecca hoped it would be soon enough.

38

R od Hammond's house was swarming with city cops as Rebecca and Locke pulled up in front of it, parking along the road with four other cruisers. They were staged near the front door with an officer at each corner.

They hadn't finished clearing the house. Rebecca slipped from the passenger seat, Locke's door closing in the same heartbeat as her own. The cop near the front door turned to look, noticed their uniforms, and waved them up to join.

Rebecca didn't even make it to the front step before the smell hit her. Decomp. Once she'd smelled it working with the FBI, she could pick it out anywhere, anytime.

"Victims?" She crouched down next to the officer who had waved her over.

"Female adult." The other officer's eyes were locked on the door.

"They have a son too."

"House is clear." The call came over the radio. The officers at the corners of the house made their way forward, moving to clear the yard as well.

Rebecca didn't wait for that. Straightening, she headed inside.

"Sheriff West, coming in." The echo of the warning ran through the house as those inside started making their way back to the front.

A man met her at the door, and Rebecca caught his name tag. "Blane." She gave him the nod all cops greeted each other with, a quick upward jerk of her chin. "Locke, wait here and keep your eyes peeled."

"Sheriff. Thanks for the heads-up. It looks like your guy was as bad as you thought. The victim matches Crystal Hammond's license photo as best as we can tell."

She understood what that meant. The body was either beaten so badly they couldn't get a solid ID, or it was so far gone they couldn't be sure. A chill ran up her spine, aiming for her heart. "And the boy?"

"No clue, but he's not here. But there's something here I want you to take a look at." He shook his head and gestured for her to follow. "We're reaching out to next of kin and the woman's boss to see if she knows anything."

The chill stopped before it stabbed Rebecca too deeply. If the boy wasn't in the house, there was still a chance he'd gotten out in time. She focused on her job and what she could do.

The house was a disaster. Dirty dishes, takeout boxes, and stacks of mail were scattered around the small space. And each step she took made a soft crunching sound. She looked down, hoping it wasn't cockroaches again.

"Oh, yeah. It's kitty litter. It's tracked all over the house. Was like that when we got here."

"They have a cat?" She glanced around but saw no signs.

Blane ducked down a hall. The thick haze of rotting corpse grew stronger with each step, and it mixed with the awful fake floral scent of the kitty litter that announced their every move. "No. From the looks, he was using it to cover up the smell. It's poured all around her body and on the floor." He led her into the main bedroom, and she could see it for herself.

The room was trashed. It was easy to see a huge fight had taken place. Furniture was broken, knocked over, and in the case of the bed, slid out of place, leaving heavy scratches on the floor. Clothing was spilled out from the broken dresser. Several drawers were busted, some of the wood splintered.

She glanced around and saw a big piece, like a stake. Covered in blood, it rested on the bed next to the bloated corpse of Crystal Hammond. Liquid from her rotting organs leaked out of the slash in her throat and onto the pillows. More of it had dried along her lips.

Rebecca took slow, careful breaths in through her mouth, trying to keep the stench out as much as possible. It wasn't as bad as it should've been, the clay-based litter having soaked up and dried most of the decomp. However, it wasn't doing anything for the gasses that expanded what was once the living, breathing body of Rod Hammond's wife.

"He sliced her throat with a broken piece of furniture?" She kept her words measured so she wouldn't inhale too deeply.

"That's what it looks like, yeah. That's not what I wanted you to see, though." He stretched out a hand, pointing. "That is. Do those people look familiar to you?"

When she followed the direction of his arm, an electric shock zinged through her. Pictures were cut out and stuck to the wall. She recognized them easily.

A photo of Amy and Buzz Washington had been torn from a newspaper. They were smiling beautifully at the camera. Sebastian Drysdale's picture appeared to be his glossy staff yearbook picture. Both images had red lines slashed through Amy's and Sebastian's faces.

There was one more photograph in Rod Hammond's creepy shrine. Carol Krieg, smiling from the booth of a book fair. There was no red line across her photo.

Yet.

39

"Really, Miss K is still alive?" Hoyt felt incredibly old as Viviane shook her head in innocent wonder. She laughed. "She was ancient back when I was in school. I just kinda assumed she'd bitten the dust years ago."

"Yes, she's still alive." He thought back to how the librarian hadn't changed in the slightest and chuckled. "Still as fierce as ever. And not nearly as old as you seem to think."

Viviane cradled her chin in her hand, eyes wistfully wandering. "I'd like to go see her. I didn't even know she worked at the library."

"That's because she mainly works in the kid's section, and you usually live in the reference section." Greg grunted, not looking up from his Kindle.

Viviane wrenched her chin from her hand to stare at the older man, who was leaning his chair against the wall at his desk. "How am I the only person who didn't know about this?"

"You don't have kids." Both men spoke at the same time, then shared a knowing look.

"Hey, Vi." Elliot wandered back, holding some papers in his hand.

"Yeah, what's up, Dispatch?" She grinned, and Hoyt could tell she genuinely enjoyed being able to call someone else that.

Elliot didn't seem to notice her mirth, too caught up in whatever he was holding. "Should I let you guys know that Sheriff and Deputy Locke are driving out to Coastal Ridge to pick up Rodney Hammond?"

"Who's Rodney Hammond?" Greg dropped his chair down onto all four legs, setting his Kindle aside.

"Rebecca and I had him and two other witnesses in to corroborate Melvin Drysdale's alibi. Hammond plays poker with them." Hoyt faced the new dispatcher. "Walk us through what happened, starting with when the sheriff called in and what she said."

Elliot took a breath, settled himself, then told the entire tale, including his screwup and learning about the missing Crystal Hammond. His eyes were on Viviane for that part, but otherwise, he kept them fixed firmly on Hoyt.

The dispatcher glanced at his watch. "That was just a few minutes ago. As soon as I hear from her again, I'll let you all know."

"I'll be." Viviane turned her monitor around. "Boss got some new evidence. Look at this picture."

Hoyt leaned over. She'd opened the active file, and sure enough, there were images he hadn't seen yet. A yearbook picture of an aggressive-looking young man. "She cracked the case."

"Or maybe Locke did." Greg gave a snorting chuckle, which mangled his words.

Viviane was quick to jump to his defense. "Hey, he's been working really hard."

Raising his eyebrows, Hoyt could only shake his head.

"That's neither here nor there. Did the boss ask for us? Or ask for backup?"

It took Elliot a few seconds to realize the question was directed at him. "No. She's meeting up with officers from Coastal Ridge. They were already on their way."

Hoyt nodded and stood, checking the time. "Send her address to my phone, will you?"

Viviane frowned. "What time was that children's story hour?"

Grinning, he headed toward the door. "Looks like you're going to get your wish about seeing Mrs. Krieg again. She might know the name. If we hurry, we might still be able to catch her before she leaves."

Abner knocked on his desk. "Guess that means I'm babysitting the grieving drunk?"

Shit. Hoyt had almost forgotten about Melvin Drysdale. "Yeah…that'd be great."

Waving a hand at them, the older man picked up where he'd left off in his book. "You go talk with the librarian. Tell her I said hi."

"Will do."

When Hoyt nodded at Viviane, she dashed out ahead of him. She was so happy to be the one driving the cruiser, and he didn't mind at all being chauffeured around. It'd sucked when he wasn't allowed to drive, but now he was starting to enjoy it.

On a Sunday evening, with most of the tourists already gone for the season, there was hardly any traffic.

Hoyt kept his mind occupied on the short trip, thinking about whether he should press his luck, talking inside the library after hours, or concede to the inevitable and ask Miss K to step outside for the chat. Hell, he could even ask her to come down to the station.

"Is that her car?" Viviane's excited voice brought him out of his fantasy, and he turned to where she was looking.

"It matches the one she has registered with the DMV. Just park in front of the door." He pointed to the spot where the sidewalk sloped down to join the parking lot, giving wheelchair access. It was another thing that Viviane, being an impressionable rookie, still got a kick out of doing. And in truth, he didn't blame her. These were the things that had thrilled him when he first started too.

Of course, now that he was older, wiser, and more stressed, he rather relished the door-to-door service. He slipped out of the cruiser and swung the door shut without looking back.

Viviane's hurried steps raced to catch up with him, eager to see her old librarian. As a study-aholic, she probably viewed librarians the same way most people idolized superheroes.

A few of the lights were still on in the library, so that was a good sign. Hoyt pushed tentatively against the door, and it swung open. There was a loud crack, and he froze, his hand jumping to his gun.

"Mrs. Krieg! Are you in here?" The yelling brought a strange taste to his lips, one he recognized. Drywall powder. What the hell was going on?

"Help! Hoyt, I'm in the cage! Rod Hammond is trying to kill me!"

Hoyt took off running, his boots sliding on the aged carpet tiles worn smooth by countless feet.

Viviane caught up with him, her face grim and her gun held in a low, two-handed grip. "Reference section."

They dodged and wove through the bookcases to the back corner.

"He's running out the back! Hurry!"

Hoyt made the last turn, pushing to put himself half a step

ahead of Viviane. The faint smell of drywall dust and the chalkiness in the air clued him in that something was wrong, but it had not prepared him for what he found.

The wall that blocked off one side of the reference section had a sizable hole carved into it. Pieces of wall were all over the floor. And Carol had stuffed the hole with a table lamp, numerous large reference books, and some seat cushions. Rod had tried digging his way into the room she'd locked herself in. And the crafty librarian had been packing it with anything she could move to keep him out.

"Out the back! Hurry! That way!" Carol stood at the locked gate, pointing and hopping in place.

"Stay here!" Hoyt turned to follow the librarian's gestures and pointed for Viviane to stay. "He might loop back around. Keep your head up 'til I get back and call it in. Now!"

The glowing exit sign hanging from the ceiling told him exactly where he needed to go, and he ran as fast as he could. The heavy back door was closing yet not fully latched by the time he crashed into it. Stomping footsteps resounded from around the corner, and he raced to follow after them, gun clenched tight in his hand and pointed at high ready.

Anyone who was willing to carve down a wall to get to his victim was willing to do almost anything.

Hoyt veered wide as he came to the corner, slicing the pie as he approached. From his position farther away from the exterior wall of the building, he could see across the street. He caught the unmistakable glint of a blade in Rod Hammond's hand as he flung open a car door to hop inside.

There was no way Hoyt could make it to the vehicle before the man took off. Giving up on that idea, he ran for the cruiser parked out front. Hammond's car, a mid-nineties, model-gray Ford Taurus, peeled out, heading southwest.

Ripping the driver's door open, Hoyt flung himself inside, reached for the keys, and came up with nothing. There were no keys in the ignition. Viviane had taken them with her instead of leaving them like she was supposed to. A rookie mistake, but one that was allowing the killer to get away.

"The first two are his victims. And I suspect the last one is about to be." Rebecca's phone rang and she looked down at it. "West."

"Sheriff!" The word burst from the phone like a tidal wave as Elliot nearly busted her eardrum with his enthusiasm. "Frost found Hammond, but he got away. He was at the library, trying to kill—"

"Carol Krieg. I'm at his house in Coastal Ridge right now, looking at his murder board. Which way was he headed?" Rebecca turned, waving for Blane to follow her. His eyes were wide as he trailed behind her, summoning his men as they raced from the house.

"Frost said southwest. He's chasing him now but got held up securing Krieg. I've already sent you the vehicle details."

"He might be trying to come back home." She gave the officers around her a pointed look.

They scattered, running back to their cars. If they could set up a trap at his residence, that would be best. Far better than trying to take him down while he was driving.

"I'm heading back now. I had to turn my radio down while we were infiltrating his house, but I'll have it on. Keep me updated."

"He's coming here?" Blane moved up next to her as they stepped out onto Hammond's front porch.

"Sounds like it." Rebecca looked around at the officers waiting for orders. They weren't her men. This wasn't her jurisdiction.

"Get that door back in the frame! Move those cars up the

street and park on the adjoining ones." Blane gestured, driving the uniforms around him into a frenzy of preparation. "I'll send a guy down to the bridge. Do you have a vehicle description?"

Rebecca checked her phone and read him the make and model. "There should be an APB going out on it now too."

The cruisers were already pulling away, moving up and down the street to hide and wait for Hammond to arrive. Two officers struggled to lean the door against the frame in a way that looked natural.

"I need to get back to my side of the bridge. Let me know if he shows up here."

"And let us know if you run into him."

"Will do!" Rebecca waved a hand at him, rushing as well as she could manage to her SUV, where Locke was waiting.

40

With the cruiser's lights flashing and siren wailing, Locke tore down the island-bound lane of the Shadow Way Bridge. The Coastal Ridge cruiser that had been following them from Hammond's house made a wide swing, the officers setting themselves up on the shoulder where they could keep an eye on the approaching traffic.

Rebecca was belted into the passenger seat, and her aching ribs reminded her with every erratic turn that she'd probably returned to work too soon.

The bridge arced up, ever so slightly, giving the impression of driving into the sky before flattening out again.

Frost's voice rang out over the radio clutched in Rebecca's hand. "Boss, I don't see him anywhere. I think he made it to the bridge."

"Roger that, Frost. Locke and I are on the bridge now. Will keep an eye out." Rebecca released the button but held onto the radio, her eyes glued to oncoming traffic.

It was after dinner and traffic was thin. Most of the tourists had already left town for the season. A few cars still spotted the roadway, each one standing out as they trickled closer.

"Gray '93 Ford Taurus," Rebecca mumbled, leaning forward. They were already more than halfway over the bridge.

"That one's gray or silver." Locke pointed to the car that had popped up over the slight rise leading from Shadow Island.

"And a Ford. And speeding."

The driver must've seen them because the car lurched forward as it accelerated.

"A Taurus. That's gotta be him." The words had no sooner left her mouth than she was finally able to see the man behind the steering wheel. It was the same man who'd casually spun lies in her station, attempting to frame Melvin Drysdale for his own brother's murder. She wondered if he was winking now. "That's Rodney Hammond."

The fleeing vehicle whipped past them.

Locke spun the Explorer around, bouncing Rebecca off the passenger door, sending pain searing through her chest. The car was now ahead of them and pulling away, with them having lost momentum in the turn. The few other cars on the bridge slowed down, giving them plenty of room. He slammed his foot on the gas pedal, taking off after Hammond.

Rebecca squeezed the radio button. "Dispatch, we have subject in sight, heading westbound on the bridge. Advise Coastal Ridge we're coming back to them. And have them ready to toss a spike strip too. He's running fast."

The much larger engine of the sheriff's SUV closed the distance between them. She didn't know if Hammond got spooked, if there was something wrong with his car, or if he'd managed to hit the expansion seam of the bridge perfectly, but the Ford suddenly lost control. The back end kicked out.

Hammond overcorrected, setting the vehicle to fishtailing wildly.

Then he did what any driver knew not to do. He yanked the wheel hard to the opposite side of the skid. The Taurus spun out. The front driver's side tire hit the concrete shoulder barrier. Sparks flew as Hammond's tire either folded under or snapped right off.

Locke hit the brakes.

Hammond's car rolled.

Pressing her feet hard against the floorboard and gripping the grab bar, Rebecca braced herself. She triggered the radio. "He's flipped. Send officers."

When the SUV slid to a stop, Rebecca flung open her door, pulling her weapon free with her left hand. As she stepped around the nose of the cruiser, she transferred hands.

Though the Taurus had managed to roll back to its upright position, it was angled halfway in both lanes. Traffic screeched to a halt all around them.

Rebecca rushed forward.

"Boss, no! Stop! What are you doing?" Locke was climbing out from behind the steering wheel.

The windshield and front windows of the Taurus were pushed out and shattered all over the road in front of them. And Rod was nowhere in sight. Oil leaked from his car, and the smell smacked Rebecca hard.

Raising her gun, Rebecca pointed the muzzle at the interior. Her eyes raked the scene, checking the ground and the underside of the car while keeping track of every vehicle around them. One truck, unable to stop in time, roared past the wreckage.

Loud crunches reached her ears. Grit, like cat litter, was

under her sneakers as she moved closer, kicking the safety glass away. "Rod Hammond, come out with your hands up."

Despite her words, Rebecca wasn't even sure if he was *in* or *out* already.

Locke slipped to the left as Rebecca continued right. They circled around so the fugitive had no place to run. People stared as time slowed. She even saw a window, in front of a young boy's face, start to lower.

As she took another step, her gazed shifted back to the interior of the car. The driver's seat was visible. No one was in it. And there was no blood. She stepped forward again.

Locke disappeared around the back of the wrecked vehicle. He'd have to get past the crumpled mess of a guardrail and the rear bumper.

Rebecca noted smears of red on a sheet of broken glass on the road.

With a roar like a maniac, Rod Hammond launched himself over the crumpled hood of his vehicle. Blood trickled down his forehead onto the bridge of his nose. The knife in his hand held a dull reflection of the lowering red sun.

Rebecca's finger started to pull the trigger.

Behind Hammond, the boy in the car stared in fascination.

Blood on the tiles...

Rebecca hesitated, her finger locking tight, unwilling to make the final movement.

Hammond's shoe slid on the roughened surface of his hood.

Brains exploding in a hot wave and falling into the cool ocean...
How many people have I killed now?

Her body count had surged since arriving on Shadow Island. Was she ready to kill another? She was capable. But...

Staring down the sights of her gun, she only had milliseconds to decide.

The field behind him wasn't clear. If she missed, she could kill that child.

Even as she stepped sideways to change the angle, Hammond lunged.

Rebecca jerked back, throwing her arms to the sides to avoid the sharp edge that would have taken out at least one arm. Her right arm was still healing. It didn't need another wound.

The blade sliced down, missing her chest as she dodged backward, pulling her right arm back defensively. She backpedaled, jumping out of his reach, trying to get enough space between them.

Rebecca was grateful for both the power of adrenaline and Bailey's suggestion to wear the Kevlar vest. Even with the protection, though, she knew Hammond preferred to attack the neck.

"I will not go down for this!" He flailed wildly at her face, and she dodged easily, twisting her right hip back to spin out of his way. As she did, she realized his knife was the same kind that came from any sporting store or military consignment—a basic Ka-Bar substitute sharpened to within an inch of its life. Scary and sharp, it could no doubt slice through flesh, despite the poor craftsmanship.

"You won't ruin my life." Rod gritted his teeth, his jaw clenched tight as he raised his knife once again.

A loud pop announced Locke's arrival to the battle as he stepped around the front of the Taurus.

Rod Hammond jerked upright, stretching so tall he bent over backward as the Taser rammed electricity through his body. His jaw snapped shut and his face contorted as every muscle went taut and out of control. He spilled backward, landing hard on his side like a felled tree.

After kicking the knife away, Locke rolled Hammond over and knelt over his hips. Hammond's arms shook as

Locke twisted and secured them against the small of his back. He pulled the handcuffs from his pouch and slapped them on him.

"Thanks for the backup." Rebecca gazed at her deputy, who was focused on the sweating mess of a man he'd tased and cuffed.

"Anytime, Sheriff." He glanced up at her and showed the tiniest of smiles. "At least this time, we didn't both get cracked in the head."

Rebecca laughed as four Coastal Ridge police officers ran through the stopped traffic to join them. "Yeah. I don't think Frost could handle it if I had to go on leave again."

41

"Let me get this straight." As Rebecca watched, Greg Abner rocked back his chair in the bullpen, lifting the front legs off the ground as he did so. He scratched his jaw. "His wife was an incessant nag and he just snapped and offed her?"

Rebecca smiled, thinking that Greg had spent too much time in a rocking chair. Or maybe it was the rocking of a fishing boat he was trying to recreate. "That's what the mom said. She admitted her daughter had been in a marriage of convenience after she got pregnant at seventeen. She'd used the intentional pregnancy to get away from an abusive father."

Leaning against the table, she sipped her coffee. As nice as it was to have her own office, it was also a relief to get out of her chair to hang out with the rest of her team in the bullpen.

"What happened to their son?" Greg's chair came down with a clatter as he shook his head.

"Apparently, the wife had contrived the trip every year for a while now. Hammond was a real ass to his son, beating him and shaming him for the smallest infraction. Crystal would send the boy to spend the last week of summer with her mom up in Nova Scotia so the boy could experience some normalcy. They'll be sending the kid to counseling to work through losing both his parents, one to jail and the other by his own father's hand."

"Poor kid."

"Yeah...poor kid indeed." Rebecca lifted her coffee mug and savored the hazelnut scent. "Hammond admitted he and Crystal fought often, not just yelling and screaming, but that he would lash out. And I quote, 'put the bitch in her place.' This time, they broke a piece of furniture, and he used the jagged shard of wood to slice her throat open."

Locke twisted his chair around to face them. "He said it was such a relief to silence her, he didn't even feel bad about it. The euphoria didn't last long, though, because he saw the notice in the local paper about Amy Washington's retirement party and became furious when he read about how perfect and happy her life was going to be."

"His trigger," Rebecca murmured.

"In his opinion, she didn't deserve happiness if he couldn't be happy. Which was when he got the bright idea to start killing all the other people in his life that had, as he put it, held him back." Locke rolled his eyes. "I say they held him accountable for his actions and that's why he hated them."

Rebecca waved her cup at that. "No. I mean, that might hold true for Sebastian Drysdale, since he stopped Rod from attacking Mrs. Washington. But Amy and Carol Krieg only stopped going above and beyond for him after he showed them his true self."

Locke grunted, dropping his head. "That's not how a lot of guys would see it, you know...the ones who think they're better and more deserving than everyone else."

"People, Locke." Greg knew as well as Rebecca who Locke had been talking about. His old childhood friends who'd turned on him as soon as he stopped helping them. "It's not a guy thing or a woman thing. It's a people thing."

Rebecca jumped in. "There's always that fraction of people who see others as mere stepping stones or building blocks to their own ambitions. A woman is as likely to stab you in the back as a man is. But generally, with the figurative knife before resorting to violence."

Greg slapped a hand on his knee, erupting in laughter. "Isn't that the God's honest truth!"

"What is?" Hoyt walked in from the lobby.

"People suck." Locke leaned his forearm on his desk. He was starting to droop after being at work all night, then filling out paperwork from taking down Hammond the previous day. Greg had gone over it and sent it back to be corrected twice before allowing him to submit it.

"Not most of them. Take it from an old man, most people are good, if a little stupid or unsure. And when given an obvious choice between helping or hurting someone, most people choose to help."

Hoyt's words, spoken so simply, seemed to revive Locke somewhat. There was only a decade of difference in their ages, but a lifetime of experience separated them.

Rebecca remembered the first time she'd looked at Locke's date of birth on his personnel file and realized he was six years older than her. She'd assumed from the way he acted and his baby face that he was in his mid-twenties. Instead, he was forty-one. Now that he'd lost the thick beard, he looked even younger.

Strangely, being taken in by the über-rich of the Yacht Club crew had left him fairly sheltered. She knew that was something he was still struggling to deal with now that he no longer had them giving him "presents" or taking him on luxurious vacations and weekend getaways.

Locke had managed to deal with the culture shock fairly

well so far. She hoped he would continue. And that his descent back into reality didn't break him or leave him bitter.

Or worse, convince him to revert to his old ways of being a stool pigeon for the Yacht Club.

Considering how much self-loathing he had over Wallace's death, she didn't think that was possible. Which didn't mean she wouldn't keep an eye out for it.

Rebecca pushed off the table and walked to his desk. "Go home, Locke." She picked up the report he'd struggled with. "You've done enough for today. Get some rest. You've got ten hours before you need to be back here for your next shift."

The deputy didn't need to be told twice. Not on this, at least. He popped out of his seat, again making him seem decades younger than his age. "Yes, ma'am." Turning to Greg, he gave a little salute. "Thanks for all your help."

Greg grunted and shooed him off. "That's what us old men are for. To teach you younger ones."

"When they'll listen." Hoyt stepped around Rebecca, heading for the coffeepot. "Speaking of not being able to get through to people, Melvin was bitching the whole trip home. He said he was going to sue us for false imprisonment."

"Whatever you might think of him, realize this. That man was napping in an unlocked interrogation room and never even tried to leave." Rebecca headed to her office. "I hope he reconsiders, because I don't need more paperwork."

"Better get it done fast." Hoyt chuckled as he settled down at his desk. "You've got an appointment this afternoon. Vi's not going to like it if you're late."

"I won't be."

It would take a disaster of epic proportions for her to miss her date today.

42

"I've missed you." Viviane gazed down at the name of the man who'd been her mentor, her hero, and in every way except blood, a second father.

The gray headstone stared back at her dully.

"You did an excellent job when you picked Rebecca as your replacement. Did you know it would turn out this way?" She knelt, pulling the wilted flowers from the vase perched on top of Alden Wallace's grave. "Was this something you planned? Obviously, you didn't know she was coming to the island. But did you plan to talk her into helping you with everything you couldn't handle because she was ex-FBI and knew how to deal with organized crime?"

Taking the green tissue paper from around the bouquet, she placed the fresh flowers into the emptied vase and adjusted them so they sat prettily. "Or did you pick her because you knew I needed a female role model to convince me that I could do the job I'd always dreamed about?"

Using both hands, she reverently smoothed down her uniform. "Well, it worked. I did it. You weren't there to swear me in, but Rebecca was." Tears trickled down her cheeks, and she couldn't tell if they were from the loss she still felt every day or from the pride that filled her since she'd taken the oath of office. Regardless of their source, they made her voice squeak. "It was almost as good, but I still miss you. I hope you're proud of me. I..."

Viviane choked, and this time she knew it was grief. A warm hand fell on her shoulder, and she reached up blindly to take it, appreciating her friend's silent support. "I never would've been able to do this without you. I hope you know that. You're the one who gave me direction. Rebecca," she squeezed the comforting hand, "helping push me over the finish line. We'll make you proud, Alden. And we'll finish what you started."

That sentiment settled like a solid core in Viviane's heart. She didn't know when or how, but they would put an end to the group of men who'd taken Alden's life and nearly ruined his reputation. That was yet another thing Rebecca had managed to save.

The Yacht Club, a group of white, rich assholes, were going to be taken down by two women. She could picture it —slapping the cuffs on some potbellied old Boss Hog fanboy, and him looking up at her, a Black woman with the full force of the law behind her. The tables were turning, and she was here for it with her entire family at her back.

"Is the cemetery always this messy?"

Viviane giggled, wiping the tears from her cheeks, and turned to look up at Rebecca, who was frowning as she took in the landscape around them. "No. It's usually kept very neat. I think the hurricane damage is probably requiring extra time. Or maybe the caretaker hasn't reached this section yet. Trust you to be the one to notice something like that."

"I'm sorry, Vi. I didn't mean to intrude or take away from this. Ignore me. It's not important. This is." Rebecca flinched, and her eyes pinched with emotional pain as Viviane stood.

One of the things Viviane loved best about her new friend was how easy she was to read. Viviane had known where she stood with Rebecca the first time they'd met. When Rebecca smiled at her the first time, she realized she'd been like a lost soul being seen for the first time.

"No, it's fine, hun. I just wanted to show him my new uniform and let him know how thankful I am for what he gave to me. And I did that." Unable to help herself, Viviane embraced her friend gently, fully aware of the delicate state of her ribs. "Thanks for coming out with me."

Rebecca squeezed her in response. "Of course. I was honored you asked me to join you."

Viviane straightened, looking her friend in the eyes. "Now, let's go find someplace to dispose of these. The groundskeeper clearly has enough on his hands if he let the flowers wilt this badly."

Before answering, Rebecca gazed down at Alden's grave, and Viviane wondered if she said her own heartfelt words silently. "There's a work building over that way. I bet we'll find a garbage can there, at the very least."

Looping their arms together, Viviane hefted the desiccated flowers she'd left more than a week ago. "I'm pretty sure you're right. Bye, Alden." She gave the tiniest wave before walking the short distance to the oddly shaped caretaker's building.

Rebecca rapped on one of the double doors even though it wasn't latched. "Hello, is anyone—"

Viviane gasped when the door swung open on well-oiled hinges, revealing a pair of feet, clad in heavy leather work boots, dangling above the ground. Her eyes shot up the man's limp frame.

The rope that was twisted around his neck creaked softly as the breeze at their back caused him to sway.

Viviane didn't need to see his face to know the man was dead.

The End
To be continued...

Thank you for reading.
All of the *Shadow Island Series* books can be found on Amazon.

ACKNOWLEDGMENTS

How does one properly thank everyone involved in taking a dream and making it a reality? Here goes.

In addition to our families, whose unending support provided the foundation for us to find the time and energy to put these thoughts on paper, we want to thank the editors who polished our words and made them shine.

Many thanks to our publisher for risking taking on two newbies and giving us the confidence to become bona fide authors.

More than anyone, we want to thank you, our readers, for sharing your most important asset, your time, with this book. We hope with all our hearts we made it worthwhile.

Much love,
Mary & Lori

ABOUT THE AUTHOR

Mary Stone

Mary Stone lives among the majestic Blue Ridge Mountains of East Tennessee with her two dogs, four cats, a couple of energetic boys, and a very patient husband.

As a young girl, she would go to bed every night, wondering what type of creature might be lurking underneath. It wasn't until she was older that she learned that the creatures she needed to most fear were human.

Today, she creates vivid stories with courageous, strong heroines and dastardly villains. She invites you to enter her world of serial killers, FBI agents but never damsels in distress. Her female characters can handle themselves, going toe-to-toe with any male character, protagonist or antagonist.

Discover more about Mary Stone on her website.
www.authormarystone.com

Lori Rhodes

As a tiny girl, from the moment Lori Rhodes first dipped her toe into the surf on a barrier island of Virginia, she was in love. When she grew up and learned all the deep, dark secrets and horrible acts people could commit against each other, she couldn't stop the stories from coming out of the other end of her pen. Somehow, her magical island and the darkness got mixed together and ended up in her first novel.

Now, she spends her days making sure the guests at her beach rental cottages are happy, and her nights dreaming up the characters who love her island as much as she does.

Connect with Mary Online

Made in United States
Troutdale, OR
02/16/2024

17736245R00149